Tendence and Cavile

D. T. Kastn

ISBN-13 978-0615651118
ISBN-10 0615651119
Copyright © Leeftail Press
June 2012

Printed in the United States of America

For the kids.
All three sets of them.

Chapter One

This is how it happened.

Sev had given up on the myth of an intelligent, handsome man and was instead looking for one who could count to ten and wouldn't frighten small children. She knew the rule: you always find something in the last place you look. Car keys in the freezer, adoptable children in Tibet, Grandma in the duck pond, prospective mates in retail clothing stores. Supposedly he was buying ties but she found him inexplicably hanging out in the misses section, just next to her size on the rack, bobbing back and forth with a hopeful smile.

Matthew was clean cut, handsome, witty and apparently intelligent. He showed not only signs of the ability to be half of a worthwhile relationship, but the apparent inclination to start one at the earliest opportunity. It was a nice quality, Sev thought, reaching irritably for the phone to call her parents on her thirty-seventh birthday, cursing the shattered remnants of her biological clock. She, blindly, called what she felt "love," and decided his strange eagerness to share his life with her was not frightening, but endearing.

Matthew was handsome, witty, and intelligent. And he was willing.

She fell.

The falling wasn't hard, but the landing was awful.

Dinners with Matthew were a series of mediocrities, chain restaurants and toothy waitpersons who insisted their specials were, ludicrously, both taco salad and lobster. Sometimes, taco salad with lobster on it.

"How's yours, Sev?"

"An incongruous mix that seems destined to end in gastrointestinal distress. It's surprisingly tasty. Yours?"

They never shared. She'd taken a french fry off his plate once and his face had frozen so quickly she thought he'd had a heart attack.

Now, his answer was a smile shared across the dinner table, the restaurant a quiet buzz behind the ringing in her ears, a slight glint of light off one white tooth (peculiarly sharp), that twist to his smile that was his only uneven surface. Sev didn't think much about the possibility of being in love with a dangerous idiot any more than she thought about the possibility of being in love with a potential lunatic. All men were probably lunatics on some level, anyway. She was almost certain she remembered her mother telling her so.

So any doubts were stillborn and buried. Matthew told her about his work; she discounted it easily, let it pass, didn't let it get to her. Time machines were impossible. Time moved in one direction, measured out by ticks and tocks and spaces of silence. He was an eccentric genius, possibly, but no hint of geekiness dulled his smile, and she liked it that he shortened *Sevannah* to *Sev*. Not that it hadn't been done before, but he hadn't met any of her friends and family. He called her *Sev* without any prototype and therefore it seemed thrillingly fresh and new. He tried to explain time as a subway station to her over dessert, but he'd ordered low-fat ice cream and she just assumed it went to his head.

They watched reruns of the Mary Tyler Moore show, and fed each other popcorn, and she let her mind slip lightly over how corny it all was and then allowed her mind to connect the corniness with the popcorn and then reprimanded herself sternly for the ridiculous pun. She wondered briefly if the punning was a result of how disgustingly sweet life seemed to be all of a sudden. She listened hard for a laugh-track, and was momentarily disconcerted when it came, but it was only Ed Asner being clever. *Or so he thinks*, she thought darkly, aware of the deep rumble of laughter from Matthew, vibrating in his chest under her head and hand.

He was just crazy enough that she didn't think about it much. And it was *good*, it was how she liked things to be. Effortless, easy, with a thin veneer of enjoyment over the top; scratch away at the surface and who knew what you'd come up with, but it was thick enough to fool all but the most keen observers. Sev didn't have a plethora of intelligent friends, and her last remaining relatives lived three states away (the states of Washington, Oregon, and Ignorance, specifically). The keen observers were limited to strangers who passed her by on the street, got little creases of worry between their eyebrows, and went home with a nagging sensation of concern that they couldn't fully explain.

Sevannah wasn't paying attention, and she fooled easily. So, as it wasn't pleasure but at least an absence of pain, she enjoyed it.

Things weren't so bad after all. They could be much worse— and had been, not so very long ago. If she wanted to be overly romantic, she could refer to Matthew as her savior, as he'd nursed her gently out of a bad relationship with Torrance, who was much flashier and more noticeable than Matthew, but who also hit her on occasion, such as if he'd had a bad day. Torrance had been rather upset with her when she left and called her, among other things, an enabler.

"True," she'd agreed thoughtfully. "I enable you to use your fist."

"I never used my fist."

"That's wonderful, Torrance," she said methodically, "that the difference between me and the punching bag at your gym is the way your hand is positioned."

"The punching bag and you," he corrected automatically.

"What?"

"Your grammar. You come last in the list."

She squinted at him. "That only applies to proper nouns."

"No, actually. It applies to everything. It's basic grammar, okay? You're supposed to be last."

"I think," she said, "that just illustrated my point."

No witnesses. She'd kicked him on the kneecap as she left. Could he show a bruise anyway? His entire leg was intricately tattooed. She was scot-free and his lawyer was a moron anyway.

In the end, maybe it wasn't the being hit, but the endless harping on proper grammar. It could have been more than that, even, but the relationship post-mortem was never something that appealed to Sev.

And so there was Matthew, and they were piously good to each other, with some sort of unspoken pact to make no off-color jokes, nothing politically incorrect even if it was funny in context, no capering, no annoying puns, no frightening display of affection in public or private, no bringing out the camera and taking nasty close-up blackmail shots of the other's nostrils, no pointing or laughing when one of them tripped and fell. It was a stretch of humanity for Sev, this tacit agreement not to let the gloss disappear from their relationship. Secretly she believed it was good for her, in some arcane, unknowable way. But certainly she had her doubts, however neglected they were, about Matthew.

When he proposed and they became officially engaged she fought off the nagging feeling that this didn't feel like a beginning, but more like an end; or, more properly, a means to an end. There was something perfunctory about it. They had dated for three months, and in all that time she heard not a slip of the tongue, not a burp, not a half-uttered oath, nothing to betray any sharks circling beneath his surface smoothness.

She could deal with smoothness, she thought, almost fondly.

All in all, she had herself pretty much convinced that it was a bad thing when he disappeared.

What surprised her most was that the police were so willing to help. They were practically falling all over themselves. She'd grown up the love child of a slightly deranged British-expatriate hippy, and was used to hearing soliloquies on the deviant propensities of "pigs" which, once she understood that "pigs" in this sense meant "police and other government employees," lost its barnyard appeal. Her rebel-teenager stage made things more clear. Brought home at two in the morning with flashing blue lights, she invariably found her mother coming soberly out to meet them and her father flipping the officers the bird from behind the gauzy curtains ferociously adorning the front window.

Eventually, of course, she grew out of these assumptions about law enforcement— at least, she thought she grew out of them, although it turned out they'd lurked in her psyche, coloring her perception, along with the childhood suspicion that her father was really John Lennon, or at least Rik Mayall.

The police were nice. They gave her a Coke they'd confiscated during a drug raid as a result of a simple misunderstanding. She didn't want it— carbonation was one of the things she was truly against, also due to a childhood experience better left unexplained— but she wanted to show willing. So she drank it, lips curling slightly in disgust at the taste, which was scarcely concealed by the fact that she tried hurriedly to force it down her throat as swiftly as possible. At the second swallow she tried tucking her tongue to one side to preserve her taste buds, but this only succeeded in blocking the liquid from making it down her throat at all.

After a prolonged coughing fit, she set the can down on the desk and focused as much intensity as she could muster on the policeman seated across from her.

At this point she still expected a challenge.

"I *know* that he is missing," she said with unnecessary fervor, "because he used to call me twice a day, and I haven't heard from him in a day, a day and a *half* actually. That's *three* calls he's missed, and that never happens."

"I understand completely why you're concerned," said Officer Walsh. "He's being put on the list of missing persons as we speak, and the picture you brought in—"

He gestured tentatively at the small photo she'd handed him. In it, Matthew did a very small and decorous mug for the camera, one corner of his thin-lipped mouth crooked a little higher than the other, but everything else perfectly symmetrical. He wore a brown shirt buttoned close to his neck and his hair was newly shorn to half-inch bristles that, he'd told her excitedly, meant he *never had to comb.*

"—will be put on a wall in every grocery store, gas station, post office, heck, we'll even nail it to telephone poles if we have to!"

Sevannah recognized the sincerity on the man's face, but her mouth kept moving without checking with her brain for the go-ahead first. "It's absolutely imperative that we find him, I don't care what you say, I *know* he's gone, I can *feel* it, we have this *connection*—"

An utter lie. They had no connection. She became very gradually aware that the warmth on her hand was the ineffectual patting of Officer Walsh.

"There, there," he said, conscientiously. "There, there."

There was a small, embarrassing part of Sev that

hadn't made a stupid joke in a very long while. It chose this moment to pipe up with, "Where? Where?"

Even this made her miss Matthew harder, since he wasn't there to shake his head in his gently disparaging way at her ridiculousness.

"We'll find him," said Officer Walsh, ignoring her. He probably thought it was just the worry talking. His blue eyes were kind, his snub nose was freckled, and she assumed he was Irish. "Don't you worry, ma'am. We'll find him."

She tried to fight past paranoia just enough to feel reassured and, after a moment's struggle, achieved it. Officer Walsh stood, prefacing her movements with his, and sheltered her towards the door. She glanced back over her shoulder before hoisting her purse over it, and disappeared onto the sunlit summer streets below.

Officer Walsh exchanged glances with a few of his comrades.

"Poor woman. What a nut."

"Guy got cold feet," suggested Lewis.

"Probably."

"Ah, well, some people will do anything to escape commitment." Lewis actually was Irish. He'd proved his comfortableness with commitment by having been married five times, with another on the way.

Officer Walsh folded his arms and shook his head. "She's kind of hard, that woman," he said. "And sharp. Like a broken pair of scissors."

"You think she'll find him?" asked Kowalski.

"I hope she does," said Walsh thoughtfully. "I know for a certainty she'll try."

Two weeks went by, and Sev was sure it was heartbreak. She knew things were bad, because she put in a long-distance call to complain to her older sister. It was never a wise decision.

"I know something's drastically wrong, because he never mentioned anything and he never would have left without letting me know he'd be gone—"

"Can you stop shouting? I'm in a restaurant. People are taking an interest."

"Sorry." She squinted at the phone. "You're talking in a restaurant? Don't you know how rude that is?"

"Well, I'm not with anybody, am I? This one guy keeps leaning over in my direction. But that could just be the cut of my shirt."

"Taylor, I'm thinking I've got to—"

"Sevannah, what's your opinion on dark-haired guys?"

She blanked for a moment, could only see the nondescript brown of Matthew's careful hair, before he cut it and inspired the one almost-terrible argument of their history together.

"Because this guy has a friend," said Taylor. "If you wanted to come up this weekend, I'll go ahead and wrangle us a double date. No problem. Easy. Pushover. Sound good?"

Sev stared in utter horror at the phone for a moment. Then she said, rapidly and without pause for breath, "This isn't *high school*, Taylor Mark, and you're not seventeen, you're forty-one. And my fiancé is missing, and can we have a little *perspective*?"

The phone was hung up decisively and Sev ruthlessly quashed the small voice in the back of her head that was asking, perkily, "*Dark hair? Intriguing. How old? Does he look smart? I don't mean is he drooling or anything, but does he look even remotely capable of holding an intelligent conversation about anything other than himself or stock car racing?*"

She'd reached a decision, but was presently finding it difficult to put into words.

The police, helpful as they'd seemed, had been all loudly-voiced good intentions and no action. Matthew's father didn't seem at all concerned when she finally reached him; in fact he hadn't much appreciated her interruption of his fishing trip and, while he was polite in the extreme, he very politely asked her not to bother him again.

"He'll show up," was how he signed off. "He always does."

This possibility was something that hadn't occurred to Sev. Had he disappeared before? Was this going to be a regular feature during their relationship? Strange as it seemed, it was more of a relief to Sevannah than anything else, to realize that apparently Matthew did have at least one annoying habit. It made her breathe a little easier.

The question remained, however, of just what she was going to do about it. What could she do? Options were limited. She'd gone to the police, she'd gone to his father, she believed private investigators to be paragons of unmitigated idiocy, and she was fast running out of ideas that didn't involve curling up on her bed with ice cream and whimpering for about four days.

In the end she settled for breaking into his house.

The few months and even the engagement ring hadn't led to an exchange of keys, but she'd visited the house enough to know there weren't any security systems in place that weren't capable of being surmounted by a five year old. She avoided the front door. Matthew always locked it religiously. Not even being abducted would interfere with that.

She hadn't meant to actually think the word "abducted" but it was a little late for that. The house felt quiet, but not abandoned. It felt like more of a voluntary-vacating-of-the-premises type situation, and she couldn't really fathom anyone nabbing a quietly insane scientist who's byword was "inoffensiveness." Unless he'd been arrested for being un-American.

She skirted around to the left side of the house (two bed, two bath, no pets, hardwood floors, mysteriously low market value) and glanced timidly into Matthew's bedroom window. A split second while her eyes adjusted to the dark within, and she ran through the possibility that he'd hired a hooker and been done in for his pocket watch and electronic equipment. No, the bedroom was empty, neat and clean. Her minor experience had taught her that he had a bed, a dresser, and a desk in his room, and nothing on them. It was blank and fastidiously clear, something of a void. Even if there'd been a struggle, there really wouldn't be any way to tell short of the furniture actually being smashed up. It wasn't.

The window was not locked and rose easily when she bit her fingernails into the wooden frame and tugged upwards. It squeaked slightly as it reached the top of its rise, and she shushed it with a finger against her lips before realizing how ridiculous that was; huffed out a breath of amusement and hurriedly shushed herself the same way. She extended one leg into the window carefully, gritting her teeth, bent down and angled her torso in, got her foot on the hardwood floor, leaned, overbalanced, and fell over.

No one inside, so the noise was not an issue. But she felt like a fool and that made her irritable. Casting arcane curses at Matthew and his inconsiderate, disappearing ways, she got up, brushed herself off, and marched out of the room. Clearly, nothing interesting ever happened there anyway.

The hallway was dark and quiet. No lights had been left on anywhere in the house. Sev, inadvertently rising to her tiptoes and sneaking down the hall, glanced quickly into the kitchen −clean, bare, boring− and then perused the circuit of the living room, clutching her arms about herself as the chill started to get to her. It wasn't all that cold, but there was something about a dark empty house when it wasn't her own. She didn't turn the lights on, and things presented themselves to her in the form of unexpected furniture. Even in her own house, she frequently came downstairs for a drink of water and ended up tripping over a random ottoman or something, so this wasn't surprising. It just reminded her that, like other things, the Redecorating Elves only came out at night.

She doubled back quickly and went for a scrutinize in

his refrigerator.

Well, his milk was bad. Definitely off, well off. She wrinkled her nose at it. His refrigerator was predictably neat and very nearly empty: a few eggs and a cube of butter lined up neatly on the door, three beers in a row, half a head of wilted lettuce, the aforesaid milk and twelve large D batteries. She blinked at these. They did nothing back. She grabbed a beer from some default impulse, closed the door, then changed her mind and put it back, meekly.

Closing the door neatly once more and moving on, she walked back through the hallway, steps weighed down by the lack of clues. Nothing to indicate where he'd gone, or why he'd gone. No bloodstains on the carpet, no decapitated heads in the freezer, no suggestion of drugs or any other sort of contraband anywhere she'd looked.

There weren't many nooks or crannies in Matthew's simple and uncomplicated house. There weren't a lot of places to look because there weren't a lot of places that he could have hidden anything. Sev walked back through the house, thumping listlessly on walls in the hopes that she'd discover a secret room, a cloister, a hollow, maybe a safe. Nothing.

In a last ditch effort she attacked the notoriously sticky door leading to the basement. In Matthew's initial show-the-girlfriend-around-the-house tour, when they'd reached this door, he had tugged and pushed and pulled and grunted and sweated before finally shrugging and declaring it unopenable.

"Oh well," he'd said. "Not like there's anything in there anyway."

A clever piece of misdirection, she found out. She hurled herself at the door and it gave way immediately, sending her through it and partway down unexpected stairs. The house was out to get her, she reflected as she picked herself up, as though it knew she didn't belong here when its master was away.

There was in fact something in the basement. Lots of things. She'd assumed that he had a laboratory somewhere— probably government-funded, because the government likes a laugh as much as anybody— but here it was right in his house. Home-grown. If the government had given him money, he must have pocketed it, because nearly everything looked as though he'd been dumpster diving for it. Things looked ratty and used, as though they'd been there for years, although Matthew himself had only moved in only ten months ago. Or so, at least, she'd been told. In the light of things, perhaps that wasn't entirely accurate either.

There was dust everywhere; Sevannah fell victim to a surprise sneeze attack, and things lit up and made noises as if in response. Loud noises, siren-like and querulous.

When finally they stopped, she came out from behind the chair to which she'd retreated. The lights remained on, picking out the outside lines of a larger heap of junk. It took her a moment of incredulous staring before she realized that there was, in fact, a basic structure to it. It took the form of a rough pyramid, made from banks of cannibalized computer towers. The structure had wires leading to and from it, and huddled around a kitchen chair, looking rather incredulous and frankly confused at its role in all this. The chair, in turn, had a railing around it which gave it a forlorn feel. It reminded her of the way pony rides made her feel as a child. Sad, yes, but she had a sudden deep desire to sit on this strange, sedentary pony and see where it took her.

Not that it would take her anywhere, she hastily assured herself, and breathed a sigh of relief. But since that was the case, there was no reason she shouldn't give it a try.

The room must have been alerted by her footsteps and weight rather than the sneeze. The floor lit up as she walked across it, giving her a path to a truncated set of stairs that led to the chair. Underneath the faux-leather seat was a portfolio full of notes. She pulled it out, glanced at them, then stowed them back because the sight of all those numbers and mathematical language made her ill.

She sat swiftly on the chair, crossed her legs and looked nonchalantly at the piece of paper that was pinned on a bulletin board leaning against the railing.

Operating Instructions:

To operate this machine, please enter the desired year in the Year/Destination Indicator, then press the Enter button. To return to your time, press the Return button twice.

Very user friendly. The consumer magazines would have a ball with this one. That was about it, apart from the very small letters at the bottom that said,

For Your Safety, please keep arms and legs inside the Time Machine at all times.

"Redundant," said Sev aloud, without thinking about it, and quickly considered just how ridiculous this whole thing was: time machines, instructions on operation and safety when doing so, disappearing boyfriends and broken biological clocks. And if it were true, if time travel existed, shouldn't it be more *complicated* than this? Shouldn't there be cogs and levers and life-or-death situations and black helicopters and government conspiracies? Fox Mulder? James Bond?

Then again, who, she thought, was to say there wasn't? She didn't know for certain. She didn't know anything for certain, not even whether or not this time machine actually worked. Since that was the only thing she could determine with any sort of clarity, she was sort of obligated to try it and find out, wasn't she?

She was, she decided.

She wondered what would happen if you pressed *Enter* without specifying a year first.

Chapter Two

One of the virtues of time travel, as Sev found out, was that it was fast— practically instantaneous. Inasmuch as she had expected anything— she hadn't, really— she'd thought it would take some time to warm up, maybe spin around in circles, make some whirring noises and beeps perhaps. She expected caricature, science-fiction, a time machine cliché. But, she supposed, if you were going to create an impossible machine you might as well create one that worked smoothly. The look of the thing had been deceiving. Almost as soon as she hit the button she found herself somewhere *other*.

It was more like an unusually clear acid trip than time travel, she decided. Colors were brighter, sounds were at first watered down, then sharpened to an almost visceral clarity. An unusually clear, and historically sound, acid trip. With all your friends and all the strangers and everyone in the world dressed in odd clothes.

Historically sound, as far as she could tell, anyway.

At this point she was finally forced to admit what she'd suspected about herself all along: she knew nuts about history. Less than nuts. She couldn't identify an out-of-place nut in this scenario if she saw one, which was going to make it hard to spot Matthew. She had no idea where she was, or, more appropriately, when she was. Though, "where" applied too; she wasn't sure which year or even century this was, but she was fairly sure Big Ben had never been in Matthew's basement.

England then. England— maybe Dickens' time, she thought, but she was only judging based on the high school performance of *Oliver!* she'd attended a year ago. The women wore dresses, bonnets, shawls, gloves, boots with tiny buttons, and the men wore suits, or things that looked like suits, with vests and dignified expressions. More beards than she was used to seeing, as well. Things looked complicated and dingy. People milled around the streets talking excitedly— not about anything in particular, she thought, catching words here and there, just talking excitedly for the sheer joy of it, apparently. Horses tramped by looking footsore and weary. Cart wheels flung mud at random on the passers-by. Sev had taken a few inadvertent steps away from the chair and she now glanced down at the streets and wrinkled her nose. The cobblestones here and there in this quarter weren't doing much to assist with the mud problem. Mud and— well, not only mud. The horses were a dead giveaway.

She cast a glance back at the erstwhile time machine. In this setting it looked as incongruous as minced lobster in a taco salad, a yard sale kitchen chair with a cobweb strung underneath it from seat to left front leg, a slight tear in faux-leather fabric cushion. The Year/Destination Indicator turned out to be attached by a wire to a small round black electronic thing like a smoke detector— in fact she was pretty sure it had been a smoke detector in a previous life— which was in turn attached to the bottom of the chair. The tear in the upholstery had been from Matthew, putting reciprocal attachments on the inside of the lower fabric. The tear also made for slightly uncomfortable sitting, she thought reproachfully, but perhaps he just hadn't gotten around to patching it yet. He was too busy being missing.

She wondered if there was at all any chance that he

would turn up here. That he would come waltzing around the corner, expressing surprise and delight at seeing her, congratulate her for her intelligence and persistence in finding him, show her around a little, and take her home. Highly unlikely. Matthew didn't know how to waltz. But, as she turned back to historical London and looked around with wide eyes, she really could have used a hand to hold.

Not only that, she realized as she took another few steps and started attracting strange looks from the population, she really could have used period dress as well. She glanced down at herself. Jeans, a worn t-shirt, one of those thick-banded black-and-silver-studs wrist-watches that make you look like a punctual hoodlum. Standard breaking-into-Matthew's-house wear, sure, but she wouldn't have passed for an *Oliver!* extra. This was probably not going to go over well.

But she was here now, and as there was just the slightest possibility that her missing boyfriend/fiancé might be here, she couldn't very well turn away.

She could, however, attract the attention of the police, and did, almost immediately. She'd never managed this before with so little effort, and in different circumstances this might have made her proud. A policeman, emerging from a tea shop on the corner already staring, hesitated only a moment before advancing on her. He stood just in front of her with his hands tucked behind his blue-clad back, and his highly-polished buttons winked at her fiercely in the dim sunlight. He wore a heavy frown, and with the strap of his high-domed hat underneath his chin, his jaw jutted forward in order to keep the hat from falling off.

"Now, miss," he said, severely.

Sev coughed briefly.

"I'm sorry, Officer, was I doing something wrong?"

This appeared to disconcert the policeman, who had taken it as read that she was a crook and would not only know it but confess it immediately. He had the look of someone who had just joined the force and was as yet ill-equipped to deal with innocent women, though his older brother had promised to show him how one day. He rallied magnificently however.

"Well, I think we both know the answer to that, my lad— er." He bent down slightly and peered at her. Sev stared back, baffled. The idea of being taken for a man just because she was wearing pants hadn't occurred to her. The idea of her being a woman of her age without a dress on hadn't occurred to the unfortunate policeman either, but something about her shirtfront and hairstyle was nudging ineffectually at the edges of his mind.

"I think we'd better take you into custody until we get this sorted out. I seem to remember," he went on, gaining strength and conviction as he got back on solid ground, "a face like yours 'anging around the Bishop's Park doings of a fortnight ago. Caught up with yer mates yet, 'ave you? We knowed there was another man, wot passed the goods along."

Sev had broken into a wide smile. "That's great," she said. "Fantastic. Okay, say, 'What's all this then?'"

He didn't appear inclined to indulge her. "Come along then, my lad."

"Am I nicked?"

She'd succeeded in irritating him, but that was his fault for being a walking cliché. He reached round, caught hold of the back of Sev's shirt and yanked her towards him, now definitely disturbed by the presence of something underneath it that probably shouldn't have been there. Hormone therapy at this stage, she figured, was at best experimental.

"Hey!" said Sev angrily, thrashing around and trying to escape. "Let me go!" The policeman caught hold of her arm as well, and propelled her bodily along the sidewalk, informing the watchers on the street that there was nothing to see here, move along, move along.

"Ouch!" he added, as Sev kicked him on the shin.

At this point a man who had been watching with the sort of detached amusement that is an offense to all sensible, right-thinking persons finally went and caught up with them.

"Hold up a moment, Harry."

The policeman gave off haranguing Sev about her criminal tendencies and poor choice of company and/or clothing, and turned towards the interloper obediently. Sev twisted in his grip and wished to be taller. The other man caught her attention by bending swiftly, catching her chin in his hand and staring her right in the eyes for a moment, narrowing his own and grimacing.

"I recognize this one, Harry," he declaimed, straightening up. "Where'd you pick him up?"

"Just on the corner, over there," said Harry obediently, gesturing back where they'd come from. The newcomer turned his inimical stare on the area, noted the lone kitchen chair standing at the back of the alley, nodded decisively, and turned back. " 'Ad him down for the Bishop's," said Harry helpfully as soon as he'd regained the man's attention.

"Bishop's? Nonsense. We've got them all. No, PC MacReady, this one's due for much, much worse." The man bent down again slightly till he was right at eye level with Sev again, and spoke slower, for emphasis. His voice was deep with oddly feathered edges, tending to whispers, and what she thought of as Very Proper British. "Much— *much*— worse."

"Really?" Harry was intrigued. "What's that then, Mister Simon?"

"*Murder.*" The word dropped into the policeman's inquisitiveness like gin into tonic; Harry jumped, looking surprised and gratified all at once. "And," Mr. Simon went on, "burglary, vandalism, banditry on the King's Highways, refusal to admit personal gender, bathing too frequently, arson, and crimes of fashion."

Sev was now staring blankly at him. He stared impassively back at her. She narrowed her eyes at him, in response to which he widened his and threw in a raised eyebrow for good measure. Thus reassured, she relaxed into the policeman's grip and gave up struggling.

Harry looked at her as well.

"It's a fair cop," said Sev.

" 'Fraid I'll have to take custody of this one, PC MacReady," said Mr. Simon gravely. "He's wanted on trial in the King's Court at once, and I'd hate him to be late for his own execution."

"Of course," said Harry importantly, and transferred the grip on Sev's shirt to the other man's grasp. The unlucky bobby glared at her. "He kicked me, you know," he informed Mr. Simon.

"Believe me, that will be added to the list of his charges," said Mr. Simon with immense gravity. "The King, being a fair-minded and just man, looks on all crimes as one. That is enough to hang him, even had he not committed all the others."

Harry nodded violently, and lost his hat in the process. He began backing away, still nodding and trying to get his hat back on, then stiffened his spine, saluted, and marched away. Mr. Simon took a harder grip on Sev's shirt and yanked her back with him as he walked backwards.

"Okay," she said, trying to turn around. His fingers were clenched too tightly in fabric of her t-shirt to allow it. "Who are you, really?"

"All in good time," he said, and then he sat down and perforce she did too, abruptly, on his lap, leaning back against him. One of his hands found her wrists and held them tightly while the other found the YDI and fumbled with it. He muttered, "Ye gods, how primitive," in her ear in an accusatory manner, growled at the Indicator, and they were back in Matthew's basement.

She stumbled up and off his lap and leaned against the railing, feeling as though she needed to get her breath back even though she hadn't really done anything worth losing it in the first place. *How nice to be back in the basement*, she thought, her thoughts a bit scattered. *How nice not to be in whenever that was just now.*

When she at last turned around the man had crossed

his legs, folded his arms, and was sitting with an easy nonchalance on the time-traveling kitchen chair as he dedicated a thorough stare to Sev herself. He was somewhere approaching middle age, though in a vague and indirect manner, sidling towards it hoping it wouldn't notice. Black hair was lightened here and there with grey and his eyes looked like they'd earned their lines by much staring at unsavory sights. Such as this one. She straightened up.

"So I guess I owe you a thank you."

"I suppose you do," he said, and stared harder. His voice, now that they were away from the past and into the present, suggested a former accent that was not only nearly unrecognizable but clearly beyond repair. She wondered if he'd really talked with that heavy, heady British accent, once upon a time.

She shifted uncomfortably under his gaze but couldn't think of much else to say, so she shrugged and leaned back against the railing. "Well. Thank you."

"Who are you?" he demanded. "Other than so obviously new at this you should be embarrassed for yourself. *I'm* embarrassed for you and I don't even know you. What's your name and your call number?"

"Sevannah Carlson, but look, what—"

He'd whipped a small notebook out of the pocket of his now out-of-period suit and was scribbling her name down as well as, by the look of it, a few choice observations. She frowned and tried to look at what he was writing. He hunched his shoulders over it and barked, "Call number?"

"I don't know what that is."

He glanced back up at her, incredulity in his eyes. "Did no one explain anything to you? You didn't even read the FAQ?"

"Well," Sev said with a poor attempt at unconcern, "there's a sheet of paper with operating instructions over here but other than that— what do you mean, did no one explain anything to me? Who would have explained? What's to explain? What's going on? And what is that?"

He'd apparently found the call number on the back of the left rear leg of the chair, and was scribbling that one down as well.

"You have to be a little specific with these machines," he advised her. "When it comes to recall, getting it back to your home base, it can be like elevators."

"They go up and down?"

He stared at her a moment longer. "You hit the button and wait to see which one shows up first. If you don't call your machine by its personal ID number, you're liable to get whichever machine is closest; and if you get a machine whose owner is large and prone to irritability, you can end up in a lot of pain. Not to mention, a home base like this, some of the machines aren't even going to fit in here," he added, glancing around the room. "Having your house displaced by a temporal-real time machine that looks like a submarine is not an experience easily recovered from, especially if you get crushed underneath all the rubble."

"So— hang on a minute," said Sev, shifting to climb onto the metal railing and sit down, "you're trying to tell me that there's all these other time machines out there—"

"Tons," said Simon easily, with a shrug.

"Wow," said Sev. When he looked at her she blinked rapidly and said, "I mean, it's just, you're right, this was my first trip. When you suddenly go for a ride and discover that time travel isn't just science fiction, and then you get told it's as common as, as *popcorn*— I just wasn't expecting this whole—" It took her a minute to find the proper word for what she meant and she gestured gymnastically to try and give him the unspoken scope of her idea. "Shebang."

He stood up abruptly. "I knew it. This isn't your machine, is it? You didn't build it."

"You're absolutely right."

"Who did?"

"My boyfriend."

"He must have gotten in touch with the Corporation," he said, emerging past her through the railing and starting to pace. "Not rich, your boyfriend? Or if he is, he's stingy."

"Not rich. Definitely not rich. A little stingy. We always eat at chain restaurants. Why?"

"Couldn't pay the Corporation fees," said Simon triumphantly. "But then, isn't that the plight of most of us? Couldn't even manage the retainer probably, rushed home and decided to build this. No wonder I don't recognize the call number, it wouldn't be in any of the books."

"He," said Sev, remembering suddenly, "gave me the impression that he'd come up with all this on his own."

The man gave a brief, dismissive hand gesture. "He was lying. Probably trying to impress you. There's plans available on the Internet, if you know where to look. A very basic five-century free one, and three upgrades of increasing price and scale. Not a patch on what the Corporation offers, though, for a mere paltry eight million or so." He smirked, and shook his head. "One of these days, I swear, they'll hack that design too."

"Corporation," prompted Sev, returning to one of many things he'd said that she didn't understand.

"Rechtzeitig Corp.," said Simon promptly. "Their motto is 'In Good Time'. They're bleeders. They'll suck you dry. You know, it's not just eight million for the plans. God knows if it was *just* that we'd have all those American millionaires flying through time so fast we'd have head-on collisions on a daily basis, and it's difficult to have an accident when you're talking about practically instantaneous travel. But eight million for the plans, *and* a fee each time you travel anywhere, and let's not get into the roaming charges. It mounts up, do you see? No one could sustain that. Well. Almost no one. Certainly not me."

"But— you were time traveling. I saw you."

"Aha," he said, and he gave a wide grin, ducking down to put his finger in her face and shake it at her. "Therein lies the secret of my continued existence, as a matter of fact. How do you manage to escape the petty bureaucracy of everyday life in the nineteenth century? Discover how to time travel without a machine. Only those of us who are very very clever can figure out how." He stood and just grinned at her for a moment, eyes half closed, savoring his long-ago victory of intelligence. The smugness was so palpable she itched to hit it. "The rest of us just turn Anarchist and build cheap machines. Still need a call number but they're randomly assigned by a site on the Internet; if you can hack it to access it, you can hack it to not inform the Corporation that you hacked it, therefore your number doesn't go in their books, therefore they can't type it into their recall and yank you out of whenever you've gone and lecture you to death before they slap you with a hefty fine of, let me see, eight million dollars. That's just the first time, of course— legitimate businessmen like the Corporation's suits like to think of themselves as principled. After that, for repeat offenses, you get beaten to death. But hey, all in the game—"

"So let me get this straight," said Sev slowly, shifting on the railing which wobbled beneath her. "Time travel is real. It seems to be run by some Corporation the name of which I can't pronounce. They charge you a lot of money to travel. Some people pay it. The rest of you form secret societies on the Internet like any good subculture and skip around in time avoiding the Feds."

"Well, it's not anywhere near that simple."

"Simple?" she repeated incredulously. "I had to imbed a corkscrew in my brain to get it around that. *Simple*, what are you talking about? How could it be any more complex than that without being a Robert Altman film?"

He just grinned at her and she shook her head.

"Okay, so how does it work, then? It's a chair. It doesn't look anywhere techy enough to actually be a time machine."

He waved a hand dismissively. "The chair itself isn't the important thing. It's just the vehicle, connects to the main hub."

"I don't see any connections."

"We're not Philistines. We've gone wireless."

"Wireless. That's all I need. What's wrong with plugging things in, is what I want to know." She folded her arms. "So it's not just the past, then?"

"Definitely not. The future is extremely popular, as a matter of fact. People vacation there all the time."

"So." She hummed to herself, thoughtfully. "Can you tell me what's going to happen, then?"

"For starters," he said slowly, looking her up and down, "that railing's about to collapse."

The metal had been vibrating and moving in an agitated way for a while now, but she'd been too distracted to notice. She leapt off it and stood before him.

He grinned at her. "After that, it's pretty much up to you. Not everything of course— but it's all to do with what you let affect you. And what effect it has."

"What is—" She paused, and shook her head. "No. I don't quite. Look. Matthew tried to explain it to me. He used all sorts of long words that I didn't understand."

Mr. Simon stood up, and looked thoughtful. "Well, how I usually go about it is explaining it as time," he used some demonstrative hand gestures, "being like a river."

"Isn't that a song?" asked Sev.

He went on, anyway, ignoring her. "You see, it's not so much moving forward and backward as moving upstream or down." More demonstrative hand gestures. Sev crossed her arms.

"So what's the present then?"

"The present?" He wrinkled his nose. "Sort of near the bank, as it were. Moving slowly. Time travelers move fast. Up and down, back and forth, zipping by."

"And what if you're stuck without a paddle?"

"Honey," he said with a snort, "you've just described the plight of mankind in general."

She stood before him with a slight frown— the *honey* was, she thought, uncalled for— trying to take this all in and deciding to focus on something more easily understood. "What's your name, anyway? Really Simon?"

"Sort of really Simon," he said, fumbled in a pocket, and handed her his card.

It said, merely,

Sime (In Time)

"Hmm."

"I take it you don't have eight million dollars," he said thoughtfully, turning away from her and perusing the interior of the basement with the air of a connoisseur.

"Well, you're right about that. What do I do, then? Join the Anarchists?"

"Sure, if you want," he said, with a shrug. "Every little bit helps. The Corporation's been running their crooked business for hundreds of years, you know. That's the benefit of a business in time travel, I suppose. Always allowing for inflation of course, or the fee would still be one pound six in England and a handful of beads and a deer here in the US. It's like everything else now— nothing but an industry, and one that turns a tidy profit. It might turn an even tidier one if more people knew about it, but it's in the Corporation's interest to keep it as quiet as possible. Keeps their business exclusive."

"How you suppose Matthew found out?" she asked listlessly.

"Matthew is the boyfriend?" He waited for her nod. "Well, if he had any sort of creative-science bent he might have supposed it and worked towards finding whether or not it was true. That happens a lot, actually, more than you might think. Or he might have had an encounter with a big-mouthed time traveler himself. That happens even more than the other. Why can't you ask him yourself? For that matter—" He glanced around the room. "Why didn't he take you on your first trip? Or at least tell you about period dress— look, there's a costume closet over there in the corner. That would have come in handy, don't you think?"

"He's gone," said Sev, shrugged, and shook her head. "He disappeared about two weeks ago. Everyone's looking for him, the police are being disturbingly helpful, my worldview is all challenged, and I just— I broke into his house, and this is what I found. He'd told me that he was working on a time machine, but that's it, and I never even saw all this." She waved her arms around the shabby, overcrowded basement with its confusing contents. "Here I am, I take a nice rest on a kitchen chair, hit a button, end up in wherever— or whenever, sorry— that was."

"London, England, 1856," said Sime. "Good going. Lucky for you I found you before the Corporation's watch dogs did."

Sev heaved a sigh and sank onto the cement floor, her back against the railings. "Can you help me find Matthew? I mean, you know your way around, right? Or maybe you could sort of direct me through a network of your friends, the Anarchists I mean, and someone else could help me? I'd do it on my own, but— you saw what happened in 1875."

"1856."

"See!" she said, spreading her arms. "That's exactly my point. I'm lousy at history. I failed all through school, and that's been longer ago than I care to think about. I don't do dates. I couldn't even remember when my own birth date was until I was about twelve years old. People kept asking me if I felt any taller and I was just all confused."

"I've always said that an amateur historian is a terrible thing to turn loose on history. I suspect you're even worse." He rubbed his chin. "You certainly gave that poor bobby a few worrying moments. Talk about having your worldview challenged."

"That's another thing," said Sevannah. "Why are all British cops called Bobby? Is it a law?"

"Now you're just being ridiculous." He sat down beside her and turned to her seriously. "Look, Sevannah Carlson, there is something about this that doesn't sit right with me. Your Matthew's been missing for two weeks now?"

"Yeah."

His eyelid twitched. "Time travel is a wonderful thing, you know. There are practically no limits on it, once you get past the Corporation and if you have an adequate machine, which despite the appearance of this one, it certainly is." He smoothed a hand over the top of the chair's back. "Not only can you do wonderful things with it, you can do them and return home the exact moment after you left, and no one would be the wiser. If Matthew was just off gallivanting in time like a good little Anarchist, thumbing his nose at Tendence and Cavile and interfering with established historical events, he should have been back. In fact, you should never have known he was gone."

Sev looked at the cement floor, carefully noting the crack in it that looked like the outline of Texas. She was quiet and thoughtful. None of what Sime was saying seemed to be leading up to anything good.

"And not only that," the time traveler went on, "but he's not like me. He needs a machine to travel or he wouldn't have wasted time building one. And if that's the case—" He paused, and looked over his shoulder at the chair. Sev froze and then looked slowly in the same direction, as though expecting the chair to suddenly be doing something horrific. Sprout teeth and wings, maybe, and start chasing them around the basement. "Then what's it doing here?"

She waited a moment.

"So what are you telling me?"

Sime sighed.

"Well, either he got to some nice year he's going to enjoy for a while and the machine malfunctioned and got called back here, thereby stranding him in whenever— or— Sev—" He took her chin and turned her to face him. "Or someone caught up with him."

"And by someone, you mean the Corporation," she said steadily.

He nodded.

"Meaning a fine and— let me guess what happens if he can't pay the fine. Which he can't."

Sime nodded again.

"Meaning—"

"We can go and look for him," Sime offered hurriedly.

"Usually if someone is captured there's some sort of notification to his home time."

"Like a letter?"

"Nooo," said Sime, looking a bit worried. "More like— remains. But don't— don't look like that, Sev. Two weeks is much too long a time to torture someone for. There is very, very little chance that he got caught after all, now that I think about it. Which means that he's somewhere out there enjoying some nice time period. Like Hawaii. In the 30s." He stood up, and held out his hand. "Come on."

"So what do we do, then?"

"Try and figure out where he is so we can go and bring him back." He entered the railing again and advanced on the machine purposefully. "It's at times like these I really wish these things had a black box—"

Chapter Three

Sime was rambling.

"The rules are somewhat amorphous. We hack a signal from the mainframe and we're at where and when we want to be. Most travelers tend to stress the 'when' part, but really, when you're doing research on the French Revolution and you end up checking out 1790 in the Catskills instead, I think the 'where' is important too." He frowned thoughtfully. "Then there was that disastrous Beatles concert. The balcony would have been fine. Getting trampled outside by fangirls who were unable to secure tickets was not."

"Sime, I'm getting flashbacks to the Eternal Professor. It is not pleasant."

"The Eternal Professor?"

"My social history teacher. His lectures lasted forever and hit everything. Our other nickname for him was 'Drunk Grandma.' Look, can't we just check his browser history, or something?"

They were sitting on the floor in front of the machine, sifting through the folio of papers that had been shoved underneath it. It wasn't so much that there was a lot of material to search through for clues as to Matthew's whereabouts; it was deciphering Matthew's college-trained handwriting that was providing the problem.

Sime gave her a pitying look. "Any Anarchist worth his salt turns that option off, first thing. Nothing's really secure, you know? Anyone could hack in and see what medieval porn he's been watching."

"Just, ew," said Sev, wrinkling her nose, but Sime went on obliviously.

"You say *browser history* like you want to say *rap sheet*. Clearly you don't have a lot of experience with technology, and an innovation like time travel is enough to blow the mind of even the most hardened geek. You should probably lie down for a while. Drink some chamomile tea."

"Who are Tendence and Cavile?"

Sime looked up at her briefly, then swiftly back down. He didn't say anything, but frowned and laid another paper aside.

"I can't get this one— it's like he's born in America but educated on Mars."

"You mentioned Tendence and Cavile," pursued Sev. "You mentioned them in a way that didn't sound like you liked them all that much. It was Tendence and Cavile, right? Funny names."

"Funny guys," said Sime under his breath.

"They work for the Corporation?"

He looked up at her again and seemed to reach a decision.

"They do. They're the enforcers. And not only that, the custodians, jail-watchers, judges, jury, and executioners. All in a day's work to them. Not nice people to know."

"Do you?"

"Do I what?"

"Know them?"

He paused. "I've had run-ins. Never up close, but they've been on my tail."

"How come not up close?"

"I know it wasn't up close because I'm not dead yet. They are vicious, Sevannah Carlson. It's all a matter of fact to them but it just—" He shook his head. "We're going to try and stay out of their way. Okay?"

"Okay. Sounds good." She shifted through another paper and ran a finger down the list of— well, it was hard to tell what it was a list of, exactly. "What exactly do they do?"

"Sevannah."

"I'm curious."

"You're morbid, is what you are."

"I'm not being morbid. I just want to know what I can expect if they've caught Matthew," she said steadily, and this time when he looked up at her it was not brief. His gaze locked with hers, and he seemed to be feeling her out, determining what exactly she wanted out of this conversation: the truth, or comforting lies.

She faced him, chin up, eyes only slightly crossed from the close proximity.

"The Corporation employs scouts, sort of like moles, that infiltrate the Anarchists' Trust, find out call numbers, and inform the authorities. If you travel fast enough, especially if maybe one of the numbers is off, you can stay just ahead of them, but they'll follow you. They follow any Anarchist they get wind of, through any times he travels, and they follow fast. They're like me, they're adepts. They travel without a machine. There aren't very many of us— Tendence and Cavile were the firsts. They're not like normal police, Sev. They're—" He paused. "Sadistically intelligent."

"That's a weird phrase."

"It's accurate. They're bloodhounds. They can smell you out no matter where you are, and once they're on the case they'll follow you anywhere. Through time, through space, through a vacuum, into a black hole."

"Really? A black hole?"

He paused a moment, then recanted. "Well, no, not a black hole. They're not stupid."

"And when they catch you?" she prompted.

He took all the papers he'd gone through and shook them together, tidying up the corners briskly and laying the stack neatly to one side.

"They take all the years you've traveled, add them up, and tack them onto your present age, effective immediately. That's how I'm pretty sure your Matthew hasn't been caught by them. Not yet."

"How are you pretty sure? I don't think I understand."

"Because there's not a mummy in the kitchen," said Sime briefly.

Here is Cavile, looming, broad-shouldered and nattily dressed, toting an out-of-place umbrella, smiling his gentle smile. Here is Tendence, a bit smaller, in a pin-striped black jacket with a purple tie, square-rimmed hip-young-school-teacher glasses, really great cheekbones and a ravenous mouth.

Someone has tried to run far away, but they've caught him.

Tendence writes the man (puddled on the floor, shaking, whimpering, wetting himself in terror) a ticket. Neat copperplate hand, the result of practice, the hand of one who means there to be no mistake about what's being written.

He tears the slip off and shows it to Cavile, who shakes his head— "How many years?"— and tsks.

Tendence tries a few times to hand the man his ticket, but gets no cooperation and ends up pinning it to his lapel.

"It will be just one moment," he informs him politely.

The illegal time-traveler comes back to himself at the breakfast table, with his wife and son. The ticket begins to take effect immediately; his punishment ticks away as he ages rapidly, and more rapidly dies. He stiffens, decays, rots, and becomes a husk in a matter of minutes, but because of the two hundred years he's swindled, it's nearly half an hour before his bones become a pile of dust on the dining room chair.

"I think I've found it," said Sev at last.

"Better you than me," said Sime, wearily. He rubbed both hands over his face. "It's to be expected, after all, since I can't even read his writing. One would hope you'd have learned, being his girlfriend and all."

She didn't bother to correct him with *fiancée, actually.* People who were too specific about relationship titles, she'd always felt, probably had something to prove.

"It's a list," she told him, and scooted over to sit next to him so they could both look at it. "Look, it's got years and names."

Sime looked them over and whistled slightly. "He's inquisitive, isn't he? Look— what's that one say, there?"

"Um— Robin Hood, circa 1224?"

"Good. Not what it looks like then. Your boyfriend's handwriting leaves something to be desired. A lot, in fact."

"He trained as a doctor for two years before he flunked out of college," she said matter-of-factly, and Sime smiled crookedly.

"Doesn't surprise me in the least. Look at this. Your boyfriend was eager to seem with-it, wasn't he? King Arthur, Edgar Allen Poe, Albert Einstein. When in fact he was passively bourgeoisie and outrageously cliché. Matthew," he added in an explanatory way in response to her blank stare, "not Albert Einstein. Any idea what he was planning to do when he'd visited these historical luminaries?"

She shook her head mutely, turned over another few pages from the folio, covered in Matthew's beautifully ornate and exquisitely indecipherable handwriting.

"Half the people on this paper are fictional," said Matthew. "Some are agglomerations, of a sort;

hodgepodged personas."

"Hodgepodged," repeated Sev, biting her lower lip to keep from laughing and not knowing why this was so funny.

Sime was a fast learner. He ignored her.

"All created from several different aspects of several different real people. Legends, you might say. If he intends to go after the truth he's going to find himself with a harder job than he suspected, probably. Unless he's got a healthy dose of reality as well as an unhealthy one of optimism. Jack the Ripper? *Really*. What's he doing, writing graphic novels?" He snorted and carried on running a finger along the letters. "Reading this is like decoding Soviet messages. I don't understand it, and I get the feeling someone's laughing at me."

Sev controlled herself, and concentrated on the papers she hadn't gone through yet, scratching at her ankle absently. She couldn't figure out why it smarted so much for several moments before she remembered that she'd biffed it on the leg of the chair in 1856. Matthew's papers were not exactly fascinating. No true confessions, no plans for world domination. No plans for Sev domination, either, and she twisted her face wryly as she went through page after page of scientific jargon with no mention of who she'd hoped would be an important person in Matthew's life—herself.

"So where do I fit in to all this?" she said, quietly. Sime looked up at her for a moment.

"Sometime in the early twenty-first century," he said shortly, and then, "Here's something sort of intriguing." He handed the paper back to her. "Take a look at one of the last names on the list. Three up from the bottom."

This one was fairly easy to decipher, and only threw her a little because she wasn't expecting it. She looked back at him in confusion.

"But—"

"Yes."

"It's you."

"That's right."

"It's even phrased exactly the way it is on your card. Sime and then 'In Time' in parentheses. Italics and all."

"That's because it's my name," said Sime, getting up off the floor and stretching before settling his three-piece suit more neatly around his spare frame.

"Your last name is 'parentheses, in time, parentheses'?"

"Well, I did have another one," he said with a shrug, and offered her his hand. She took it, still looking at him in confusion, and he pulled her up. "But it's been so long ago, no one remembers it. Not even me."

She looked back at the paper, looked back at him. "Maybe your parents—" she offered. "Just a suggestion."

"My parents have been dead for hundreds of years, now, which is a bit of a problem."

"What?" She dropped the paper and had to bend and pick it up. "What do you mean, hundreds of years?"

"Just two hundred. I was born in 1802. They died when I was three. The orphanage doesn't keep the best records and I wasn't at my most alert at three, you know. I was too busy preparing for my life of being Oliver Twist."

"I've seen the musical."

"Still—" He took the paper from her and looked at it again. "It's interesting he should have me on here. Clearly he's fascinated by the history of time travel, and is looking for someone non-Corporation to set him straight."

"But—" said Sev. "But— I'm confused. You were born in 1802?"

"You want the story? Fine. Sit a moment." He pushed her into the kitchen chair and shoved the YDI away carefully with his foot. "I was born at a very young age to very rich parents who subsequently died of unknown causes. Being heir-apparent and not old enough to be actually heir, my aunt took over the fortune and, as soon as she decently could, claimed I was too much trouble for her to take care of and put me in a local orphanage for the next twelve years. Upon emerging once again from the creaking and rust-encrusted gates I went home only to discover that the house had been sold and most of the money had been used by my aunt, who was living it up during those twelve years. They really didn't care much about fraud in those days," he added ruminatively. "In fact it may not have even been properly discovered yet."

"You were sixteen and broke? What happened to your aunt?"

"She discovered time travel." He made an impatient gesture with his hands. "Not actually 'discovered' it as in 'pioneered it Wright-brothers style'. 'Discovered' as in she heard about it while she had the money to pay for the trips. Took the trips. Didn't come back from the trips. Don't know for sure what happened but I suppose it's possible I might still run into her some day."

"How? If that was hundreds of years ago— surely she'd be dead by now."

He tipped his head to one side and regarded her seriously for a moment. "You're not kidding, are you? You don't actually know?"

"Know what?" said Sev, tiredly, dropping her head into her hands. She was becoming disgusted with this recurring feeling of ignorance and felt that it was time she started discoursing on something she understood very well, like the politics of sale-shopping. Just so she could stop feeling so much like an idiot.

Sime went slowly to his knees before her and looked up into her face.

"Listen carefully," he said, "because I'm only going to say this once. Are you listening? Good. Time travel means never having to grow older, and never dying."

She dropped her hands into her lap and stared at him. "What?"

"I said I was only going to say it once," said Sime airily, and stood back up, brushing off his pant legs with both hands.

"Time travel means you don't die? Time travel is like the Fountain of Youth? I don't get this one, I really don't.

Do you know how *sick* I am of not getting things?" Her frustration showed clearly in her face, voice, and the manner in which she had leapt out of her seat, grabbed him by the lapels, and started shouting in his face.

"Alright, alright," said Sime, smiled indulgently as though to a child, and covered her hands with his own. He made no attempt to prise them from his person, though, possibly because he probably would have lost half his suit in the process. "Alright. You know how I said that Matthew could have gone and come back and you would never have known the difference?"

"Yeah. I got that part. That's straight out of every time travel book or movie I've ever seen."

"Well, *think* about it," he cajoled. "If you lived all the time that you traveled through, how quickly the age would mount up! And if you actually were that age, obviously people would know the difference when their beloveds suddenly turn geezer and lose their teeth. So the only thing that makes sense when you're traveling all that way is to suspend your personal aging process. Which means, my dear Sev, no matter how much time you spend in a year that is not your own, you never get any older. At least," he added thoughtfully, "it hasn't happened yet. *Quod erat demonstrandum.*"

"It isn't either *demonstrandum*," said Sev stubbornly. "How in God's name can you 'suspend' your 'personal aging process'? It isn't possible. It can't be done."

"Said the woman who just hurt her ankle in 1856 while scrambling to get on a time-traveling kitchen chair."

She sighed and resisted the urge to bite him. "Alright. *Demonstrandum.*"

"How's your ankle, by the way?"

"It'll heal." She let go of him and sat down again. "Rrrrrrrgh!"

"What was that?" asked Sime, nonplussed.

"A noise of extreme frustration. Is that how you look like you do, even though you were born so long ago?"

"How old do you think I look?" asked Sime, a pleased

smile appearing on his face.

She shrugged. "Forty-eight. Fifty."

The smile faded.

"I started traveling in earnest when I was forty-one. I can't have changed much since then as I haven't been back to my own time since then."

In response to his stare she said placatingly, "That's what I meant, of course. Forty-one."

He sat down cross-legged in front of her and said conversationally, "I've known people who went forward one year and lived their lives from then on, always moving forwards. Never got older because they were out of their own personal time, but still lived with their friends and family. Managed to do it without telling anyone, though that's a bigger secret than I'd like to keep, personally. Of course, they started losing friends when no one could figure out how they were getting all these face-lifts on the sly. No one likes to have friends that look better than them all the time, you know. It's just— not friendly." Sev waved a hand in agreement. "And if you went back in time and started living forwards, eventually you'd reach the exact time where you left originally and start aging again, so it pays to be alert."

"Well, I can see that."

"But that's what Tendence and Cavile do, you see," he said thoughtfully. "Take you back to your own time and reverse the process so you get all those years all of a sudden. It's not a pretty sight." He smiled slightly. "I wouldn't like it to happen to me."

"Me neither," she agreed solemnly. She folded her arms. "So why are you out of your time, Sime (In Time)?"

"Very good, with the parentheses pronunciation and all!" She plastered a facetious beamy grin on her face, which he mimicked briefly. "I am out of my time because at a certain point I just decided to take advantage of what I learned to do when I was a child. I spent a lot of time when I was growing up traveling around, back and forth. I was always partial to other times anyway, and eventually I just decided I'd better make use of what strength and good looks I had left and embark on the greatest journey of all time— everlasting life." He grinned at her. "At any rate I expect you're probably keen on going to save your boyfriend, aren't you?"

"Oh, yeah!" she cried, startled. Had she forgotten about him? Had she actually *forgotten* about Matthew? How horrible of a person did that make her? And what was she supposed to do about it? "How are we going to find him?"

"There's a meeting of the Anarchists in 1607. Called the Assembly of All Saints, because of where it takes place— All Saints, Ireland, though it wasn't called that then— but might as well call it the Assembly of All Anarchists. More appropriate. True to life. We are not and never have been saints." He chuckled slightly.

"I don't get the joke," said Sev.

"Never mind. Look. We can give that a shot, see if anyone's noticed him. I've already been two or three times, so don't be surprised to see me wandering around. I won't know you."

"Shouldn't we hurry?" she asked, standing up and brushing herself down. She jittered her foot on the floor, suddenly feeling the urge to run. Run through the city, run through time and space, it didn't matter— it was all the same, apparently. "To find Matthew I mean. We don't have any idea of where he is or what's going on, or what could be happening to him— anything could be happening to him!— he's practically helpless without me around."

"If it happens in the future," said Sime patiently, "we've got plenty of time to get there. And if it happened in the past, what do you expect to do about it?" He smiled at her, and it was reassuring, comforting, and unexpected. "It's really all a matter of timing."

She gulped, and nodded.

"First things first," he told her admonishingly. "What did we learn from our little trip to 1856?"

"Don't harass policemen?"

"That too. But before you even leave for whatever time period you're planning on—" He gestured toward the wardrobe in the corner. "What do you reckon they dressed like in 1607?"

Chapter Four

"The great thing about this is that we only have one meeting." Sime was clearly excited about this. He was almost bouncing. "We'd thought about scheduling several throughout history but then we thought, hey, why bother? If there's unfinished business, or if there turns out to be more to talk about later on, all we have to do is show up and talk about it. Often someone will have a different perspective on it, depending on what time they're from. Or two or three different perspectives on it, depending on how many of themself are here. I know, I know, 'themself' isn't proper grammar. It's not my fault the English language isn't equipped to deal with past preventatives and present-future plural honorifics."

"I wasn't going to say a thing," said Sev gratefully, who was not at her best with grammar anyway and hadn't actually noticed anything untoward. "What are you doing?"

He had in fact written "Newbie" on a sticky note and stuck it on her forehead.

"Just so people know," he said, patting her on the arm. "Just so they don't expect great things out of you. Things you're not equipped to handle."

"Like time-traveling while sitting on someone's lap?"

"Oh, much worse," he assured her with a vivid grin.

The Anarchists were gathered in a large stone hall somewhere in Ireland. It was decidedly cold inside, wind whistling through gaps in the roof somewhere high above them. The floor was strewn with dried rushes that were getting increasingly stained and nasty with each set of boots that tramped over them. There couldn't be too many Anarchists, Sev figured, because most of the ones she could see were replicas of other ones she could see; some were enthusiastically greeting themselves and others were politely trying avoid their own questions about what happened later on. Everyone here, she decided, must be incredibly well-adjusted when it came to their own self-image. Personally, she feared, she would be exchanging comments of, "Am I really that fat?" with herself.

"Everyone's in and out of here all the time," Sime went on, gesturing around the hall. "As more and more issues are brought up, the meeting gets longer and longer, but that's not too much of a problem as you can just show up for the more interesting parts."

"How do you know when the interesting parts are going to be? Or— have been?"

"Very good," he said approvingly. "The trick is to get a copy of the minutes every once in a while and see what's been added. See the woman sitting to the right of the head of the table, messing with her PDA? That's Anastasia, the secretary. She's in charge of the minutes so she's the only one who actually has to be here all the time." He shook his head. "I do feel sorry for her. She's been sitting there for three years now, more or less."

"That's got to be tough. Do you feed her?"

"Throw her scraps every now and then," said Sime vaguely. He seemed a great deal more interested in looking around at the assembled Anarchists. "See anyone you'd like to meet? If not, tough luck. We're probably going to have to talk to all of them, just in case."

The Anarchists appeared to take it as a matter of extreme importance that they be dressed for the period.

Sev, quite naturally, had no idea when these periods were, but none of the costumes were anything less than drastic and some of them were verging on frightening, like Halloween at Salvador Dali's house. Ducking and weaving through the crowd for a moment while Sime tossed off-hand greetings here and there, she looked for someone a bit more normal to try and talk to.

There was a man standing just to one side, looking like he was guarding a chair at the left corner of the table. His hair was long and dark, and he wore a shirt with lots of buttons and plaid pants, but he was probably as close to normal as she was going to get. She nudged Sime in the ribs and pointed him out.

"That guy, the one dressed as a pedantic golfer. He looks like he might speak English, at least."

Sime gave her a high-handedly amused look.

"Everyone here speaks English, Sev. I know it'd be kind of conceited to just assume that, so thanks for the effort to display your larger world view, but language barriers aren't a problem here."

She blinked. "Why? Don't any other cultures learn how to time travel?"

"All sorts. It's just— kind of like a country, where you have the main language and then any offshoots form communities. Well, there aren't really enough of us to form communities, but we've all learnt English. Among other things. Some of us, it took longer than others. But one thing we've got is time."

"Alright. Point taken. Sounds good. Who is he, anyway?"

"Barnaby Barrowman," responded Sime promptly. "Expatriate from 2378."

"From that long ago? Really?" She twisted to face him, incredulous.

Sime chuckled and turned her by the shoulders to face front again. "From the future."

She stood in frank amazement and watched the man, who was now picking his nose in what he probably hoped was an unostentatious manner. "I see. We don't evolve much, do we?"

"You don't evolve at all," said Sime, and laughed. "Think of all those hopes held out for your parents or grandparents, in the Roaring Twenties and the Screaming Thirties and the Boring Forties, of the flying cars for everyone, the rocket-ships, the colonies on Mars, the television in every room. The only one they got right was the TV, wasn't it? Think that's going to change? There's not enough money in flying cars and rocket-ships and colonies. Alright to stick advertising on them, but think anyone can read them when they're going by at three hundred miles an hour?"

"So we— stall? That's it? That's all she wrote?"

She had turned to look at him again. Sime watched her with his eyelids drooping at half mast for a long moment.

"That's for me to know," he said, "and you to find out."

She turned away from him and faced front once more. "So. Barnaby Barrowman?"

He shrugged. "Barnaby Barrowman."

They approached him carefully; nobody likes to be surprised with guests when they have their finger in their nose.

"Barn!" said Sime.

"Sime!" roared Barnaby, turning to him and opening his arms widely. Sime obliged him by doing the same and they stood in an attitude of mutual pre-embracement before, since neither moved forward, they dropped their arms and just grinned at each other. Sev rolled her eyes.

"So, how's our favorite Adept?" asked Barnaby, twinkling at both of them. "And who's his pet? Found a Newbie, have we? House-trained it yet?"

"Barn, this is Sev," said Sime easily. "Ignore her glare. We're looking for her boyfriend and have no idea when he's at."

"Tough luck," agreed Barnaby with hardly any sympathy at all. "I'm waiting for my girl at the moment, as a matter of fact. She went to the ladies' room about four months ago and I haven't seen her since. I'm beginning to think she met someone on the way. What's your guess?"

"Never give up," said Sime solemnly, and nudged Sev in the ribs. "Right?"

"Right," said Sev, putting a hand on her wounded ribs. "The longer you wait for a girl, the more impressed she is if she comes back. Giving up implies a lack of interest."

"Interest and stick-to-it-iveness," said Sime, grinning hard. "Two things we've got in abundance, right Sev? Looking for her boyfriend, for instance, is likely to be hard work, but we're definitely determined."

"No idea where he's at?" asked Barnaby, looking over their shoulders in case his missing companion was trying to sneak away while he was distracted.

"He left a sort of laundry list of places he wanted to go. No idea why, of course— he's a mysterious guy, eh Sev?" He nudged her again. She reflected on the tendency of men to turn annoying in the presence of other men. It seemed to happen no matter what time period they were from. She wondered if there was any way to circumvent it and decided, isolation.

"What's he look like? Maybe I've seen him around."

Sime went to nudge her again and Sev caught his elbow and pushed it away, hard. She took a deep breath. "He's tall, with short brown hair. Sort of handsome, in a fairly conventional way. Always neat, always put-together, always symmetrical."

"Symmetrical?"

"I don't know how he manages it."

"Perfectionist?" suggested Sime.

"Probably. Anyway, I think there was a period in the future that he wanted to go—" She dug in her pocket for the paper and unfolded it, slipped a finger down the list. "2019? That's not very far. Why would he want to go there?"

"No reason I can think of," said Barnaby thoughtfully, "but I'm not that up on my history, really."

"We'll give it a shot and find out," said Sime.

"Hold on a minute. 2525's on here too."

"There was a song about that," offered Barnaby advisedly.

"Maybe he just likes it for its symmetrical value," suggested Sime, and his smile was less than genuine.

"Well, it couldn't be for the song."

"Will we go there too?" Sev asked, turning to look at Sime. "I mean, he could be there. There's no particular reason for it— at least, none written down. It's not like '1815— Napoleon', or '1840— Edgar Allen Poe.'"

"We'll go. If nothing else, to satisfy my curiosity." Sime glanced at Barnaby again. "No idea? 2525?"

Barnaby shrugged. "Could be the aliens, I guess."

"Aliens?" repeated Sev, her eyes wide.

Sime nudged her very quickly before she could stop him. "Guess your guy's more of a geek than you thought he was, eh?"

She dropped her head in her hands. "Oh, let's go ask someone else."

"Let me know if you see a girl named Carol," Barnaby called after them as they walked away.

But neither a girl named Carol or a hint of Matthew turned up. They talked to Anarchist after Anarchist, sometimes to different versions of the same one, and no one seemed to have noticed anyone who answered Matthew's description. Sime gave Sev a significant glance after each denial, and eventually she had to stop pretending she knew what for and ask what that meant.

"He probably got trapped in the first time he traveled to, is what it means," he proclaimed. "No one recognizes the description, and let me tell you, Newbies such as yourself are extremely easy to see, usually because they tend, if you'll pardon the expression, to completely bollocks things up."

"I pardon the expression but not the underlying insult."

"Good. Just so we know where we stand. Of course it's also possible," he added grudgingly, "that he's done this a few times by now and is getting good at it. How long has he been working on the machine, do you know?"

She shrugged. "We've only been dating a few months. And I only met him the day he asked me out." Sime nodded encouragingly and she went on. "He seemed peculiarly interested in me. I say this not because I've never had guys interested, but because he was *very* interested. We met out shopping. Then he followed me around at work, is what I mean."

"Where do you work?"

"I manage a dry-cleaning business in the city."

Sime looked aghast. "And risk all those chemicals? You know ten years past your time they discover that those chemicals lead to brain cancer, spontaneous combustion, and asexual reproduction?"

"What?"

"Okay, it was just the one time in the study," said Sime, shrugging. "But still, are you sure you want to take that chance?"

She lifted her hands toward him in a cease-and-desist gesture, and closed her eyes briefly. Unfortunately, when she opened them he was still there. "Anyway," she went on helplessly, "what I'm trying to say is that Matthew pursued me openly, and it was so unusual. Unusual from what I learned of his character later, I mean. Wouldn't say boo to a goose. Wouldn't say egg to a chicken."

"Weird," said Sime, looking around again. "Huh." He caught the arm of a passing Anarchist. "Where's Weaver?"

The Anarchist shrugged and said, "Hasn't been here in any recent millennia I think. Last time he showed up was the version from 1908, and that one didn't stick around long. Had to get back to his run for president."

"Ah." Sime nodded. "Thanks. Will you tell him if you see him to watch out for me? Got a question for him that no one else seems to be able to answer."

She nodded back and walked on.

"Who's Weaver?" asked Sev.

"Aren't you mighty inquisitive," said Sime, and

ignored her.

She was about to ask him again when there was suddenly a great deal of exclaiming and uproar going on, centered around the middle table. Papers flew as Anastasia the Secretary tried simultaneously to get things out of the way, clean things up, and keep notes on what was happening. Apparently a traveler had appeared in midair and, having fallen, landed on her PDA and effectively squished it. He was now sitting on the table, hair streaming wildly and eyes wide, telling anyone who would listen that he was being followed.

Sime forced his way through the crowd to reach him. They obviously recognized each other, for the man stumbled off the table and towards him.

"They're coming, Sime! They're coming!"

"Who's on your track, Oedipus?"

"They—"

"Just tell me who and I'll fix it, okay?"

The old man looked suddenly even more haggard, and stared at Sime wordlessly. Sime sighed harshly and ran his hands over his face before he stepped forward and offered one to Oedipus.

"Come on. I'll get you out of here."

The man took Sime's hand without hesitation. It echoed Sev's own situation, and forced some introspection that she did not quite feel ready for. In the middle of her own insane experience, she had trusted Sime without question. Was it just some indefinable quality the man exuded? Was it charisma? Was it virtue? Was it just basic old-fashioned trustworthiness? Whatever it was, she wasn't the only one to feel it. The crowd stepped back as he led Oedipus through the room, murmuring slightly about how Sime would make things better; Sime would make things alright.

Sime stopped in front of Sev, briefly.

"May I borrow your machine?"

"Why—"

"I can't travel without one if I'm carrying someone

else," he told her quickly, leaning down to speak directly to her, "and I need to take him far away from here."

She looked in his eyes and there it was again— *trust me*, they said. *Believe in me.*

"Alright," she said, and he was gone immediately.

She stood alone in the room and glanced around at all the people, still watching her eagerly. There were murmurs here and there of, "Sime's pet," and "Sime's Newbie," and, "Another stray he picked up, no doubt." There didn't seem to be any surprise among any of them, and she wondered how often her savior did this: jump time-lines to reach the unreachable, and reach out.

Sime was back with a suddenness that made her stumble backwards, clutch wildly at air for a moment, and then trip over someone's shoe. He glanced down at her curiously as he addressed the crowd.

"We made it to 5801. There's air, and a little plant life, so maybe."

He let the sentence hang there open-ended. Everyone nodded as though he'd given a thorough explanation, leaving nothing out, instead of a cryptic half-finished remark that left Sev completely and utterly confused. He offered her his hand and she took it.

"What do you mean, air and plant life? That's all? In 5801?"

"B. C." said Sime, shortly.

Sev deflated. "Oh." There was a pause. "Oh!"

"It's one of the years we've never seen Tendence and Cavile," he explained. "We don't know why. But there's a chance they won't be able to follow him there. He also probably won't make it very long," he added grudgingly. "He's an Adept, but he can't risk traveling on his own. He'll be caught in no time. He's got no machine and nothing to make one with, and there's a limit to how long you can last on algae." He frowned. "I think. I admit I've never tried it myself."

"*Algae*? Can't you just, you know, go back and get him?"

"Of course not, Sev. That would just be stupid."

"I mean, *wait*, you know. Wait till Tendence and Cavile would be gone, or have, I don't know, moved on or something, and then go back and get him!"

He looked at her as though she wasn't the brightest freak in the circus.

"There's no way of knowing if they're there or not. I didn't set up a video camera, you know. And it's— Sev—" He leaned closer again, speaking quietly for just her to hear. "It's quite likely— it's very likely— that they found him immediately after I took him there. I've told you before, they're bloodhounds on the trail. They'll tree you every time. This is not the first time I've had to do this."

She stared at him. "Then why couldn't you have left him here?"

"What?"

"Yeah! Left him here, and we could all fight them!"

"No, you don't understand, Sevannah. No matter what, we can't risk them finding all of us. It would only be a matter of time." He laughed a little, ruefully. "Just like everything else."

"They can't take all of us at once!"

"They don't need to. *Time travel.* I keep trying to tell you. They have ways."

Sime." She faced him seriously. "That man was terrified. I've never seen anyone look like that before. How could you just leave him there, on his own?"

He'd been looking at the floor, studiously. He raised his head swiftly now and caught her square in the face with eyes suddenly narrowed and piercing.

"I did what I had to, because there was no other choice. That's an end to it. If we're to prevent the same thing happening to Matthew, we'd better get going. It's up to you."

She stared at him for a long moment and he only looked back at her, not giving an inch. No matter how hard she tried to cow him into shame with her glare, it wasn't working. He'd seen so much more than she had— far too much to be gotten at now. She was never going to catch up. She folded her arms; no effect.

Finally she closed her eyes and sighed.

"Alright. Where are we going?"

"We're going to assume he's somewhere in that shopping list he left for you," Sime told her, gesturing to her pocket. "As it doesn't really matter where we start, pick one at random or a time you've always wanted to visit or something that looks appealing or, I don't know, do eenie-meanie-minie for all I care. Just pick one and we'll be on our way."

She dug the paper out and looked it over dubiously.

"Time and space," she said. "When we get to the time, how will we know where he would be? You don't have a time-traveler locator or something?"

"Unfortunately I left my radar in my other pants pocket," said Sime dryly. "We're just going to have to do our best, aren't we? Come on, Sev. Give it a shot."

She shook her head, closed her eyes, stabbed with her finger at one of the times on the list. She opened her eyes in a squint and looked at it.

"You've got to be kidding me."

"Robin Hood it is, then," said Sime grimly. "How on earth he expects to find a fictional-though-fact-based character or even what on earth he expects to do with him when he finds him— well, lets go ask him, shall we?" He sank back onto the time machine and beckoned Sev towards him, casting a final glance at the inside of All Saints. She sighed, put the paper back in her pocket, and watched as he flipped the YDI. He hesitated perceptibly, but went along with the date on the paper— 1224.

"Well," he said lightly, "we're off on another whirlwind adventure."

And they were gone.

Chapter Five

"And they can understand us— how?"

"I keep trying to tell you. Look, this is my patient voice."

"I think," said Sev, "that's actually your condescending voice. I may be wrong."

Sime shrugged and pulled her along. "Same difference."

She dragged her feet till a root tripped her and took the fun out of it.

"Sime, I'm just trying to get this all straight in my head. I know it's probably a losing proposition, but I'd like to try. We go to different times, different places. Obviously not everyone's like the Anarchists, and not everyone's learned English, right?"

"Right. There are no hard and fast rules for this. Time travel is a series of small re-writes. Now, it's a nice idea to try and avoid the butterfly effect—"

"Or at least that awful film."

"—but impossible, in the face of it. Look. We speak English, more or less, and they understand us, more or less, because that's what happened, and they did, and we did, because they do, because we do. Little nonsensical time loop, all wrapped up."

She detached her arm from his hand and rubbed at her eyes. "Contrariwise," she said, feeling exhausted already, "what it wouldn't be, it would."

"Well, that's taken out of context," said Sime, "but yes."

"That just feels like a huge cop-out to me."

"It is what it is. Like it or not, we all benefit from things not being logical."

"Oh, good," said Sev, sadly. "I always thought there must be a reason for it."

The woods were unexpectedly beautiful. Not that Sev hadn't seen woods before; even being something of a city girl, her parents had dragged their two daughters up to the closest national forest nearly every summer of her early life. But, she thought, it had been quite some time since she'd been around wood that was living— not cut, stripped, and nailed to a bunch of other planks with sheet-rock over it. As a matter of fact she was a great deal more used to metal, which hadn't ever been alive in the first place, and so she stood in the middle of this archaic forest and told herself to breathe deep: it was unlikely she'd get exactly this chance again.

Especially if the Corporation found them.

Everything was twisted and Edward Gorey-like, dark and strange and stately. Not exactly what she'd pictured as the setting for Robin Hood and his Merry Men. Not that she'd had much occasion to imagine such a thing until now.

Sime stood beside her and sniffed the air, narrowing his eyes and looking very professional at all this.

"They've killed a deer somewhere. This would be their cue to advance on the castle, interrupt the king's party, and throw the deer on the table. Poor thing."

"The king?" she asked, nonplussed.

He looked at her blankly. "The deer."

"I knew that."

He shook himself and went on.

"Then they could have some witty banter, you know. 'Why you speak treason!' and 'Fluently' and things like that—" He trailed off. "That's really all I remember from that film."

"Me too," admitted Sev. "I never particularly liked Errol Flynn anyway."

"Mm. At any rate," and he gestured around himself, widely, at the surrounding trees looming over them. "They must be close. *Avanti.*"

He hooked the chair higher over his arm and strode off through the woods, looking like he'd been looting someone's house while there was a garage sale going on. At least, she thought, the cobwebs had been knocked off at some point. The stuffing was beginning to come out of that slit, though, and she wished she'd thought to stick some packing tape over it when they were at home.

They'd taken a few moments to return to the basement and put on what she thought of as costumes— tights ("Hose," corrected Sime indignantly, "this isn't a Mel Brooks movie.") and tunics and about three extra garments for Sev, one after another, over the tights ("Hose!") and the tunics. Two of these extra were petticoats, or so Sime informed her, with vertical slashes here and there so the underlying colors could show through, and the top one was more like a tunic again, bodice and tails. She had a lot of cloth on and felt like she'd have to be cut out of it if they ever wanted her to change again. She'd said as much. Sime said not to worry; he had a knife.

It occurred to her to wonder why Matthew had stocked his wardrobe with women's clothing as well, and though on the face of it this seemed fishy to her suspicious mind, eventually she decided it was flattering. It meant, she told herself, that he had intended to take her with him one of these days, and only the curious circumstances of his going missing had interfered.

With this settled to her satisfaction, she concentrated on not tripping over the roots of the trees, which twisted in a manner that suggested, if Edward Gorey hadn't been involved, it was only because Tim Burton had taken over before Gorey could get there from the Great Beyond.

She tried to keep up with Sime, who, being more sensibly dressed, could actually see his own feet and where he was putting them.

"How do we expect to find this guy?" she asked, panting.

"I haven't a clue," he called over his shoulder. "If a team of historians from 'In Search of Robin Hood' couldn't do it, it's not entirely likely we'll succeed. Still, not to be a pessimist, because remember we have something they didn't."

"What's that?" She was panting harder now, finding it increasingly difficult to get her breath. Sime had laced her up in back, and she had a feeling he'd pulled things tighter than they should have been. Something she was going to have to get him back for later on, because she certainly couldn't reach him now.

He stopped, though, and turned to face her, smiling kindly as she wheezed up to him.

"A time machine," he reminded her gently.

"Oh yeah," she said, bent over and put her hands on her knees. "There's always that. Interestingly enough, since we have a magical machine anyway— I would have thought we could just land right next to this guy? More to the point, right? Less hassle, easy timing?"

He tossed her an amused glance.

"What's the matter? The pace doing you in?"

"No. It's more the costumes." She stood up straight and jerked at her skirts irritably, trying to disentangle them from around her legs. They had a mind of their own, apparently, they fought her strenuously and just went back to their original positions as soon as she let go. "This is ridiculous. I feel like a very high-fashion pincushion, right before they stick in all the pins. And all my clothes are dirty."

"It's authentic. All clothes are dirty in this century. It's authentic dirt."

"But *I* didn't get them dirty. Do you understand how much this disturbs me? And why doesn't it disturb you, too?"

"Well, it won't be a worry much longer," he assured her, patting her shoulder and walking on. "Legend has it he tends to divest visitors of their clothes anyway."

"What!"

"I did say di*vest*, not *digest*."

"I know what it means," she snapped. "Don't patronize me."

"Fine clothes are pricey these days," he told her, grinning. "And let's face it, they live in the middle of a forest— they're probably pretty starved for entertainment." Seeing as she'd stopped dead, he was forced to take her arm and pull her along with him. "Don't worry, I'm here. I'll protect your virtue."

"But—"

"Come along, Sevannah. How many people do you think get the chance to meet the man who inspired all the Robin Hood legends?"

"I don't know," she grumbled, tripping and holding onto his arm more tightly. "How many?"

"Not very," he answered promptly. "Legends are notoriously difficult to track down. Like I said before, they tend to be a mixture of several different stories, some from different places, some from different eras entirely— nothing really matches up. It's like the saying, 'Never meet your heroes'. There's a reason for it."

"There's always a nasty truth?" suggested Sev, leaning heavily against him as she attempted to navigate the area of a fallen tree, the branches reaching out to her with vigor and animation. They snagged on her dress. She growled at them and pulled away, and sure enough there was the sound of a rip. Several rips in fact. She heaved a sigh and Sime grinned at her again.

"Yes," he said, "always."

And twenty men in period dress dropped onto them

from out of the trees.

"So how close to the legends are we going to get?" Sev whispered to Sime as they were led through the clustered forest.

"I don't know. How close do you want to get?"

"Well— don't you have any idea how similar reality is to the stories?"

"I've been baffled by that question for years."

"Sime!"

"Look, Sev," he said, and apparently would have gestured if his hands hadn't been tied together at the wrists. As it was, he tugged them up and down a few times to illustrate. "Just because I've been traveling for hundreds of years doesn't mean I know everything there is to know. I have in fact never met Robin Hood or any of his equivalents. As for reality, I haven't a clue. I'll tell you my best guesses though. There probably is no Maid Marian."

"Really?"

"Really. There may have been several maids, but no one involved in any way with royalty. If anything Robert will be trying to subvert the sheriff by conspiring with his house-staff to not bring him breakfast on time."

"Robert?"

"Yes."

"Not Robin?"

"Almost certainly not. Maybe not Robert either. Maybe John, or Thomas, or," he did that ineffectual gesturing thing again. "I don't know. Tinnitus."

"That's when your ears ring."

"So?"

"So why not Robin?"

"Sevannah, don't you know anything?" he said with the first sign of irritability and impatience she'd seen in him since she met him. "Do you think people actually get named things that fit? Do you think, Wow, what a coincidence that someone who was named Robin Hood grew up to rob people? While wearing a hood?"

"I thought he maybe wore a hat," said Sev, and shrugged. "With a feather in it."

Sime just shook his head, and they were led into the camp. It was dirty and makeshift and temporary-looking, as though everyone in it was poised to shift at a moment's notice, and shift fast. She wondered how often they had to do so— once a month? Once a week? Once a day? The Merry Men came out from their slipshod shelters and stood, hands behind their backs, watching Sev and Sime solemnly. There were some very young and some very very old, but hardly any in what Sev would consider middle-age— most of them, she remembered, if this bit of the stories was true, would be off fighting a war with the king, while Prince John sat on the throne looking at himself in mirrors and talking to his pet snake.

Blinking, she decided she'd gotten the Disney version mixed up with other versions in her head, but it didn't seem any less real to her so she decided to leave it that way and try and forget about it all together.

The man who seemed to be leading their captors looked Sev over good and slow, then winked at her and went off to find his fearless leader. Sev frowned after him for a moment, then turned the frown on Sime.

"But you really were joking about the clothes? I mean, if they were going to take them, they would have taken them by now, right?"

Sime's reply to this urgent plea, if he was planning on giving one, was interrupted by the appearance of the legendary bandit himself: younger than many of the men there, he was approaching forty if anything, Sev decided. Tall and dark-haired, a thick beard hid the lower half of his face, through which she could make out the gleam of his smile. At least, she thought it was a smile. It was also possible he was just baring his teeth at them for effect.

He was also wearing a hat.

This he swept off in a deep bow to the both of them.

"William Redburn, at your service," he proclaimed. Sime tried to exchange a significant glance with Sev but she ignored him. "What are you fine lords and ladies doing here now, in the middle of the woods with only the two of you? It's far too late for tea; the sun is going down. Would you be looking for supper?"

"Actually we were just looking for you," said Sime. "It was— that is, Sevannah and I had been attempting to— if you don't mind— hey, look, could you take this rope off? I can't talk properly if I can't gesture."

"We're looking for a man," broke in Sev. "A handsome man, about your age, Master Redburn, with brown hair and spectacles. He is my betrothed, we are to be married a fortnight hence. My father and I," she nodded at Sime, "were a bit afraid he's lost his way in the woods and, since you know everything that goes on in your woodland, we thought perhaps you had seen him, or could tell us where he is."

"Father?" said Sime under his breath.

"Shut up," said Sev under hers.

William Redburn laughed. "Aye, to be sure. At your age, my lady, you would want to keep fast hold on the man who's to marry you."

She stared at him. "*What?*"

"Payback by the god of poetic justice," murmured Sime, looking pleased.

"I have not seen this man myself," Redburn went on, "but my confederate tells me in an off-side whisper that one answering his description was seen quite some time ago, wandering the forest to the deep south, bumping into trees and cursing. After a time, he appeared to grow tired of this plane of existence, and vanished completely."

"Cursing?" repeated Sev incredulously. "Really?"

"My confederate tells me further that it has indeed been longer than a month since this occurred."

"Can your confederate take us to where he saw Matthew?" asked Sev eagerly. "If we got this first try it would be great."

The confederate was a lean and elderly man with wrinkles like a Shar Pei. He leaned forward and stood on his toes to whisper in his leader's ear.

"My confederate tells me, no, he cannot."

Sev waited for more than that, but seeing as none was forthcoming, she pouted and frowned.

"Why not?"

"Because there'd be naught to see," said Redburn, spreading his arms majestically in a poorly-timed gesture as it wasn't a very dynamic pronouncement, and he really should have saved the majesty for later, "and we— Ro and I, at least— are not in the habit of wasting time."

"Yes you are, what else have you got to do?" started Sime indignantly, but Ro the confederate had decided to speak.

"Are you going to look for ectoplasm?"

There was a momentary pause.

"What?" said Sev.

"Ectoplasm. Are you going to the site to look about for ectoplasm?"

"I didn't know they had that word back then," murmured Sev. "I mean, back now. For that matter— why aren't they saying more thee's and thou's? What happened to the King's English?"

Sime, ignoring her, said, "Why would we need to? Our man is alive, right enough."

"He vanished straight off this plane," Ro reminded him.

"And straight onto another, no doubt," said Sime in response to the worried look Sev was giving him.

"Are ye sure he won't be dead?" pursued the eager confederate. "People often turn out to be, you know, when they wander this forest. Either they are with us or they are with You Know Who." Redburn looked slightly annoyed at even this vague reference to his enemy, and Ro plunged on. "Sometimes they get on the wrong side of an arrow."

"Is there a right side of an arrow?" asked Sev, who was not as up on archery as she could have been.

"Aye, the non-pointy side," said Ro.

"Why would you think he was dead, other than him vanishing?"

Ro had the grace to look somewhat abashed.

"Well, and I did fling an arrow or two at him as well. He ducked behind a tree but there was a yell. I thought perhaps I'd hit when he stumbled back out and disappeared before my very eyes."

"You shot him with arrows?" said Sev, horrified.

"Now we see whose womb a legend springs from," muttered Sime.

"What are you implying?" snapped Sev.

"Nothing!"

"So, ectoplasm?" asked Ro avidly, and he gave them a smile that was more gum than expected.

"No," said Sime firmly, and would have patted Sev comfortingly on the shoulder had he not been tied up. As it was he knocked her a few times on the elbow with his joined hands; she rubbed at it and glared at him. "He is not dead, and would have no ectoplasm to leave behind anyway; why are you so interested?"

"I collect ghosts," said Ro promptly. "There are many in this forest, many in the castles. I see them wandering about and then disappearing, such as my lady's lord did. There were two such, skin pale as the sunlight and clothes black as a grave, came wandering over the ground where the young man had been. Such callings! Threats against the young man's soul."

Sime had stiffened and Sev looked at him in worry.

"Is that—"

"My lord Redburn," said Sime, and bowed deeply. How he managed it without losing his balance on account of being tied up, Sev would never know. "We have learned what we've come for, and must hasten onwards. Those were not ghosts, but men. My— daughter's intended is in grave danger, and we must pursue him forwards at once so as to warn him."

Redburn rubbed at his beard and looked them over

seriously.

"Aye," he agreed. "It does not sound like a very safe or tenable position for my lady's lord. Be you on your way then, and we'll sound the alarm should he come back this way." He gestured to his minions, and they hurried forward to cut the captives' bonds from off them. Sev rubbed at her wrists gratefully, and Sime bowed once more, this time with sweeping hand gestures to rival Redburn's as well.

"Just one last thing," Redburn added as they turned to go. He smiled crookedly at them both. "Those are very nice clothes."

Sev glared at Sime, who just closed his eyes and waited for the inevitable.

"So I'm guessing the reason for your sudden hurry was that those two were who I think they were," said Sev, somewhat intelligibly.

Sime took a moment to sort this out.

"If you mean, was that Tendence and Cavile on the track of your Matthew, the answer is, probably yes."

"And that makes you worried."

"Why? Doesn't it you?"

"Well, yeah." She struggled through a particularly difficult clump of bushes. "But I mean, I know less of what they can do than you do. I've had less, I don't know, experience."

"No one has experience with Tendence and Cavile," said Sime wearily. "If you get any closer to them than their reputation, the echo of them through time, you don't have a chance."

"But having them pursue you is closer, isn't it?"

"Don't go looking for trouble, Sevannah. The fact that they showed up after Matthew means they're at least a step, if not more, behind him. If he's got any intelligence he'll be running as fast as he can, and if he runs as fast as he can— he's got a chance. Maybe."

She walked on for a bit without saying anything, before finally breaking down and pointing out the unhappy obvious.

"But we've got his time machine."

"That's why I hope he's running," said Sime briefly.

"Couldn't we just go back a month or whatever and look for him here?" asked Sev, feeling as though struck with a bright idea. To get it right the second time but at least in the same first place, to have all this finished and Matthew safe home again— it sounded good to her. She liked it. Sime ruined it immediately.

"No," he said.

"Why not?"

"We don't have any idea where he was, to begin with. Or when, exactly. So if you want to spend weeks squatting on the ground in the company of a guy who collects ectoplasm like it was stamps, be my guest, but you'll be doing it without me."

"You never like any of my ideas," said Sev, and proceeded to sulk.

"Like the one where I'm your father?"

"Oh, will you give it a rest?" She stopped and spread her arms out, looking all around her. The erstwhile Robin Hood and his Not Particularly Merry Men had left her only the first garment she'd put on, a beige-ish yellow linen shift. She hoped devoutly that the color was from age or design and not from use. Sime was trudging along stoically in his tights. "Look, we're not doing all that well, here. We go search for Robin Hood; instead we find William Redburn, who steals our clothing and has the audacity to imply that I'm too old to be desirable anymore, and his ghost-hunting assistants who creep me out with their no-teeth thing they've got going on. We miss Matthew by a mile and now he's being followed by the Time Police! May I remind you that this is partially your fault?"

"Really?" said Sime, looking intrigued. "What did I do?"

"You let me choose where to go!" she bellowed. Even as she said it she realized that this was neither wise nor fair, and she folded her arms immediately thereafter and stared at the ground.

Sime, however, laughed.

"What's amazing," he said, "is that you don't seem to get this. Sevannah—" He stepped closer to her and put his hands on her shoulders, bending down to look her right in the eyes when she finally looked up at him. "Sevannah, you are the only person I've ever met who, when they're time traveling and meeting historical characters and seeing different places and changing history with their very presence, the only person who looked around them and said, This isn't going well because we're not immediately achieving our objective. The only person who hasn't found the least little bit of fun in time travel. *Time travel, for God's sake*," he bellowed at her suddenly, a grin still on his face but his tone implying that he wouldn't hesitate to slap her around if that would bring her to her senses. "Instead you're worrying about a man that you don't seem to like all that much anyway— you're doing this out of a sense of obligation when in fact you're kind of relieved that he's disappeared. You're doing this with your eyes blinkered on either side, not looking at any of your surroundings and only seeking out this man who's made his mark on you but without any passion or higher intentions. And that, Sevannah, makes you *the dumbest person I've ever met.* And I," he added as an afterthought, "have met quite a few."

She glared at him.

"Are you finished yet?"

He breathed in deeply, and shrugged. "Sure."

"Good. Should I be sorry for disappointing you?"

"If you like."

"I don't like. But I'm not— it's not that—" She stopped a moment, then walked resolutely onwards without looking to see if he was coming after her. But he was, of course. She trusted in it. She trusted in him. He stayed close enough to hear her, even as her voice grew low.

"I keep forgetting him, Sime. I keep getting caught up in the moment and forgetting why I'm here— and I am here to find Matthew, and when I find him I will gladly go home and try to put this in the past, and we'll get married and I'll make him promise that if he's going to time travel he has to do it with a leash around his neck. That's all."

"And you expect to be happy, living like that?" said Sime incredulously from somewhere behind her. She stopped and turned to look at him.

"Not particularly," she admitted. "But I'm thirty-seven, Sime. It's not like I haven't had a chance to do some living yet. And I don't want to be like my sister, who gets all her experience at someone else's expense. It would be a good life, with me and Matthew, and I would be content with that. Contentment, you know," she added, "is not to be overlooked or underrated."

He came up to her and nodded seriously.

"You and Matthew. I can understand that. I don't necessarily agree with it, but I understand it." He bent down and kissed her on the cheek. "Come on then," he said solemnly, "let's get you and your lord home."

It occurred to her to wonder who he'd left behind in his own time. Who had turned out to be less important than his continued existence, rambling haphazardly through time, never to return? She wanted to ask him, but the words wouldn't come. The moment was too fraught, too heavy. She put it aside for later.

"Sime," she said, slowly, "what happened to all the *thees* and *thous*? There were significantly fewer of them than I expected."

He laughed at her, but she was starting to expect that.

Chapter Six

They had pursued their prey through an eon, over mountain ranges and the sullen sea. Arriving next in the Dark Ages, Tendence breathed deep and smiled lustily. "I think," he said, "I smell—"

"Potatoes," said Cavile, stomach rumbling, nostrils flaring.

"No," said Tendence, and then, thoughtfully, "well, yes. Someone is indeed cooking potatoes."

"Boiling," said Cavile petulantly.

Tendence made a brief, impatient gesture with one lithe and long-fingered hand. "That's not what I was talking about. I smell blood— the blood of an Englishman." He tapped the back of his hand against Cavile's vest. "Try it."

Cavile, obligingly, sniffed deeply. Tendence watched him eagerly until he relaxed, smiled, and nodded. "Ah yes."

"Smell that?"

"That unmistakable Anglo tang."

"Wooden teeth," said Tendence triumphantly. "Early 1800s."

"What a bizarre society," said Cavile politely.

"1800's wooden teeth in the Dark Ages—" Tendence breathed even more deeply, diaphragmatically, as his doctor had shown him. "How beautifully out of place. Ah, the Dark Ages— I love the Dark Ages! They're my favorites." He was nothing if not gleeful, hands in his pockets and bouncing on his heels. "How often does this happen, that business and pleasure coincide like this?"

Cavile considered this with gravity. "Quite often, really," he hazarded, and Tendence grinned and nodded.

"Now for the next part of the chase— finding our man— it is a man, isn't it?— among all this." He gestured around himself at the gloom and mud and desecration. "It looks like someone had a grave-looting party, and invited all his aunts and kiddies but didn't invite us. Isn't that rude of them? Nod once if you agree."

"Very rude," said Cavile patiently.

Tendence swung round to look at him, to see if he was lampooning. His associate, though, looked as serious as ever, so Tendence faced forward once more and slapped his hands together briskly like he'd seen game show hosts do on American television. They seemed to have located the site of a plague of some sort or other, what with all the bodies lying around; or failing that, shortly after a major bomb blast, which was unlikely considering the historical period. Undoubtedly, for anyone with lungs like a normal person it was a dangerous place to be. Even for a time traveler, who was somewhat protected from things like this just by foreknowledge— well, it was possible to die from something other than old age, if you weren't careful, before you got back to your own time. And Tendence was determined that this man should get back to his own time.

"After all," he said aloud, "why should he escape the Outreach Program? Did I tell you that's what they've decided to call it— the Outreach Program? And we are the Outreachers. Outreach Associates. Outreach Enforcers. Outreach Agents." He smiled winsomely at thin air. "Outreach Care Providers."

"Outreach Police," submitted Cavile, and Tendence nodded deeply.

"Perhaps. Perhaps. Only, it's not quite as friendly as

we would have hoped. The aim here is misdirection, not of the eye, but of the mind. Can't it be something that sounds all sweetness and light but is really dangerous as a carefully thrown brick, like a phantom ninja with flowers?"

"Hmmm," rumbled Cavile. "Are we the phantom ninjas?"

Tendence's smile was a knife-edge, a shark's tooth, the grin of a killer rabbit as it goes for your throat. "We are indeed. We are the ninjas. And we are the bricks. And, thanks to a wonderful PR system, we are the sweetness and light. We are everything that is good about time travel. We make this world safe for your children. We work towards a better tomorrow, a brighter future, and a cleaner Earth. We will wipe you right off of it." He turned around and inhaled deeply again, his eyes fluttering shut in something approaching ecstasy. "Mr. Wednesday," he called in sweet treble tones, like a bugle boy. "We've got something for you, Mr. Wednesday, which has your name on it."

Indeed, he'd written the ticket out about two hundred years ago in the future, when they'd been on a boat through shark-infested waters and Cavile had protested the danger of falling in was too great if they confronted their quarry in his stateroom. Tendence had contested that the shock value of their showing up, when Mr. Wednesday had assumed he was safe and sound on this steel boat would far outweigh any possible problems. Cavile maintained that it was an infraction of their duty to the client, to put this man in any harm's way before it was due and right and proper, and furthermore it was a ship, not a boat. Tendence had leaned over the railing, glanced this way and that, looked back at his confederate, asked *Are you sure?* and when he had nodded, heaved Cavile over the railing and into the water that he might get a closer look at it.

When Cavile had climbed back aboard, sopping wet and still toting his umbrella, walking to the tune of wounded sharks hauling fluke far, far away from here, he had said it wasn't funny. But Tendence had disagreed. Eventually they had compromised and Tendence had used the cruise-time to figure out Mr. Wednesday's multiple sins of making free with his chronological state and how much, exactly, he owed the Corporation. Cavile had played endless games of shuffleboard.

Now, of course, the ticket was ready and waiting in Tendence's thin, eager hand. All that remained was to locate their quarry here in a place that, if it was a theme park, would be Deathland. They were reverse ghosts, the long-living among the recently dead. Tendence and Cavile moved at a sedate pace through the piles of things and bodies and things that were also bodies, or had been. Tendence hunted under every nook and cranny and Cavile decorously turned things over and poked at them with the end of his umbrella. He poked a little longer and harder at a suspicious-looking corpse that he was sure had winked at him, until the umbrella broke through and it was evident that it had not. He had to tug quite hard to remove it.

At last there was nowhere to look except a large rock that stood to one end of the preemptive graveyard, and Tendence heaved a disappointed sigh.

"The Corporation isn't going to be very happy with us, you realize," he told Cavile woefully. "Failing in our job at a time like this? With everything in flux?"

"Watch your language," Cavile cautioned him, folding his arms with the bloody umbrella sticking out like a broken bird's wing.

"I said 'in flux'. 'Flux.' Everything is changing, the new President coming into power, the old President dying so mysteriously like that, money changing hands, energy and electricity being used in new and exciting ways, draining the public coffers, filling the executive coffins, manhandling the personnel, laying new carpet and fiddling with the wallpaper." He sighed, if anything, if it was possible, harder. "And we've got to go to them and tell them we missed this one. Is that any track record for an Outreach Agent?"

"It most certainly is not," said Cavile definitely.

Tendence folded his arms and pointed his toes, one

after the other, at the ground, a sort of slow-motion Irish jig. "Ah well," he said at last, "all you can do is your best, is that correct?"

"So I have been told."

"All you can give is your everything."

"Indeed."

"And in the end, the love you take is equal to the love," he paused, "you make."

Cavile frowned heavily, utterly perplexed. "I have not found that to be the case."

"No, no, of course not," said Tendence. "But it scans wonderfully, don't you think?"

"I suppose."

"Still. We've done what we could here, at any rate—perhaps we could move on. What's next on the agenda? Any suggestions?"

"Why don't—" Cavile raised a cautious finger. "—we look behind the rock?"

Tendence cast him a wide-eyed glance, treated the rock to a narrow squint, and laughed derisively. "Don't be facetious, Cavile. No one would possibly be stupid enough to think they could hide behind a rock. Are we children, here? If I close my eyes, do I disappear? Do *you* disappear? Indeed not, I think you will find if you perform the experiment. We are not ostriches. We do not hide our heads in the sand. No, my loyal and ponderous associate, we will not look behind the rock. That is a good rule—" He stabbed a declamatory finger at Cavile's own, and for a moment the two digits looked ready to do battle. "Never look behind the rock. You will not like what you will find. We will now move on, to bigger and better things. We have badder fish to fry." He glanced at his wristwatch. "Rendezvous in 2005?"

Cavile nodded, and the two of them disappeared.

When it was evident that they really had gone and were not going to come back to check again, a very relieved Mr. Wednesday emerged from behind the rock and into the desolate surroundings of the unready graves. His name was in fact Wenesdell— Tendence had always had issues with words— and he could not believe his luck. To have come this close to being— well. The saying went that you could never have first-hand experience with the Corporation's watchdogs, because if you did, there was no way you'd live to benefit from it. Perhaps, he thought importantly, it was time to change that assumption. Perhaps no one had gotten close enough. Perhaps no one had thought it out as thoroughly. Perhaps no one had—

"The wonderful thing about time travel, I find," said Tendence in a friendly manner, from where he'd been hiding close behind Mr. Wenesdell all this time, "is that you can be so many places at one time. Take, for instance, your sister's wedding. Not that you have a sister, Mr. Wednesday. Not that I have one either. But say that you were ordained as a minister and asked to perform the proceedings. There you are with one job already. Say also that your father had died and your sister had no one to give her away. Say also that with the burden of these two jobs you feel you just couldn't relax and wish you could just watch and enjoy from the audience. Say also that you and your sister are the only two family members remaining and she is singularly without friends or acquaintances and yet she would love it if her side of the church was filled to capacity." He gave a wide gesture of empty assurance. "Time travel fixes all these conundrums, Mr. Wednesday; it solves these little potholes in the road of life admirably."

"Please don't back away," said Cavile kindly. "I have been running for some time now, my shoes pinch, and my feet hurt."

"I told you to get something without heels," murmured Tendence to him out of the side of his mouth.

"It says 'looming' on my job description," confessed Cavile. "I signed the contract."

"You think we are fools, Mr. Wednesday?" offered Tendence. Mr. Wenesdell didn't seem to think much of anything; or at least, if he did, he wasn't capable of voicing his opinions at this point. He sank to his knees as they advanced upon him. The safety of the rock was a thing of the past, and there was nowhere else to hide. Tendence held the ticket out to him; with a shaking hand, he took it, and looked on his sentence.

"Congratulations, you've been very difficult to catch," said Tendence.

Cavile leaned over and spoke. "You did very well, really," he informed him. "We had the hardest time we've had in a good while."

"And while it has been gratifying and rewarding, working with you," added Tendence, "we regret that our time, and yours of course, must now be terminated. But do think kindly of us; we've started a new Outreach program, you see, and we'd like it to be well received. Close your eyes, Mr. Wednesday, and when you open them, you will be at home."

The unfortunate Mr. Wenesdell disappeared with a slight pop. Tendence turned to Cavile, rubbing his hands together briskly again, because when the television show hosts did that, they got syndicated and lasted for years.

"Well, I don't know about you," he announced, stretching till his back gave a discomfiting *snap*, "but all this work makes me hungry."

"Me as well, incidentally," rumbled Cavile.

"What d'you fancy? Chinese? Dine-in or take-out?"

"Oh, couldn't we have," said Cavile, gesturing around them, "a picnic?"

Tendence glanced around, and appeared to consider it, twisting his mouth thoughtfully and tapping one finger on his pant-leg. "Well," he said at last, "it is a lovely day for it."

"Given the enormous success of our last venture," said Sime cautiously, "perhaps you'd like to let *me* choose where we're going this time."

"Oh, go ahead," said Sev tiredly. "I don't even care."

"What a brilliant attitude to take towards finding your

beloved. What drama. What thrill. What an inspiration you are to fiancées everywhere. Alright, alright." He waved his hands placatingly as she moved towards him in what was definitely a threatening manner. "I know, you've had a long day."

"I've had a long three months," she said, rubbing her eyes, then returning her arms to their original folded-defensive position. "Ever since I met Matthew, I feel like I've been walking on—"

"Clouds?"

"Eggshells."

He gave her a wry glance. "Are you sure you want me to find this man?"

"It'll be worth it in the end." She looked down at the cement floor, nodded slowly. "I owe him this much, at least."

"Sevannah. You sound like you're trying to convince yourself as much as me."

She looked at him then, the two of them standing in the middle of the mess of Matthew's basement. The shift made her look more frail and waifish by the moment, and she gave a one-shouldered shrug. "Maybe I am."

He sighed.

"We don't want to talk about this right now. We just want to keep moving. If you stop moving, you slow down, if you slow down, you stop moving. Don't ask me what that means, just take it at face value, would you? Right." He took the list from her and studied it up and down, muttering something that sounded very much like, "If I was Sev's scientist boyfriend, where would I be?" and was, in fact, that.

She stood at his shoulder and looked at it too.

"King Arthur, 516?" she suggested.

"Mm," said Sime thoughtfully. "Possibly. But I'm thinking, if you're a scientist who's not got a whole lot going on in his life other than the time machine, you want to go somewhere where men were real men, you know? Back in time to— oh, I dunno— here?" He pointed.

"1712?"

"The good old days of piracy. Sort of."

"Who's Edward Teach?"

He glanced sideways at her, smiling slightly. "You really don't know your history, do you?"

"I really don't. I told you that already. I gave full disclosure. 'I don't know my history,' I remember saying."

"Ever hear the story of Blackbeard the pirate?"

She thought about it for a minute. "He had lots of wives? Killed them and shut them up in closets?"

He had to think about this too. "I think that was a Grimm story."

"I'll say it was. He killed, like, a ton of people!"

"No, I mean— a fairy tale from the Brothers Grimm. Bluebeard. Not Blackbeard."

"Oh." She paused. "Gross."

"Yes. But I'm talking reality here. If we go to 1712 we're certainly not going to find any fairy tales. It's a rough time, and I have to warn you: as a woman you can speak your mind if you want but you're likely to get slapped for it. Doesn't mean they won't listen to you; just means it's a built-in reflex they can't seem to control."

"Speaking as someone who's knowledge of piracy is culled strictly from movies which have either Johnny Depp or Tyrone Power in them," said Sev slowly, "is this something I actually want to get into?"

"I would get rid of any romantic notions you may have," cautioned Sime. "The pirate king isn't going to want to marry you on the spot, the first mate isn't going to fall hopelessly in love with you, any battles that are fought are going to be very brief and very bloody, and no one is under any circumstances going to sing 'I Am A Very Model Of A Modern Major General.' In fact if Matthew is in 1712 it would come as a great surprise to me if he's managed to stay on the right side of cell bars all this time."

"Why? You think he'd—"

"Think he was in Gilbert and Sullivan? Hard to say. I've never met the man. But with any amateur, it's always a possibility. Just something you have to watch out for."

She looked him in the eyes, searching for something to tell her which way to go from here. He looked back at her with some slight amusement. He must have known that even with the boundless and no doubt heartfelt advice he was giving her, he really wasn't any help at all. *This man.* She kept on searching, though, looking long enough and deep enough that eventually he grew restless and gave her a wink, upon which she looked away immediately.

"Alright," she said stoically. "We'll give it a try."

"Are you sure?"

"Yeah."

"You don't sound sure."

"I'm sure, okay? I'm *positive.* Now let's go before I change my mind."

"Hang on, hang on, hang on," he pleaded, catching her arm as she moved past him on the way to the railing and the kitchen chair. She turned back to him. "Remember all that talk about being dressed for the period?"

"Oh. Yeah."

"And if you thought it was difficult in the last dress—"

Some time later, she stood in front of the full-length mirror, and said doubtfully, "I didn't think this is how a possible swashbuckler would dress."

"It depends," said Sime, "on whose swash you're preparing to buckle."

Chapter Seven

Something on the chair seemed to be working better this time; whether it was the chair itself or its expert navigator, Sev could not be sure. But on this journey, they came into existence at the edge of a dock, near where a ship was anchored, or tethered, or whatever they wanted to call it. All Sev knew was that it was strapped to a piling like a dog to a leash, and rose and fell gently in a motion that already made her feel a little queasy. She quelled the feeling firmly and stood up off Sime's lap.

He pulled her back down immediately.

"What—"

"I should have thought to mention before," he said rapidly. "Any woman who is perceived as being 'free'— that is, not belonging to or with any man, or at least, any man that is within beating distance— is automatically fair game, do you understand? I know I said all that about the pirate king and the first mate, but that doesn't mean that you're not going to have some interested parties come along. You know sailors. All after one thing and one thing only."

"Which is what, hardtack?" She pulled his hands away from her. He put them back.

"Sea biscuit," he said, obviously smothering a laugh.

"So what are you telling me?"

"Your best move is to pretend to be with me. My wife, I think."

"Really?" she drawled. "And after we get on the boat and find Matthew? What then? Might be a little confusing, huh?"

"You can say whatever you like, Sev. I'm just warning you." He stood up abruptly, and she slid down his lap too quickly to catch herself standing; instead, he offered her a hand to help her up from her semi-squatting position and she took it, irritably.

"Why's he got to go to these time periods, anyway?" she demanded. "Why can't he go to one where women are respected? Or at least not treated like dogs?"

"Perhaps he can't find one."

She glared at him. "You're from a fairly sexist time period, though, aren't you? How do you manage?"

"Sexist, racist, religionist, classist, everything-else-ist," said Sime promptly. "But it's learned behavior. All I had to do was unlearn it. You get slapped enough times by Modern Woman, you learn pretty fast. I also got kicked," he added helpfully, "if that makes you feel any better."

"It doesn't," she said, grudgingly. "But thank you anyway."

"Don't mention it."

"Is this the ship?"

They stood side by side and looked at it. It seemed huge to Sev, who couldn't remember the last time she'd been on a dock by an actual ship— it may have been never— but it was in all actuality not that big, especially when compared to the Queen's Own. It was built for speed and not for bullying, because pirates had discovered early on that if you weren't fast you couldn't get close enough to bully anyway, and speed-bullying was the only way to go. The sails were dingy once-white and the wood was salt-stained, sunburned black; the figurehead appeared to be either a constipated gecko, or a duck, but was in all probability actually a dragon. There was no name painted anywhere that she could see.

"That's it," said Sime.

She glanced sideways at him. "How can you tell?"

"See the duck on the front? Definitely Blackbeard's vessel. The only question is— why is it so quiet?"

It was silent as a ghost ship; they couldn't even see the figures of any sentries on board. The gangplank, warped and twisted in a highly dangerous way, was down and unwatched; anybody could have strolled up it and taken over. Anybody that knew how, at any rate; Sime said as much. Sev just looked at him.

"Are you telling me we're going to commandeer this ship and take it out into the wild blue yonder?"

"No," said Sime patiently. "But we could steal it."

"But—"

"But we're not going to. I know, I know." He threw his hands in the air in a gesture of helpless resignation to a final fate beyond his control. "You never let me have any fun."

"But Sime— where is everyone?"

"I don't know. Out painting the town red? Sight-seeing? I don't know." He glanced to one side, then the other. "Let's take a look."

"Fine." She started towards the town but was quickly distracted by the fact that he wasn't following her; he was, in fact, walking towards the gangplank; and very quickly, up it. "Sime!"

"Just a look, I said!"

"Sime!" she hissed from the edge of the gangplank, being singularly unwilling to go any further. "Get back down here."

"Bring the chair with you, would you?"

"No! Sime, I don't want to get on that ship."

"Ha," he said airily, walking back down past her to collect the chair. "How do you expect to be a pirate if you don't want to get on a ship?"

"Sime!"

"Silence, saucy wench!" he roared, and then grinned at

her. "I'm kidding. I didn't mean it. Just getting in the mood. Come on. You get in the mood too. Say 'Aye aye cap'n.'"

"Shut *up*, you jerk."

"Mm, close, but try again."

"Sime, what is *wrong* with you?" He walked onto the ship and out of hearing, ignoring her. Shaking her head, she scrambled to follow him, trying to be careful on the gangplank, but even the vibrations of her own footsteps gave her difficulties. This was an insane venture anyway, she decided, and falling into the water would only complete things. "Sime, come back here!"

He popped his head out from behind a man-height coil of rope long enough to grin at her as she came up the gangplank and onto the ship. "I've always wanted to be a pirate, actually. I can't believe I never gave it a shot before! Welcome aboard, lassie!" He crowed the last bit, rolling his r's extravagantly.

"Oh, you—" she said, and the rest was lost in an unintelligible mumble as she chased after him through the ship. He was moving rather quickly, stealthily, and appeared to be looking for something. She caught up with him at last just as he stopped walking, and ran full tilt into him as he turned around to declaim something else piratey.

"Ouch," he said, and caught her by the elbows before she toppled over. "There was no need for that. You could have broken something, or put my eye out. Or something."

"I didn't do it on purpose," she snapped. "Why are you doing this? We came looking for Matthew, not to overtake a pirate ship! You're not supposed to get on the bad side of a pirate anyway, are you? I mean, isn't that one of the things that's generally considered to be not a good idea?"

"We can't get on the bad side of a pirate if we've made off with his ship," said Sime reasonably, getting a firmer grip on her elbow and steering her in the direction he wanted to go. "He wouldn't be able to catch up with us."

"Oh, Sime, I don't think that's how it works."

"Well, I—" he started and was interrupted by the not-so-distant tramp of feet. Exchanging a hurried glance, they rushed to the railing on the deck and looked over. Sure enough, confounding hope and defying explanation, here came a group of men, swarthy with sun and salty with salt, looking as though the ground was too steady for their taste and they were wanting for lack of sea. Their conversation was too far-away yet to make out the individual phrases, though every now and then Sev caught a word here and there, and she was convinced they were speaking entirely in clichés. She and Sime crouched lower to the railing, trying to be well-hid and possibly succeeding.

She whispered to him.

"What happens now?"

"Well, we retreat and find a clever hiding place," said Sime easily, in a fluid whisper that suggested he'd done this before. "Then we wait for them to come aboard, get ready, shove off and head into the open sea before we emerge from our clever hiding places and offer to join their roguish band of salty sea dogs."

"And if we're allowed to?"

"Employed as deck hands, first. Washing the planks, polishing boots, hemming sails, sewing buttons, sweeping the decks, stealing the silver. After that I'm confident we can move up somewhat, perhaps to being lookouts in the crow's nest." He nodded deeply and somewhat haphazardly. "After that, well, and our quarterly performance review, if we've caught the eye of the boss-man and impressed him enough, there's no telling how high we can make it. The stars are ours, babe."

She smacked him. He rubbed his arm and said, "Ouch."

"Can you be serious, please? What if they don't want us as deck hands? What will they do then?"

He rubbed the back of his neck and considered this. "Kill us, probably."

"*Ohhh*," she said, and dodged back towards the gangplank, but it was too late. The pirates had approached the entrance to the ship, and the conversation could now be heard to be a mixture of complaints about the short length of their stay on land, embittered ruminations on the sea and its particular cursedness especially during monsoon season, and irritable monologues on the quality of the ale at that inn they'd just, unsurprisingly, jilted of its money. The fact that they'd announced their intention not to pay when they'd entered and then held the innkeeper at musket-point while he filled their tankards could have had something to do with it.

A woman of spirit and bravery, Sev thought, would have sauntered seductively down the gangplank and coolly informed the men she'd been waiting for them half an hour before slapping them irately and barging off, resulting in absolute freedom with a minimum of fuss. Sev found herself regretting once again that she was not a woman of spirit, let alone bravery. Furthermore, it is hard to saunter seductively while holding a kitchen chair on one arm, and she wasn't willing to leave it behind. She returned to Sime, who smiled at her crookedly and drew her into the small nesting place he'd found. It was a tight fit but the chair was there too, and this reassured and calmed Sev as nothing else could.

"They won't find us in here?"

"Not till we want to be found," he assured her.

"Sime, I don't think I ever want to be found."

"But you're my wench!" he said, grinning. "You'll have to come out there with me. I can't be a pirate and not have a wench. It goes against all the laws of nature."

"Sime. This behavior is unbecoming in someone who is two hundred years old. I hope you know that."

He rolled his eyes at her and hunkered down, peering through a crack in the door. The crawlspace he'd found was just that— a crawlspace, tucked behind a short flight of stairs. There was no wasted space on the ship; they were sharing it with extra stores, which meant gunny sacks of potatoes, wooden boxes of what she assumed was hard tack, and a few barrels of heavy, spiced wine.

"Is this all they eat?"

"Pretty much," said Sime, preoccupied with the door. His face was close enough to it to be gathering splinters every time he shifted position.

She looked around herself distastefully. "This represents a new low in cuisine, I think. Where's the fruits and the vegetables? Where's the basic necessities of healthy life? Are you listening to me, Sime? I think I'm going to have to talk to the cook about this, I mean— they're not so far in the past that they don't know about eating their greens, right?"

He swung round and pointed a finger at her. "Only *you* can prevent scurvy."

She sighed, and looked at him seriously. "That's not funny."

"Oh. I thought it was." He looked through the door again.

"Sime—"

"Sev. You can't go through time campaigning for healthy cooking. Believe me, just because you think you know what people need, because you caught gourmet at an early age and still suffer to this day, doesn't mean it's true throughout history. Yes, certainly a lot of the diseases and maladies that afflict this benighted time period could be alleviated with judicious application of something with fiber, and the entire age could use an enema, there's no arguing that. But you won't change everything, so why should you try to change anything? And," he went on just as she started to splutter in indignation at this ungenerous attitude, "even though you think of yourself as being from an enlightened time, do you actually believe that everyone in your America eats their six servings a day? That they would willingly toss their hamburgers for an apple and a carrot? That the fast food joints will ever go bankrupt?"

"I started a petition about that," said Sev, still indignantly, "and I honestly think—"

"I've seen the future," said Sime, interrupting rudely. "It involves grease."

"I said, I— Sime."

"Lots and lots of grease."

"Sime!"

"Enough grease to lubricate a nation with a steam engine in every household, which is what it takes by that point to keep things cool— oh," he said, as he finally got what all of Sev's gestures, wild-eyed faces, and shrieking was about. "Hello."

"Hello," mimicked the pirate, with admirable inflection.

In short order they'd been dragged out and stood, practically on parade, in front of the entire crew. Their master and commander emerged in state from his cabin, and stood, sturdily and frowning gently, looking them over. He was a large man with, in fact, a thicket of thick, black, curly hair that covered nearly all of his face and his entire torso. If nothing else it was a comfort to Sev that he had not been misnamed. Not much of a comfort, admittedly, but some.

"What be this?" he bellowed at last. "Stowaways? Scavvy dogs."

"Aye aye, cap'n," said Sime, and Sev nudged him in the ribs.

Edward Teach, the pirate Blackbeard, eyed him narrowly.

"Are you being facetious, man?"

"Not I, sir," said Sime stoutly, and Sev nudged him harder. He glared at her and mouthed, "What?"

"Knock it off," she mouthed back.

"Knock what off?" he mouthed.

"That!"

"That what?"

She widened her eyes and glared at him in a misguided attempt to cow him into silence. He turned back to Teach instead and said, "We're here to join your crew, Captain, if you'll have us."

"As what?" the captain roared.

Sime shrugged. "Cabin boys?" he hazarded.

Teach laughed, a bit raucously, Sev thought. But, she amended charitably, being a pirate that was probably all he could manage.

"You'll not fool me!" he shouted cheerfully. "She—" and he stabbed a finger towards Sev, "is no boy, cabin or otherwise. *She* is a woman."

"She is," agreed Sime, abashed.

"Furthermore, were she a boy, she would be a very unsatisfactory one. You cannot be a proper cabin boy in a dress," Teach declared,. "Your elaborate subterfuge does not fool me."

"It was not intended as subterfuge, Captain. As a matter of fact," Sime glanced at Sev and hesitated perceptibly before plunging on. "—she is with me. My. Er. Serving wench."

"Wench!" roared Teach, and slapped Sime hard across the face indignantly. "Show the lady some respect!"

Sime turned a wry and very pained face to Sev, who avoided his glance and said, "Actually, Captain, I'm his sister. His much younger sister. You know how brothers are. Are we out at sea?"

The enormous pirate eyed her for a moment before laughing, fully as raucously as previously if not more so. Perhaps, thought Sev indulgently, he had something wrong with his throat.

"Aye, little lass, and come see for yourself."

He beckoned her forward and she walked with him, holding herself a few steps away as they obviously didn't have shower amenities aboard the ship, and looked over the salt-stained side. It had not been long since they'd left port, but the ship was built for speed and they had a good stiff wind blowing them where, presumably, the captain wanted to go; land was already growing small and distant. She had to squint to see it, and duck around to account for the toss and bob of the ship. It was a fine, sunny day but the sea was rather playful, whipping them around at a good rate and tossing them up and down like a thrown coin. It had been years since Sev was last on a ship that was headed into the open ocean. She'd gone whale-watching with that one guy— what was his name? Hobart or something like that. Dan, maybe.

"Tell me, little lass," said the pirate Edward Teach in a ruminative, thoughtful tone, looking her over and holding true to pirate tradition despite the fact that at five foot nine she was anything but little, "does this inspire you? The only truly free and open spaces left on this earth?"

She turned a grin on him, before she could stop herself.

"Oh, yeah! I mean, yes. Sure. Apart from the seasickness, this is great. Very pretty. I'll tell you, it's been years since I was on a ship like this— or rather, not exactly on a ship like this, but I went whale-watching—"

"Then perhaps," said Teach, "you'll give me leave to strip your freedom from you, momentarily, while I decide what's to be done with you and your," he gestured carelessly over his shoulder, "brother."

Her smile faded somewhat.

"What do you mean, what's to be done?"

"Oh, you seem to be harmless enough, but we do not take kindly to stowaways aboard this vessel. Never have. Never will. It's a tradition, do you see, and one hates to make a break with tradition." He paused and looked at her seriously, obviously with something on his mind, but then turned to the first mate with a peremptory gesture. "Jarvis! Put 'em in the brig."

"Throw 'em, Cap'n?" suggested Jarvis solicitously.

"Nay! Put 'em very carefully. I'll attend to them soon enough. God bid you rest, my lady," he told Sev, sweeping her a bow. "If I can find you some breeches I'll make a cabin boy of you yet."

Jarvis the first mate ushered Sev back to join her erstwhile companion, who too had taken a glance over the side, gazed on the rise and swell, and had gotten no merit from it. In fact he looked abominably ill.

"What's wrong with you?" she hissed, taking his arm and scuttling forwards as Jarvis ushered them on with his sheer presence, like a sheepdog and his herd.

"Abominably ill," said Sime in a strangled voice, as though the words had to be forced past something unspeakable. "Always did get seasick. Could be why I never turned pirate."

The brig turned out to be not quite as bad as Sev had expected, while at the same time not as good as she could have hoped. There was moist scum and slick algae on the floor, but the narrow bench-like bunk was dry. Yellowed and rotting, but dry. They took it at face value and sank gratefully down onto it. It had been built for very short, very thin people, and they had to huddle together to keep from falling off.

"Well, here's the grand adventure of Blackbeard the pirate," said Sev, feeling more tired by the minute. "We could get out of here if we could have brought the chair with us."

"Every time you call it 'the Chair' you make it sound like we're being executed," said Sime irritably. "And anyway, we haven't had a chance yet to ask him about your boyfriend."

"And you were so sure he was here," scoffed Sev.

"What's that supposed to mean?"

"It means, 'well, obviously he's not.' It means 'you were wrong.'"

"Second strike out," said Sime miserably, sinking into himself and pulling Sev with him as he leaned back against the damp wall of the cell. His arms wrapped around Sev's shoulders, he guided her to lean against his chest instead of the wooden wall. She thought about struggling out of his unlooked-for hold, but concluded that it was an unconscious move on his part, he didn't mean anything by it, and furthermore it was all to the good since he was getting wet and she wasn't. She settled into him.

"All that talk about freedom," she said sadly. "I thought he was going to ask me to join their crew, or something."

"Yes, well. Time traveling is very freeing as well, you know. Did you ever think of it like that?"

"Of course I've thought of it like that. I've thought of it a lot, Sime, even though I don't say it. It's just, I don't think I could—" She paused. "No, never mind."

"What?"

"No, that's all I had to say. You say something now."

He sighed, creating a rumbling noise in her ears. "The Corporation wants to take everything good out of time travel. Taking away the freedom of it; freedom you have to pay eight million for isn't really freedom, is it?"

"So the Anarchists believe it should be, what, free for everyone?"

"Sure. Free as the air. Free as the sky. Free as water and light."

"I don't know where you get yours from, but my water and light comes as a result of the utilities bill I pay every month." She shook her head slightly. "Free time travel for all. Huh."

"What?"

"Well— it boggles the mind, doesn't it? It certainly boggles mine. It sounds like an ideal platform for some sci-fi political campaign."

"Hmm," he said, and she realized suddenly that the tingling sensation she'd been feeling for a few minutes now was his fingers rubbing small circles on her upper arm. He was thinking about something else, though, and after tensing for a moment she forced herself to relax again. He didn't notice any of it. "The Corporation's even figuring out a way to strip the age-delay element from it. Not just from the part they control either; from all of it. Take the science fiction out of it, they said. Make it more humane."

"Humane?"

"They said it's not human nature, not to age and die."

"Sime— if that happens, then what—"

"What happens to me? I resume. I start aging again. I'll age very quickly, I imagine— not as quickly as if

Tendence and Cavile had caught up with me, but faster than normal. I might have ten years then— I might have five— I might have one."

"*Oh,*" she breathed into his shirtfront, very quietly.

"And I'm not the only one, either, Sevannah. That's why we're fighting against it, you see. That's why we're trying to bring the Corporation down."

"So you and the Anarchists— you're an outlaw then? A renegade?"

"There's more to it than that. It's a very complex thing, Time and the management thereof. Only very special people are allowed to learn how it works."

She waited for a moment.

"—well?"

"I said only very special people." He pinched her arm lightly to let her know he was joking and she snorted obligingly to let him know she didn't take him seriously. "Really, Sev, it is very complicated. Suffice it to say, I've been time traveling for longer than all the Corporation's Board of Directors. I'm older than all of them; they were all born late 1800s and up. The earliest birth was a good forty years after my own. This kind of ruthless industrialization, with no regard for life or the way of things, is a modern phenomenon, you know. It wouldn't have happened in my time."

"Can't you do something about them, then? You say the Anarchists are trying to. I don't see why you can't, I don't know— go back in time, you're good at that, and do something to prevent the Corporation from taking control. Thwart births or destinies or something."

"Destinies." He sighed. "It's *complicated.* People know enough not to get involved in the really big things. That's just self-preservation, it's all instinct; keeping out of wars and politics, since they'll both get you killed equally dead. Doing something like preventing the Corporation— it would take delicacy, an inherent knowledge of the situation, caution and boldness in equal measure. The Corporation is wrapped through time in a way that transcends the birth dates of the leaders. It's all tied up with Tendence and Cavile, and they're older than any of us."

"What— how is that possible?"

He shrugged; she could feel it, just underneath her head. "I'm not sure. No one really knows their full history, or how they discovered they could time travel without a machine. But there's no doubt about it, they were the first."

"They didn't start the Corporation, though?"

"No. They're not like that. They're fully concerned with themselves and the honored way of things, not with making money or creating franchises. But if someone sets up rules and laws, they'll do anything to see that they're obeyed; and that's why they were perfect for playing watchdog for the Corporation. No one knows when they were born, or where they came from. All we know is what happens when we meet up with them."

"Sime?"

"Yes."

"What happened to Oedipus?"

He heaved a sigh. "I went to his house. He'd been— returned."

She was silent for a long time after that, and he sat quiet as well, stroking her arm up and down now in long slow passes that made him shiver but didn't stir her from her contemplation. His fingers circled carefully, warily, around the bump of her elbow and she shifted closer to him, burrowing in. She was fairly well the worse for wear on this trip, as on the others. Time travel wasn't the cleanest occupation. She spoke suddenly and he jumped.

"What happens if everyone discovers time travel, and the Corporation can't control it?"

"Well— what do you mean, what happens? We all time travel."

"But if they can't turn the aging thingie off. Do we all just live forever, if we want?"

He shrugged again. "Sure. Why not?"

"It does seem strange."

"Listen, Sev, do you want to die?"

"Not particularly. Why, what are you telling me?"

"Not telling you anything. Just asking. Do you want to die, have you ever really thought about it? Do you think you'll ever seriously contemplate wanting to die in the future?"

She sat up and looked at him. He looked back at her seriously.

"No. Why?"

"Neither do I," he confided. "In fact, I want not to die so much that I will travel through time for the rest of eternity trying to avoid it. Why do you think that is?"

She shrugged. "Raging against the inevitable?"

"No, Sev. Look at humanity as a whole, as a collective. We don't want to die. We want to live. We want to live so much we could die trying. Why is that?"

She dropped her hands in her lap and stared at him, perplexed. "I don't know."

"Maybe because we're not supposed to," he suggested gently. "Maybe it's not right. Maybe it's not meant to be. Maybe we're supposed to live forever."

"But we don't."

"But we could. Maybe someday we will."

They remained staring at each other for some time, Sev mulling this over and over in her mind to see if it made sense. She had reached something of a conclusion and was about to say it, but all she got out was, "Hmm," before something banged against the cell walls.

Jarvis stood there, grinning.

"I'm to take you up on deck," he announced. "The Captain's got a little surprise for you."

Edward Teach was waiting, arms behind his back and a stern look on his face, when they emerged into the bright sunlight on deck. They blinked and saw spots while their eyes took time adjusting; the pirates stood grinning loosely at them, ranged in untidy rows behind their captain, leering at Sev and making faces at Sime, who, once he could see properly, made a few back at them.

"I hope that short time stayed in my comfortable brig did not inconvenience you none," said Teach politely. "I had been meaning to further furnish it but was precluded by lack of interest."

Sev blinked. Sime smiled broadly.

"Aaargh, me hearty," he said, "'tis a terrible job, interior decorating."

Edward Teach stared at him.

"Ye put me in mind," he said, "of a man I once knew. I took this man under my wing, so to speak, and taught him the trade of pillage and plunder. He went around with his mouth agape, so, always saying 'Aaargh' and 'Avast' and 'Shiver me timbers.'" Teach snorted. "Dumb puppy thought he was speaking Pirate."

Sime sobered considerably.

"Indeed," he said with dignity.

"At any rate," Teach went on, rededicating his attention to Sev, "my lass, I've a proposition for you. If ye would come with me."

He beckoned her forwards and led her away from the rest of the crew, which closed in on Sime, walling him off from Sev. He folded his arms and tried to look over the heads of the crew to see where she was being taken.

It wasn't very far away, in fact. The Captain's quarters weren't all that large, reminding Sev again that this was a pirate ship and not something belonging to the Queen's navy, which would undoubtedly have housed its commander in a much larger stateroom. As it was, the room was both sleeping quarters and office, as the untidy bed shoved in the corner attested. There was a small desk as well, looking forlorn and relatively unused except as a dinner table. Clearly, writing was not so much a feature on this ship as it possibly was on others.

Teach gestured to Sev to seat herself in one chair, and took the other across from her, grinning yellowly through his beard.

"Do you enjoy the sea, lass?"

"Very much," she said politely. "I was actually raised

around it for a few years, before we moved inland to the city. I kind of miss it."

"Hrrrm, just so." Teach nodded. "You are a woman after my own heart, no doubt, and a ruffian of a sort."

She didn't know what this meant, and so she smiled politely. It seemed to be an acceptable response, and Edward Teach went on.

"Would you like to see the sea every day of your life, lass?"

She tilted her head to one side and widened her eyes at him as innocently as she could. "Are you asking me to join your crew?"

He hesitated a moment, then grinned at her and nodded.

"As what?" she prompted. "Cabin boy?"

He did the laugh again, so loudly this time that she had to sit back hastily to avoid being blasted in the face by flying saliva. "Nonsense, lass! Can't have you cabin boy-ing in a dress! And I've no trousers that will fit such a dainty thing." Sev snorted violently at this and had to cover her mouth with her hand and pretend it was a cough. "So the question is," said Blackbeard cunningly, "what is it ye can do, that you'll not need neither trousers nor skirts for?"

It took her a flabbergasted moment to realize what exactly he was implying.

By that point, of course, he had her on deck already and was encouraging his cheering crew to gather round for the wedding ceremony.

Chapter Eight

Sime, quite naturally, looked as surprised as anyone. He even said as much, in case it wasn't clear from his expression.

"I thought you told me this wasn't going to happen," Sev whispered testily out of the corner of her mouth. They'd allowed her supposed brother to stand by her for the ceremony, which was predictably without pomp and circumstance. Sev had been given a white apron for her pains, or at least an apron that presumably had been white some time long in the past, and was told to stand between the two sets of stairs. The door to the captain's quarters was nestled behind them, and Edward Teach was apparently busying himself inside with pre-marriage duties.

"I didn't *think* it was going to happen," whispered Sime back. "In all reasonableness, how on earth could I expect this was going to happen? I didn't expect you to be quite this irresistible, I guess."

"Why *is* this happening?"

"I have no idea."

"I mean, why couldn't he have gotten a bride when he was on land just now?"

"Bad breath?" hazarded Sime. Sev glared at him.

"Alright, alright. If I really have to guess, I would say it's because he's too well known at that particular port. You'll notice they didn't exactly sack it." He shrugged. "Maybe it's like a safe house of a sort, maybe he's got an agreement with those townspeople. He won't rape and pillage, they won't arrest him."

"Is that *likely*, or are you just trying to sound like you know what's going on? As usual?"

"You wound me, lady," Sime said, and folded his arms staunchly.

Sev said, "Grrr!" and did the same.

The pirate Edward Teach emerged humming cheerfully from his quarters, closing the door gently behind him, and advanced on Sev purposefully, holding his arms out.

"Aarrgh, me lady," he said. This was such cliché dialogue for a pirate that Sev automatically assumed it was part of the accepted ritual of the marriage ceremony. She wondered how much more to come there was. Any minute now he'd say something about shivering timbers and swabbing the deck, and then it would be too late. Just before Teach swept her up in his great arms, she whispered frantically out of the side of her mouth to Sime.

"How do I get out of this?"

Sime winced. "I don't think you do."

Teach engulfed her in his embrace, and for the moment, everything he'd said was true— with those brawny arms around her, she feel like a dainty and delicate lass. The feeling was nice, briefly, till he laid her backwards over his arm and grinned in her face and said, "We be married."

The watching pirates burst into an unexpected round of cheers and catcalls. Some of them more enthusiastic than others and started what looked like a very early version of the wave; others just jumped up and down yelling happily like they were '60s girls at a Beatles concert.

"That's it?" said Sev. "That's all? That's the whole thing?"

" 'Tis official," agreed Teach.

Sev narrowed her eyes at him. "Look, you don't have any other wives stuck in a closet somewhere, do you?"

"Aaarrgh," said Teach once more, with feeling, "it be a lonely life as a pirate captain. I am obliged to have a girl in every port."

"Oh God."

"Yes," said Teach, smiling faintly at the recognition.

Sev fought a bit out of his arms and tried to stand aside a little. This proved to be difficult. He had latched tightly onto her elbow, fingers encircling it completely, so there was a limit to how far away she could get.

"Listen," she said, "not to tarnish such sacred proceedings, but while I've got your ear, if I could ask you a question."

"It be your right," he said indulgently, "on Maiden's Eve." He paused a moment and looked thoughtful. "Actually, Maiden's Eve be yesterday."

"But I didn't know I was going to be married yesterday. Not to you, at any rate."

"Aye. Then you can have the privileges of an unmarried woman this eve, to compensate."

"You mean I don't have to sleep with you?" She raised her eyebrows at him.

"All except that," amended Teach. "Ask your question."

She took a deep breath and let it out slowly. "Do you know, or have you heard, of a man named Matthew, tall and brown-haired?" She really needed to find another way of describing him one of these days. "He might have come here looking to meet you, perhaps to join your crew as I did."

Teach looked thoughtful behind his beard. "If there be such a man, would he be accompanied by a woman such as yourself?"

"No. He would be traveling alone."

"Ah." The thoughtful look disappeared, to be replaced by one of dismissal. "Then he would have been thrown overboard once we discovered his presence. I am in no need of new pirates. I have my hands full with the ones already in my crew; always fighting when I say peace, and all layabout when I say fight. If a man stows away on my ship and is not accompanied, as I say, by a woman, he is got rid of."

"Jeez," said Sev, aghast, "you're a tough potential employer. You actually threw Matthew overboard? Before or after you left port?"

"How should I remember?" demanded Teach.

"Well, there either would have been a splash, or a solid thunk."

"Look, my lass," said Edward Teach, putting his hands on his hips. "I grow tired of your questions. I do not cannily remember this Matthew, and beg leave, my princess, to ask what he is to you, that he so importantly displaces more usual activities."

She wrinkled her nose at the suggestion and though Sime tried with numerous face-twistings, eye-rollings, and frantic wavings to get her to shut up, said, "Well, for starters, he's my intended husband."

Teach went quite still.

"What 'twere that ye said, lass?" he breathed.

"I was going to marry him at the earliest opportunity," said Sev in a rush. "It was going to be a big wedding, too, not this slipshod ship-side recognition of a piratical union which isn't even real let alone official. In fact I intended to marry him, I wanted to marry him, I am going to marry him and I would even say 'I do' which is something you didn't give me a chance to change to 'I don't' probably because you knew I wouldn't. Would. Wouldn't." She paused for breath. "I mean, knew I would change it to 'I don't' and knew I wouldn't get married— that is. Not to you. Why are you poking me, Sime?"

"You mean, you're to be married to another man?" said Teach, who at this late date was proving to be slow on the uptake.

"I most certainly am," said Sev.

There seemed to be something hypocritical about

pirates; they apparently loved to disrupt lives and pacts and ceremonies, and would look for any opportunity to do so. But they absolutely hated to have it happen to themselves. Teach, clearly considering himself well married to Sev with no chance of annulment and no escape for her without the outside chance of death, appeared highly indignant when she proclaimed her plot to marry another. Despite the fact that he had summarily married girls all over the world he traveled as was his whim, he was loathe to have any woman do the same to him. Like all pirates, he most likely suffered an inferiority complex. Sev's favorite psychiatrist would have had a field day with Edward Teach.

He took a deep breath.

"*Wench!*"

"Hey!" said Sime, and then, seeing this wasn't the time for indignant feminism, grabbed Sev by the hand and bolted. The captain's quarters were admirably placed for running into, and he did so, yanking Sev in behind him and spinning around, looking for something to put against the door. He had seized upon a heavy battered tallboy that looked completely out of place on a pirate ship, and was trying with exhausted exertion to push it towards the door when Sev discovered the deadbolt and calmly shot it through.

He let go of the tallboy and sagged against it. "I guess I need to go back into training. Can't even move furniture."

"I think it's bolted to the wall," Sev told him. "To keep it from falling over out at sea."

"Ah."

"So I'm married to a pirate." Sev thought about this for a moment. "What will my mother say?"

"Probably ask how soon you intend to give her grandchildren," said Sime. "I know that's what mine said." Without pausing to let Sev pursue this thought-provoking remark, he started knocking against the far wall of the cabin.

"What are you doing?"

"If I'm right," he said, "and I know I am, through this wall is the store room where we left the machine."

She heaved a sigh. "Oh, man. Are you *sure* you're right?"

"I know I am. I told you so."

She sank down into a chair and put her head in her hands. "How on earth are we going to get through the wall and get at it, though?"

He turned to face her, still knocking, and grinned at her.

"It depends," he said. "Are you prepared to make somewhat of a mess?"

She lifted her head slowly and narrowed her eyes at him.

"What kind of mess?"

"The best kind," he told her, walking towards her and ducking his head cajolingly. "The kind we don't have to clean up, and someone else does. Probably the cabin boy, God rest him. God bless and keep him! Do you know Teach was going to throw me overboard?"

"Just like he did with Matthew," said Sev despondently.

"What?"

There was a very loud bang. They looked desultorily at the door.

"Someone wants to come in," observed Sev.

Sime seized her hand and pulled her up beside him; losing her balance slightly, she grabbed hold of his shoulder and held on. He grinned hard at her and chucked her under the chin, earning a glare.

"Ever notice that pirates keep tons of extra weaponry around? I mean, literally tons. There was a whole room on the way to the brig. Did you notice that? And here we have, oh, lots of things— scimitars. Sabers. Daggers. Dirks. I always was partial to axes, myself." He located one and hoisted it onto his shoulder. "Does this make me look like a woodsman?"

"Yes," admitted Sev.

"Great. That's exactly what I was going for."

So saying, he swung the axe mightily and it bit deep into the wood of the wall; he struggled briefly to get it out and then on the second swing it angled, bisected, and brought a neat chunk of age-weathered wood with it when it emerged. Sev stood up as another set of blows rained on the door, and gave a fierce grin.

"Is there another one?"

"Be my guest," offered Sime, pointing with his elbow towards the racks of weaponry, since his hands were otherwise occupied.

She grasped a huge double-headed axe and lifted it, straining. It weighed approximately a third of her own weight, and she stumbled with it towards the wall. Sime glanced up to see her and advised, "Don't give yourself a hernia."

"I'll try to avoid that, thanks."

She struggled the axe upwards, gritted her teeth and swung it towards the wall as hard as she could. It struck the wood and bounced off, landing on the floor before she could get control of it again. Sime looked down at it thoughtfully.

"Trade you," offered Sev.

In short order they were both at work, chopping through the wood of Edward Teach's cabin, while on the outside of the door the pirate captain Blackbeard himself howled curses and terrible piratical invective. They made a hole in the wall big enough to crawl through just as the crew burst through the door at last and swarmed into the room; Sime yanked Sev through the hole, located the kitchen chair in the dim light from the hole, and sat down abruptly. He pulled her down with him and wrapped his arms around her, holding her tightly in the dark as outside, the pirate hordes raged.

"Aaargh!"

"Avast, ye swine!"

"Shiver me timbers!"

"*Aaaargh!*"

When they faded back into view in Matthew's basement scant seconds later, both of them were giggling madly.

Chapter Nine

"There is no reason time should re-write itself for pirates to sound like that." Sev folded her arms. "It's just ridiculous."

"Oh, clichés have to come from somewhere."

"Yeah, well, the suspension in my suspension of disbelief is sagging, okay."

"Ought to get that looked at. So what do you reckon?" Sime's finger paused at the top of the list as he prepared to lead his eyes a wending, merry way down.

"Somewhere I don't have to get married," she teased him. "Once was enough, thanks."

"Well, that could be difficult," he muttered jokingly. "I didn't know when I agreed to help you that I was going to have to protect your virtue and keep you away from all men."

"Except the one we're looking for."

"Except that one," he agreed.

"I don't care where we go. I just want to know if we're going to find him soon. I'm getting a little tired of all this, you know?"

"Well," he said reasonably, "historically, it's always in the last place you look. Of course, if you look there first, that'll make that the first place you look, and the balance of the entire universe will be thrown off."

"That's comforting, thanks. You're not helping."

"I'm not really trying to," he responded, shrugging slightly. He ranged his eyes over the paper, following his finger over the cryptic lines. "What's that one, again?"

She leaned closer and squinted. "Vlad? Something?"

"Vladislaus Dragulia?" he said.

"Um— could be."

"His spelling is horrible. Vlad. Vlad the Impaler. You boyfriend wanted to meet Vlad the Impaler?" He shook his head. "Tell me, have you, at any point, noticed any other signs of insanity or any suicide attempts on his part, or anything?"

"Why? Who is he?"

He stared at her blankly for a minute before shaking himself. "Right. I forgot about your history impairment."

"You make it sound like some kind of disease."

"For my money, it is. It's Dracula. Basically. Real Dracula, although the stories are all somewhat—" He paused.

"Stories of his death are greatly exaggerated?" hazarded Sev. Sime laughed.

"Something like that. You know humans, everything has to be sensationalized." He waved a diffident hand. "Dracula isn't all he's cracked up to be, you know. He was basically just a murderous nymphomaniac really. But 'excommunicated and condemned for being a blood-sucking spawn of the devil' sounds so much cooler than 'excommunicated and condemned for being a right horny bleeder.' The press had a field day and Bram Stoker had an epiphany."

"And a thousand different versions of the world's favorite vampire were born," murmured Sev.

"Such is life," said Sime equably.

"Such is life."

"Such is life after death."

She tilted her head to one side. "Was Vlad the Impaler

ever really dead, then?"

"Well, yeah. Eventually." He gave her a sidelong look at this question and smiled fondly, like he would at a child that is trying its level best to amuse the adults in the room by using long words. "It does happen."

She gave him a wry smile in response to this look of, in her opinion, decidedly premature affection and stared back at the list. "So if we rule out Dracula—"

"We don't have to rule him out," admitted Sime. "There's a possibility that Matthew was just stupid enough to go pay him a visit. But I'm hoping, for your sake, he shows more sense than that. And if he does, then he should take something. Always polite to take something to a visit, especially unannounced. Flowers could work. Lilies would be appropriate."

Another of those sidelong glances and a downright impudent grin. Sev snatched the list away from him and wandered off with it, perusing it on her own. Sime watched her, tapping his fingers together and humming to himself.

Eventually he said, "Look, we've given the past a try, haven't we? What do you say to the future for a bit now? What's he got on there for that?"

"2525. No reason why, just the year."

"In the year 2525," said Sime slowly, thoughtfully, and absolutely deadpan, "if man is still alive— if woman can survive— they may find—"

"Don't make me hit you," said Sev pleasantly.

"Let me think. In the year 2525— ain't gonna need no husband, won't need no wife. Hey! Maybe that's why he's gone there." He grinned at her a little meanly and she treated this with the disrespect it deserved, and stuck her tongue out at him. "Maybe he's got a problem with commitment and can't bring himself to tell you about it. It must be a difficult subject to raise with your fiancée, I imagine. Me, I'm old-fashioned. I like to marry my girls." He paused. "Like Edward Teach."

"You're not old-fashioned, you're just old," Sev retorted. "Are you sure you've got no idea what happens in that year?"

Sime shrugged. "Never been there."

Sev sighed.

"Always willing to give it a try, though," said Sime encouragingly.

"But what will we wear?" asked Sev.

"Studs and leather," said Sime promptly. "Ever popular. Positively perennial." He took in the look that Sev gave him and grinned loosely, loopily back. "How about we wear some clothes? Pick out what you like. The great thing about the future is if you're dressed differently they just assume you're in some club or gang or something. Nothing to worry about."

Sev snorted. "You think being thought to be in a gang is nothing to worry about? You're showing your age, Past Man."

"Past Man? You keep dwelling on that. Anybody would think you've got an ageist complex. Either that or you're hitting on me by trying to make yourself seem young and desirable, if only by comparison. Come on, Sev. Get yourself together, here." He handed her a shirt and a pair of pants which she took sullenly, not completely thrilled at the reference to her age. He glanced up and observed this. "What, you can dish it out, but you can't take it?"

"Unlike other individuals, I don't time travel my life away. I am going to get older, Sime, and there's nothing I can do about it. It's just different from you, and you might as well realize that."

He tossed his own selection from the wardrobe over one shoulder and ducked his head to talk directly to her, to her face and to her ideas. "But it doesn't have to be, Sevannah. That's what the Anarchists are all about. Time travel free for all— life free for all."

"But that's just what it will be, a free-for-all! Don't you think, human nature being what it is, even if you figure out a way to take the Corporation down, another version of it will rise to take its place? And after that, another one? Don't you think that as long as it's up to us, if someone can figure out how to take over the system, they'll turn it back into what it is now, just to make a buck?" She thought for a minute. "It's like the Internet. Do you have any idea what I pay for my wireless? I'm paying for air, I'm paying for space. I'm paying to be advertised to. They make you pay for everything these days."

"So what are you suggesting?" asked Sime quietly.

"Pessimism!" shouted Sev. "I'm suggesting you stop talking about free life and free time and join me in wallowing in realism for once!"

"I may not be a pessimist," said Sime, thoughtfully, "but I'm not exactly an optimist either. I suppose I hold to a strict standard of meliorism."

Sev quieted and looked at him for a long time.

"That's funny," she said slowly. "That's what I always wanted to be."

Sime grinned at her. "Well, in the name of meliorists everywhere, I declare that you can be if you want to be."

She was still watching him, a tentative, half-tender look on her face. "Really?"

"Definitely." He waved her away. "Go get dressed. We've got you a husband to find."

"Fiancé."

"Why pay attention to sundry details? He's as good as ball-and-chained anyway."

She nodded. "Thank you, Sime."

She knew her face was drawn and serious— she could hear it herself, in her tone. Sime hesitated, and looked about to ask her something, ask her why, maybe; but she turned on her heel abruptly and went into the other room to dress. When she finally returned the moment had been lost. She kept that moment of hesitation in her head, though, and thought about it now and then.

After a certain point in human history, architects, clothes designers and other designing luminaries apparently threw up their hands and gave it up as a bad job. Other things were probably thrown up as well, Sev imagined. Judging by the crowd on the streets outside what had once been the tallest building in the world, it would be hard to give over to the rabble; but the thing about rabble is they've got size on their side. Probably the architects, clothes designers, etc. didn't have much of a choice.

"Well," she said, "it's very— flat."

"This is so strange," said Sime, who appeared to be a great deal more troubled by this turn of events than Sev was herself. In fact he seemed to be downright upset. "I watched them build this, you know. You know that picture of the workers eating their lunch on a beam, high above the city? I was the third one from the left."

"You actually worked on it?"

He shrugged. "No, I just knew how to find free lunch, is all. But look at this, Sev! The Empire State, brought low. Brought to nothing, brought to the dust."

"It's not like it was demolished," pointed out Sev reasonably. "It just was sort of— demoted."

At some point, it apparently dawned on mankind that tall buildings were a great deal more hazardous, expensive, and difficult than short buildings. This is just one of the many virtues of shortness. The difficulty was that architects, more often than not, had Napoleon complexes so bad that they would have arguments over it; "My Napoleon complex is bigger than your Napoleon complex," they would say. Being that a great deal of architectural design is done in bars and restaurants on paper napkins, the prevalence of alcohol made these fights even worse, and being as fights aren't always too clear when you're practically pickled, all architects go home positive they've won the brawl. As a result, the next morning they wake up and design an even taller structure to represent their prowess.

City officials had dealt with this tendency, in the light of their great realization about height, by ordering the construction companies to build these structures horizontally. This, naturally, took up a great deal of room and made the cityscape less picturesque than previously. Thinking to compensate for it, they took all the existing buildings and laid them down on their back as well, adding in doors for each floor for easy street-access. As a result of all this innovation, New York City now covered the entirety of New York State and was bleeding over into Pennsylvania. But the buildings themselves— one story tall, untold stories long— were a great deal safer. Until, that is, the stricken, thwarted architects started blowing them up.

"So do you think this is why he came here?"

"Who?" said Sime, who was preoccupied with other things right at the moment.

"Matthew."

"Matthew? No. Why would he come here for this? Why would anyone come here for this? I knew there was a reason I'd never traveled here. This is horrible. This is an affront to nature."

"Nature?" repeated Sev. "The nature that created hundred-storey buildings?"

"Why not? It created a hundred-acre wood."

"Don't be ridiculous."

"But I like it!" He glanced at her and managed to make himself smile for her benefit. "I'm sorry, Sev. I'm just— upset, I suppose. This—" he gestured around himself at the busy streets. "This just doesn't sit well with me."

She patted him on the shoulder. "I understand. It's alright. Hard to teach an old dog new tricks— hard to make a time traveler used to newfangled inventions. How many hundreds of years old are you at this point?"

"Too many," he said fervently.

"So why do you suppose Matthew would want to come here?"

Sime shrugged and looked around at the city. "Maybe it *was* just because of the song. Some sort of morbid curiosity. Maybe he—"

A small, light blue spacecraft powered down next to them, unfolding three stilt-like legs and sitting on them gracefully, like a duck on a tripod. A ramp was extended, and light showed within. Sev and Sime looked around, to see if this was now an everyday occurrence. Judging by the screams and the panicked behavior the crowd was now displaying, it wasn't.

"Maybe that's why," suggested Sev.

"Maybe so," agreed Sime.

The aliens came out shooting. Any humans nearby continued panicking and threw themselves full length on the ground, covering their heads with their arms; mothers threw themselves protectively over their children, valiant men threw themselves protectively over the nearest pretty woman they could find; children squawked in distress at being crushed by their overzealous parent, the pretty women squawked in outraged feminism at the assumption that they needed to be saved, unasked for, unlooked for, and unappreciated. Little beams of light flashed from the tips of the strange weapons the aliens bore, and as they shot merrily around them every which way they exclaimed in odd high pitched voices, apparently giving each other a running commentary on everything that was happening and their feelings about it all. Oddly enough, the people rushing by that caught the full force of some of the lights didn't stumble and fall; didn't scream any louder from pain from any wounds; didn't vanish in a flash of light or haze of red mist; didn't look electrocuted, stricken, ghastly, or purged. In fact it seemed to have no effect whatsoever.

Sev and Sime sat with their backs against one of the nearby stricken buildings, having recently recovered from a tussle after Sime had thrown himself valiantly over Sev. Sev raised one hand and pointed at the erstwhile attacking alien invaders.

"They're—"

"Photography hounds," supplied Sime.

"They're—"

"Taking pictures."

"They're—"

"What? What else are they?"

"*Tourists!*" shrieked Sev.

One of the aliens bounded up to them with all the enthusiasm of a puppy, antennae flapping here and there and a tentacle or two waving in the wind, and said, in passably bad English with an unidentifiable accent, "What is it up, man? How goeth *homo erectus*?"

"I think he's trying to hit on you," said Sime to Sev in a horrified whisper.

"How do you know he's not trying to hit on *you*?" whispered Sev back. She was not entirely comfortable with the situation.

The alien, as far as they could tell, looked insulted. "There is not a gang. We is not a gang. We is not a gangly hitting. We is are—" it struck a pose, arms wide, what was possibly a chin lifted into the air. "— exchange studentry."

"Oh my God," whispered Sev, aghast. "The aliens are high schoolers."

At this point Sime started to laugh in earnest, and couldn't bring himself to stop for some time. He laughed while a few more of the alien students joined the first and while they introduced themselves as being from the planet Possil, several billion light years away and, oh man oh *homo erectus*, it was is were the longest school trip they'd ever taken and see if they did it again without the alien equivalent of a radio. He laughed while they requested Sev to direct them to the nearest museum. He laughed while a few of them attempted to do imitations of him laughing. He sobered only when they finally mentioned that they'd always thought New York would be taller.

"It's a recent thing," he told them. "Humans are stricken with madness."

"Ohhhhh," said the aliens all together, tentacles bobbing as they nodded their heads seriously.

"Hey!" Sev hissed at him, poking him viciously in the side. "That isn't the kind of thing you want to tell aliens who just show up from nowhere. How do you know they won't take you literally and put us out of our misery or something?"

"They're *meant* to take it literally. It's the best I could do to prepare them for this planet. Sev—" He sat up straight, then leaned towards her urgently. "This is obviously, from the reactions of everyone, the first time that aliens have landed, at least with so much publicity. And now they're going to go tour the Met? What then?"

"Please yes," said one of the aliens, who was listening avidly and appeared to have some sort of notebook in one hand and some sort of marker in one of the others. "Where tour next do we go?"

"Yankee Stadium," said the one in a baseball cap, and the rest groaned.

"Havarti introduceth minimalist enterprise into we our group setting," explained the first one to the watching humans.

"Havarti?" repeated Sev.

"Like the cheese?" said Sime, momentarily distracted from what he was saying.

"Cheese?" repeated the first, and turned to his friends. "Cheese."

It took them a minute, but then they started laughing, with a peculiar honking noise like a flock of geese landing successfully just over the Canadian border. They poked at the unfortunately named alien with their tentacles.

"Cheese. Cheese!"

"*Cheese!*"

Sev turned to Sime, who was watching with his mouth open. "I have a feeling you were saying something important," she prompted him.

"Um— er, yes. I was saying, it's likely that as soon as the police discover that they aren't really armed with laser shooters and aren't going to blow up the Pentagon, they'll be taken to someplace like Area 51 and cut to pieces to see what makes them tick. The authorities will then analyze their spaceship for its point of origin and send a message to let their parents know they went down in a crash. Judging by the fact that they don't seem to be wearing any breathing apparatus, I'm guessing they can breathe the same mix as we do, and it's possible the government brains will figure that out as well, and if that happens we'll invade their planet and try to take over. We've probably already got the technology to do so, anyway."

"You sound like a conspiracy theorist," said Sev.

"I try to be."

"That wasn't a compliment."

"Weren't you just telling me to join you in wallowing in realism? I'm doing my best here. That's what's most likely to happen, so I'd advise you," he said loudly to the aliens, who had been too busy poking Havarti and teasing him about his name to listen to all this, "to be on good behavior and try to seem like you have infinite knowledge that you want to share with people. That usually goes over well."

"We are come to photo," explained the one with the notebook.

"We are come to photo lots," said another enthusiastically, who in the ten minutes they'd been here had found a street vendor and managed to buy or take a cheap t-shirt embellished with the American flag.

"That's all fine," said Sime, standing up and waving his arms at him. "Just try to establish— remember this phrase— "diplomatic relations." Okay?"

"Dippomatic relations," repeated one of them.

"Hippocratic Oath."

"Automatic relativism."

"Autocratic autism."

"Automobileic recreationism."

"Honda CRV," said one, with all appearances of a faintly supercilious smile. "Cadillacus. Porsche. Salon. El chupacabra. Ford."

"And don't worry about the language," advised Sime. "You speak it better than most government officials anyway." He stood back and watched, shaking his head, as most of them wended their merry way through the narrow streets and along the buildings, comparing notes and taking pictures with brilliant bursts of light.

"He's not here, is he," said Sev.

"Well, one thing's clear. If he meant to see mankind's first great contact with an alien race, he's missed the boat." Sime offered her a hand and helped her stand up, then dragged the kitchen chair over and helped her sit down again. "But that doesn't mean he can't go back and try again, of course."

Sev sighed, and dropped her head in her hands. "This is *so* confusing."

One of the few aliens who lingered behind stepped forward and pointed something at them. There was a red light on it, and a circular opening behind which a darker circle loomed like a watching eye. He skittered a few words out in his native language then said, formally, "Oh human homo erectus. Oh several human homo erectusi. What is thy message words? For edification of watchers on home planet, please give handful acknowledgment of your seeingship. Particularly," he added, "units of parentry origin."

Eventually it dawned on Sev that this was a video camera and he was asking them to wave and say hi to his parents. She obliged him, and tugged at Sime until he did the same.

Sime coughed in self-conscious importance and said, "Greetings, personages on the planet Perril."

"Possil," corrected the alien.

"Right. Possil. Greetings on the planet Possil from planet Earth. When you come for a visit please remember to bring proof of identification, because the border guards love that. Also maybe some life-saving medicines or something that will prove to our government that you're worth the time and effort. Under no circumstances bring any weapons. They'll just take it from you and use it before they know how it works and probably end up dematerializing themselves in the foot. Any helpful alien technology would be—" he floundered somewhat. "Helpful. Although they've already discovered TiVo. Um. Well."

He glanced around for a minute, looking for a proper and appropriately dynamic ending to this trans-universe communication, then his gaze lighted on Sev and the chair and he grinned widely and turned back to the camera.

"And finally, can you do *this*?"

He seated himself on Sev's lap and before she could do much more than give a squawk of protest at his weight, they were gone.

Chapter Ten

"Well," Sime said cheerfully as they arrived in Matthew's basement, "that's one for the books."

"You're heavy."

"Get used to it." He squirmed on her lap a little, settling himself comfortably. "We're not getting up just yet."

"Why?"

"Got to go back to the Assembly of All Saints."

"Again? Why?"

"Well, if I didn't know that 2525 was when we first made contact, do you think anybody else did?"

"A little full of yourself, aren't you?"

He wriggled again, settled his arms around her neck, leaned into her till they were nose to nose. "Just realistic is all."

"Well, Matthew knew it, O Wise Time Traveler Person," she pointed out. Sime scowled. She raised an eyebrow at him. "Don't like your thunder stolen, do you?"

"How he discovered that remains yet to be seen," he said. "But he may in fact have been told it by a future self of his which will run into me and been told it in turn. So it wasn't really him that discovered it at all, but me, even though—"

"Even though you went there because of a list he made before you went there," she filled in dutifully. Sime scowled harder.

"Yes."

"So you think we will find him, then?"

"It would appear to be the only possible course left." He bent and set the YDI, then sat back up and stared at her for long enough that she didn't notice when they arrived at All Saints. "Sevannah?"

"Yes?" she asked quietly. He sighed, and his breath brushed her face lightly like some eastern wind.

"Sometime I don't know why I bother with you," he told her, and got off her lap. The sudden release from weight was like freedom and she sprang up immediately before she could register that she'd gotten used to it.

He had already moved off through the crowd and was approaching the table. She hurried after him and caught up with him just in time to hear him informing Anastasia the secretary of their most recent misadventure.

"It'll have to be logged," he told her. "Can't have a bunch of us showing up and knowing everything that's going to happen. As it is, people panic. That's perfectly natural."

"Mm-hmm," said Anastasia solemnly, who didn't look like she'd ever panicked in her life.

"Can't interfere with that," Sime told her. He tapped at the table. "You'll have to put that down so people know they're to playact at being panicked as well. And it's not just a sort of latent post-modern anxiety either. I mean, it's not knocking at the door, it's screaming in the kitchen. Write that down."

"Are you telling me my job?"

"Just making certain," said Sime grimly.

"Because," said Anastasia angrily, turning to him for the first time and her pen finally ceasing from its hurried movements across the page, "being as I've been doing this for *years* now, I rather think I know it without your help!"

Sime stared at her.

"Sorry."

"You'd bloody well better be, buster!"

"Alright— alright!" Having decided that as discretion was the better part of valor, so placatory gestures were the better part of losing an argument, Sime raised both hands and backed away slowly. Turning to see Sev waiting for him beyond the farthest part of the series of banquet tables he was not best pleased, but grimaced and came forward anyway.

"Arrory," he addressed an Anarchist to Sev's right, who with pink-streaked hair and a multitude of piercings looked as though she'd been most recently slumming in the hipper areas of the middle 1990s despite the fact that she otherwise looked like someone's grandmother. "Have you seen Weaver?"

Behind him, Sev was mildly diverted by the sight of herself bounding through the room, following another Sime. She thought of how fresh and young she looked, all those years ago this morning, for of course it was an earlier version of themselves that had originally come here looking for Matthew. It gave her a momentary case of the shudders.

"Last I saw him was 1888," said Arrory, shrugging enigmatically.

"What was he doing?"

"Inventing peanut butter."

"Again?"

She shrugged once more. "It seems he likes it."

Sime sighed. "I suppose by the time I get there he'll have gone again."

"You're the expert, Sime."

"That I am." He sighed again and continued walking on to Sev, squaring his shoulders and looking like he was prepared for a fight. "Look, maybe we could talk about this. The longer we look for Matthew, the more irritated I get at the attitude you have towards your quote unquote 'relationship', so maybe we should just—"

"Sime, I think you'd better turn around," she

interrupted.

"I knew you weren't listening to me."

"But I'm—"

"Honestly, and they say *women* are the ones that always want to talk about emotions and whatnot." He threw up his hands and was about to turn away when he was tackled by a version of himself, shouting and swearing and tarnishing his own good name.

"Sime, you inconsiderate, insufferable, unbelievably selfish autocratic—"

"*Hey!*" said the Sime of now, hitting the ground with a solid thunk.

"Whoa there," said Sev behind him. She grinned at the present Sev, who was looking on in something like horror but rapidly approaching amusement. "I know how you're feeling. Don't worry about it. Help me get him off himself, will you?"

Together they lifted an irate FutureSime off a very confused present one, and the fighting-mad one was led off by Arrory, who apparently dealt with this sort of thing all the time— or Times, Sev amended.

Sime stumbled to his feet, released from the weight of himself, and looked from Sev to Sev.

"I hate it when this happens," he mumbled, burying his head in his hands. "It's like a slapstick comedy written by Sigmund Freud. There really is no controlling your other selves, you know. No matter how much you think, Okay, when the time comes and I feel like that, I *won't* attack myself in public. Because when it comes down to it, you did, you've done it, so why bother struggling against it?"

"Are you saying we're predestined?" asked the Sev of now. Her mirth had subsided somewhat now that Sime wasn't being throttled by himself. Watching him recover wasn't nearly as fun.

"I'm saying we predestine ourselves," said Sime, "which is even worse, because who has an accurate view of the big picture? No one, that's who. And just because we think a two-pronged mohawk and matching pocket protectors will look cool eighty years in the future doesn't mean we're *right*."

"It's interesting how you've changed over time," said FutureSev, smiling fondly at Sime. He looked at her, perplexed.

"I don't suppose you'd care to give me a hint about what you and he are doing here."

"You said that's a moral grey area and in this case it would probably be better not to let on," said FutureSev pedantically.

"Yes, well— it's not an actual *rule*, see," Sime wheedled. "So couldn't you just—"

"You said you'd say that."

"Ah. Well. I would know." Sime muttered something under his breath that sounded very much like, "Bugger me."

"You also said," carried on FutureSev, "that I should direct you to Okasina's Theory." She waved her hands in the air. "Don't ask me what you meant by that, because I don't know."

"He didn't tell you?" asked Sev.

She wrinkled her nose. "I wasn't paying attention."

Sev grinned at herself. "You really are me."

She grinned back. "Yeah, and right now I've got to go catch up with Sime. The world's ending, you know." She waved a hand airily. "He just wishes he'd done something about it."

She walked off, her words hanging in the air behind her. Sime and Sev exchanged worried glances.

"The world's ending?"

"Okasina's Theorem," muttered Sime, rubbing absentmindedly at his temples. Suddenly he grimaced. "I really got a whack to the head when I took me down, you know? Stupid bleeder."

"That's what you said about you," murmured Sev.

"Okasina's Theorem," repeated Sime, thoughtfully. Sev moved closer and took over rubbing his temples.

"What's that?"

"A useful warning for time travelers," said Sime, closing his eyes. "Actually developed by an Anarchist, but derived from the research of the Corporation's scientists. Okasina hacked into their computers on the web, stole their numbers. The police came and picked him up— actual police, not Tendence and Cavile, because it was still just a computer job at that point and didn't involve time. Well, he'd adapted a wristwatch as his machine, which is a neat trick and very difficult to do, because if you don't get the specs just right you'll just have one time-traveling arm. And some people try for a time-traveling pocket watch, which looks very cool and steampunk, except if you get it wrong and activate it in your front shirt pocket you end up with a time-traveling nipple, which is understandably confusing for everyone involved. Once I found this—"

"Sime!" He opened his eyes and looked at her. "Focus."

Sime coughed. "Alright. Sorry. Look. Okasina's been arrested. They don't take his wristwatch. Once in the cell, he goes back to his previous self and tells him how he can avoid leaving a trail, and sure enough, the police never come and pick him up, he never ends up in jail, and he never goes back to tell himself not to leave a trail. But it all holds together anyway, and this we're having trouble figuring out."

"What does it mean?"

"It means that universe exploded." He frowned slightly and she smoothed over his forehead with her thumbs. "Mm— I mean, exploded or imploded or goes to where all good universes go to die. Some sort of mysterious elephant graveyard, a wrecking yard for possibilities. I don't know. Nobody knows. That's why it's a special division of MWI—" He opened his eyes to squint at her. "Do I have to explain MWI to you, Sev?"

"Depends on what it stands for."

"Many-Worlds Interpretation."

"Is it what it sounds like?"

"It's exactly what it sounds like."

"A universe for every decision, then," she said readily. "Sci-fi. It's not as dull as history."

"Right." He looked relieved. "Which means that in every universe you're a slightly different person— which also leads to tons of philosophical arguments over whether you are in fact the same being, whether you are Sev or not, but the issue there would be what *makes* you Sev. What defines *you*. Is there one particular decision that you've made in your life that makes you what you are? Don't answer that. Every time one of those discussions gets started here at All Saints, it goes on for months and Anastasia has the hardest time getting everyone's viewpoint down. It's really not worth it. But that's still the question facing MWI and Okasina's Theorem— because if you go back to fix a mistake it will implode either your universe or the one that you were in however long ago. Sometimes it creates a new one. Sometimes it goes on with the old one. The problem is, suppose all these universes are like bubble wrap. They keep getting popped— eventually everything's going to be flat. And if they're lined up in rows like some people suggest, that means the walls between us and unreality are getting thinner. Our buffer zone of all those untaken paths is shrinking. Who knows where we'll end up? Don't answer that either, that argument's worse."

"So that applies here? He was saying that you can decide not to do whatever he attacked you for?"

"I'm guessing that was his intent— I didn't want to tell me what I'd done, because I didn't want the universe to explode, right? I mean— I don't. Still. I never have. It's a bad thing to happen. But if I discover for myself what I'd done wrong in that other universe, the future—" He paused.

"Maybe it will sort itself out?"

"Maybe so," he agreed.

"So what did he show up for then, anyway?"

"To throttle me. It happens. But also to tell me to be alert," said Sime soberly. "To warn me to watch out. I'm going to have to be very careful, Sev. Very, very careful indeed."

She dropped her hands away from his face and tilted her head to one side, looking at him. Eventually he sensed that, and opened his eyes.

"So there's a universe where I don't go looking for Matthew?" she asked quietly.

He waved one hand airily, and took her hand with the other. "There's probably a universe where you're just a brain in a vat. Anything is possible."

"But you actually think— what would happen to him if we didn't go rescue him from wherever he is?"

He stopped walking and looked at her seriously. "Sev. I doubt there's a single universe where you didn't go to find him if you possibly could. That's the decision, or one of them. That's what makes you *you*. That's what keeps you— Sevannah." She smiled at him, and he continued walking on towards where they'd left the chair, tugging at her hand to keep her with him. "Although," he added, "there's undoubtedly a universe or two where you never even met Matthew."

"But then I never would have met you either," she pointed out gently.

"That's so. It's a compromise." He sighed gustily. "The world's built on compromises."

"That's funny," said Sev. "I always thought it was built on absolutes." She grinned around her at the room, impartially. She got mostly glares back. "That was before I found out about time travel, though."

"It does tend to change your perspective," he commiserated. "Where would you like to go now?"

She pulled the list out of her pocket and scrutinized it for a moment before raising her head and looking back at him. "Weren't you going to look for someone? Weaver? In 1980 or something?"

"1888," he corrected her automatically. "It's likeliest that he's not there anymore. He tends to move on rather quickly. Restless. Can't settle down."

"Who is he?" she asked curiously.

He hesitated for a moment before he answered.

"He's an anomaly. The only one of his kind. He lives backwards."

"What, like— walks around with his skull in front, or what?"

"No, actually lives backwards. He was—" He laughed shortly. "Well, no one knows how old he was when he was born, because he refuses to tell us. But he was as old as he's going to get from his birth onwards, and as time goes on, he gets younger and younger. Presumably when he gets back to infant stage he'll either die or start over again. If it happens."

She was quiet for a moment.

"That must have been hard on his mother."

"Is that—" He dropped her hand. "Is that all you can say? Hard on his mother?"

"Give me a minute." She thought about it. "And his dad, too. Having to teach your infant son how to shave."

He laughed at that and gave her a gentle shove.

"Anyway, he usually travels with himself. So, out there somewhere, there's a young man who knows everything, and an old man who knows nothing, and they're the same person. It's pretty interesting."

"Is that why you were looking for him? Interest? A juxtaposition of stereotypes?"

"No. I'm looking for him because I think he can help me with the biggest, most dangerous job I've ever undertaken."

"Re-wallpapering All Saints?" she hazarded. They reached the chair. He sat in it and she sat on him.

"Well, I was planning on trying to take down the Organization," admitted Sime, thoughtfully, "but you're right, that would be much worse."

"Taking down the Organization? How on earth would you do that?"

"That's why I was looking for Weaver. Hoping he could help me with that part of it."

"Oh." She put her arms around his neck and held on.

"So should we go look for him?"

"Matthew first," he reminded her. "Matthew first, then the rest of the world. It'll be good practice, saving a man. Then we can move upwards in our ambition."

"Alright," she agreed. "Matthew first."

"So where then?"

"Your turn to choose," she said, even though it wasn't, and buried her head in his shoulder so it would be a surprise.

"We've been looking for you all over," said Tendence solemnly.

"You should be flattered," prompted Cavile.

Their prey didn't look particularly flattered. He didn't look particularly anything. He'd been knocked out cold when Cavile had thrown him through a wall, although, as Cavile pointed out, he hadn't thrown him all that hard.

"Some people," observed Tendence, "just can't take the heat."

"I didn't apply any heat," said Cavile.

"Not yet." It was a suggestion.

"Perhaps," acknowledged Cavile. "If the occasion calls for it. I may have to get out my recipe book."

Tendence stepped delicately through the opening in the mangled sheet rock and stood over the heap formerly known as man. He bent down and sniffed genteelly.

"No need," he proclaimed. "This man is dead."

Cavile sighed, unfolded his arms, and put his hands over his face. "I'm sorry."

Tendence straightened up and fixed him with a stern eye, like a college mathematics professor with a recalcitrant student. "I have told you and told you time and again."

"I know." Cavile's voice was muffled. "It's just hard to get the correct amount of force— if I'd thrown him a little softer he'd just have bounced off."

"You must learn not to make such a show of it, then. Throw him into a couch. Something soft. Hurl him into that pool outside next time."

Cavile drew his hands down and one eye peered at his partner over his fingers. "And get him all wet? That's not very polite."

"Neither is catapulting him through a stand of two by fours," pointed out Tendence.

Cavile drew his hands down the rest of the way and put them on his hips. "Perhaps you'd like to try for a while."

"Oh no," said Tendence, waving his hands. "You're not making this my fault, nor are you making me feel guilty. I do my part, you do yours. We work well together and you know it. How would this operation work if we were stepping out of our accepted roles all the time?"

Cavile's face set, grimly. "I want to role play."

"Oh, not again."

"I mean it. I do," said Cavile stubbornly. "You said we can do it for practice every now and then, to keep us sharp in case something happens. You said we need to know how to handle every situation that comes our way. You said—"

"I said too much. Please, stop repeating my well-articulated but poorly considered words to me. It was an error of great magnitude. I merely thought I should like to try the hands-on approach once in a while."

"Well, try it once in a while now."

Tendence pinched the bridge of his finely-drawn nose with his fingers and sighed noisily. "Very well."

The scene jumped sideways and backwards and they turned around to see their latest prey standing at his desk, going through paperwork and apparently unaware of their presence. Previously, in the earlier edition of this scenario, they'd been in front of him, and he had been very aware of them, almost painfully so. They had also been between him and any means of escape. Now, of course, they were less desirably placed, but Tendence was irritated and simply wanted to get this over as soon as possible. He strode up to the man and tapped him on the shoulder.

The prey spun around.

"Hi," said Tendence shortly, and punched him in the face.

The original punch had been the source of the problem with the hole in the wall. Cavile was a large man, with large hands, and a lot of force behind them. Tendence was smaller, thinner, and his hand had less articulatory power and force than his tongue. The man merely sat back against the desk a little faster than he would have normally. He brought his hand up to his chin and looked baffled at them. *Baffled* was not what they were used to; they'd been aiming for terrified and usually got it without any difficulty. But here they were, role playing once again, despite the problems they'd had the last time they did this, and Tendence stepped back and let Cavile take over, shaking his head.

"Now you listen," said Cavile, shaking a ponderous, admonitory finger at the prey. "This isn't your house, this isn't your time, this isn't your place, and that shirt is all wrong for your coloring."

The prey looked at Tendence, who shrugged and waved his hand in the air, somewhat apologetically.

"And furthermore," said Cavile, slowing as his imagination ran down like the sands of time in an hourglass, "your— mustache— is— silly."

The prey blinked, and as nothing more was forthcoming and Tendence didn't seem to want to jump in at this juncture, he went backwards over the desk and out of the room as quickly as possible.

Tendence and Cavile exchanged a glance.

"Told you this was a bad idea."

"Oh, hush," muttered Cavile, blushing a deep and bloody red.

They hastened after him and managed to catch him up as he reached the shed where he kept his machine. He'd very cleverly locked it to keep anyone unauthorized from getting to it and making use of it. It probably wouldn't have been such an issue if he'd chosen something simpler than a motorcycle to make a time machine out of.

"Show off," muttered Tendence.

The prey had also, quite foolishly, left the key to the shed back on his desk in the room they'd just vacated, so Tendence and Cavile had plenty of time to stroll leisurely towards him. Strolling leisurely was something they did often enough for both of them to do equally well, and required no role playing on the part of either of them. Tendence took the left side, and Cavile covered the right.

"I hope you're ashamed of yourself," said Cavile heavily. "It's just not right, stealing from the Corporation like that."

The prey turned to them, bracing his back against the shed wall, panting like a rabbit running from a hawk. "The Corporation's screwed, man. There's only so long they can bleed the economy dry. Soon no one will pay for their services."

"There are plenty of wealthy people about," pointed out Tendence.

"'You will always have the rich with you,'" misquoted Cavile in an admirable attempt at disingenuous dialogue that immediately flat-lined. The prey blinked at him, looked at Tendence, looked back at Cavile, and took what he assumed was the wiser course. He charged the smaller Tendence at the outside, headed for the narrow path that ran between the Corporation's articulate watchdog and the in-ground pool. Tendence stepped aside and, as the prey ran past, tripped him neatly. The time-traveler hit the cement first and then rolled, groaning, into the water.

Tendence brushed his hands together briskly. "And that, my friend, is how it is done."

"That's why there's that sign up," observed Cavile. "'No running by the pool'. It's just common sense, really. Safety first." He looked his co-worker, who stood with his arms folded, watching bubbles float up from the depths of the water. "Kind of cruel, isn't it?"

"Why? It's heated," pointed out Tendence.

"Oh." They both stared at the water, waiting for the prey to come to and emerge. "Explain MWI to me again, Tendence."

"Well," said Tendence, and stared into the air for a minute. "Imagine you're a brain in a vat."

There was a pause, then—

"Okay," said Cavile thoughtfully. "I'm a brain in a vat."

"Now take away the brain."

There was a longer pause.

"What do you have left?"

"—I'm a vat?"

"Exactly." Tendence went into action now, bending over, reaching in, and fishing the still-unconscious prey out. He tugged him out of the water, nearly straining his back on the dead weight. "Urgh! We'll have to advise him to go on a diet. Cavile—"

"Yes?" said Cavile, semi-alertly. He'd been pondering the meaning of Tendence's words but not very deeply.

"Get a towel."

"Here we are, then," said Sime.

Sev glanced around. She had confessed to him that she'd wanted a surprise, and he'd taken her at her word. The clothes she'd donned didn't mean much to her. As far as she was concerned, every century dressed pretty much alike until blue jeans were invented. The dress made it hard to sit in the chair, and even harder to sit in Sime's lap. The satin was slick as a water slide. She kept sliding inexorably towards his knees, and he had to hold her tightly around the waist to keep her from falling off between the basement and— wherever this was.

"Where we are, then?" she prompted, raising her eyebrows. "You know I can't tell one year from another."

"I do know that," allowed Sime, "and it's to my credit that I don't dump you off somewhere in the BC and let you learn history from the ground up. Let's give it a try. Where do you think we are?"

"Um—" She looked around her again and tried to take in more clues this time. They stood next to the chair in a land of what she supposed could be called pastoral delights; it was a sloping greensward leading down to a slow river complete with rickety wooden dock and a rickety wooden boat moored up on it. There were a few large trees further up on the slope, though she couldn't tell what kind because she was almost as bad at horticultural things as she was at historical oddities. Well, historical anything, really. There were also some sheep in the distance. She'd always mistrusted sheep, somehow. They seemed so devious underneath all that hair. She'd always mistrusted the Beatles for the same reason. Squaring her shoulders, she eyed them from afar and gave it her best guess.

"England?"

"Very good," he said approvingly. "Sommershire, England. Any guess as to the date?"

She glanced down at herself, glanced at him, shook her head. "None. Except maybe around the same time as I was here before."

"Well, it's the 1800s, I'll give you that. 1812, as a matter of fact."

"Who was on the list for here?" she asked, tilting her head to one side and finally looking away from the sheep. "I sort of thought we'd end up going to look for Edgar Allen Poe."

"1812," said Sime quietly, "I am ten years old, and time travel for the first time."

She paused and finally looked at him.

"Oh."

"Yes."

"And you think Matthew will be here looking for you?"

Sime faced away from her, faced towards the river and shrugged lightly, twisting his mouth thoughtfully. "It seems a likely place in my history. After this I experimented for a few months before giving it up after I saw something I shouldn't have seen. I didn't go back to it till it dawned on me that it would be helpful for school and completing my exams successfully—" He smiled reminiscently, and she smiled at him smiling. His face had relaxed, his eyes distant and dreamy. "And besides, what I'd seen was only a possibility. There is no point in hiding from a possibility; it won't make your life any more sure."

"What did you see?" He didn't answer and she waited for a moment before stepping up to him and putting a hand on his shoulder. "What did you see, Sime?"

"I saw a battle," he said shortly, and turned away again. "Still and all, its possible Matthew's lurking in the shrubbery somewhere, scribbling notes on things. I still can't for the life of me imagine why he wants to meet the people he does, or thinks he does, or imagines he thinks he does. It's like a schoolboy's dream."

"Maybe that's it. He is a scientist; they're a little more like schoolboys than other professions, I'd say. Them and rock stars."

"Possibly." They moved together up the thick and well-kept lawn, and she decided that it looked so much better than what she had at home that she would never use a lawnmower again. She might have to hire a troop of gardeners with long scissors, but she'd do it.

"Who does this house belong to, then?"

"It was my parents'. My aunt moved in after they passed away, and I've been put into boarding school by this point. But she still had me for holidays. This is one of them."

"What if she sees you? Or the servants, or something?"

"That's a flattering question, but I regret to tell you I've changed somewhat since I was ten. They won't know me; and I have a wallet containing credentials insisting I am a hundred different people, which is a useful thing to have in your possession when you time travel. Gets you out of all sorts of scrapes. Just don't try to use all of them at once. Remember that."

"I will."

"I think—" said Sime, and pulled out the wallet in question. He went through some of the cards, pulled one away from the rest of the pack and smiled at it. "Yes. This will impress them." He peered at her for a minute. "You're going to have to be my wife."

She *tsk*'d. "I imagine Edward Teach will have something to say about that."

"Oh yes," he said laconically, holding the card up at eye level and scrutinizing it. "Did you ever go about getting a divorce?"

She stopped dead.

"You didn't tell me I had to do that! How on earth do I do that?"

He put the card back in his pocket and grinned at her. "You don't. I just think its funny when you get affronted. Your voice goes all high and squeaky like a surprised mouse."

"Oh, you know what, Sime? You can just roll over and—"

"Watch your language," he advised her. "We're in very proper times here."

Despite her irritation, she didn't protest as he took her by the arm and led her towards the stand of trees. Inside in the dimmer light she could make out the form of an elaborate playhouse, including a platform with railings built between the branches of the largest of the trees. It looked like a childhood fantasy; the house was even neatly painted, which was more than she could say for any playhouse she'd ever had.

"I think this is where I came back to," said Sime, frowning thoughtfully. "I spent so much time here it was sort of hardwired into me. Naturally, not having to travel with a machine meant I didn't have a recall number, but if I got into trouble or just wanted to get out of wherever I was, I thought very hard about being safe. This was always where I ended up."

"Where do you end up now, when you think that?"

He looked at her, and smiled very slightly; just the tip

of his mouth went upwards. "I haven't been able to go somewhere safe for a very long time now."

She turned her eyes back to the house. "Oh."

He glanced around. "I hear voices. Let's go up to the tree house."

"Thought you were going to impress people with your credentials?"

"I'd impress adults. The child version of myself would be considerably less favorably affected. I didn't like pompous gits at ten any more than I do now."

"And that's what your card says? 'Pompous git?'"

"Get moving, if you please." Without letting her know his intention, he gave her a solid boost up into the tree. She squawked in surprise at the sudden contact, the sudden altitude, and grabbed onto the planks of the sort-of-treehouse for balance. It wasn't more than eight feet off the ground, just high enough that they wouldn't be seen. He went up the steps behind her.

"Could have used those instead of—"

"Shhh."

She mouthed, "— *instead of you putting your hands on my tush.*"

"*Ask me nicely later,*" he mouthed back, and leaned over the edge. She smacked him and then had to catch him before he fell over. He glared at her and she bit her finger to keep from laughing. Sime pointed towards a figure coming across the lawn towards them. Squinting, she could make out his features, and sure enough, in them was Sime as she knew him, in embryo as it were. Sime at ten had a petulant, upturned face, a rounded chin, a delicate mouth, and slanting wise eyes that took everything else and turned it from that of a spoiled child to that of a knowing adolescent. She grinned hard and turned back to the Sime of now.

"*You're adorable!*" she mouthed at him.

He only grimaced and, when she carried on grinning at him anyway, mouthed a long string of syllables that she didn't entirely catch and didn't ask him to repeat.

The child— approaching young manhood, yes, but a child nonetheless— walked through the trees, hugging his arms around his body and whistling in something that sounded more like a nervous habit than carefree noise. Sime sat up, tensing his back, watching alertly for what the boy did. Young Sime approached the tree house and glanced side to side, examining his surroundings for anyone watching. Seeing that no one appeared to be about, Sev could see him squinch his eyes shut tightly and murmur words to himself as though he was praying. There was something infinitely touching about him, the soft quiet syllables and the long black lashes on pale cheeks. She felt some dormant maternal urge well up in her, which was odd with the older version of the boy sitting right next to her watching himself with this indefinable look of *something* on his face. It wasn't pride. It wasn't irritation. It looked like apprehension.

She was going to ask him about it when the boy disappeared. Faded right out of view nearly instantaneously, right there in front of her. She'd experienced time travel, certainly, but she hadn't seen it happen to someone else. It gave her a funny feeling in the pit of her stomach, to think that anyone watching her and Sime as they traveled would have seen them disappear like that, so unconcerned, so unknowably ahead, and leaving everyone else behind.

She grabbed Sime's wrist, and he looked at her with amusement in his eyes.

"I'm not going anywhere."

"Just making sure."

"Well, you have made sure. I can't travel on my own with anyone else. As long as you're holding onto me, I'm going nowhere just like my aunt always told me I would."

She grinned at him. "You really are adorable, you know."

"Yes, yes, so you've said. Blame it on the youth, the age. I haven't had time to toughen yet. Still soft and cuddly."

"I didn't mean just then," she said.

But Young Sime had popped back into view, as suddenly as a Jack-in-the-box. Sev looked away from her own Sime in time to see the child clutch his arms around himself and sink down to the ground, sobbing. She moved to get out of the tree but her own Sime took her arm, held her back, stayed her flight.

"Don't."

"But he's crying!"

"I know I am," he said patiently. "But I also know that you're not the one who comes to comfort me."

"But—"

"I should know. I was there. Remember?" The sound of soft sobs coming from the foot of the tree nearly broke Sev's heart, and she gave Sime a pleading look. He shook his head firmly and carried on speaking in a low voice. "No. I don't know you when I meet you later, so you're not the one who comes to me now. Don't worry. Someone does. You—" he tucked her arm through his, doubled it up and close to his body. "— stay here with me. Comfort me."

"But you're not the one crying."

"I might well be in a minute," he said easily.

She sighed, dropped her head against his shoulder. "You're insufferable."

The slight breeze from his chuckle stirred her hair. "So I've been told. By myself, so it must be true."

"What is it that you do?" she asked, acutely conscious of both the Sime next to her and the Sime sobbing on the ground below them. "That's so dangerous to the continued non-ending of the universe?"

"I don't know," he answered. "I'm guessing we're going to find out. Whatever it is, Sev— try to keep in mind that I am just as capable of making bad decisions as anyone else. Sometimes. " He paused, and shrugged. "Sometimes I forget."

Before she could answer that enigmatic statement, she heard a voice calling in the distance.

"*Simon!*"

There were footsteps barely heard on the grass, a small shadow moving towards Young Sime, who curled himself up in a tighter ball for a moment as though he was trying to hide. But the voice that reached him now, the touch that she gave him, loosened him up and reassured him. It obviously wasn't who he'd thought would come for him.

"*That wasn't who I thought came for me,*" said Sime of now, as the Sime of then sat up and wiped his eyes, and his voice was hollow and strange, echoing and cobwebbed as though unused for a very long time.

Sev peered over the edge and looked at the two children. The newcomer was a girl not more than five years old, half Sime's age and absolutely tiny. Her hands and face were extraordinarily delicate; her hair was long and dark and thick, held back in two braids that reached her waist. Her hands as she patted Young Sime's shoulder were unexpectedly clumsy, though obviously well-meaning; Sev got the feeling that she was much more used to being comforted than being the one doing the comforting. Which, for a five year old, was as it should be. Young Sime appeared to be taking it better than most ten-year-old boys would, considering a little girl had found him crying and was trying to make him feel better. Presumably the inherent machismo hadn't fully kicked in yet.

"Where have you been?" the girl asked him. Young Sime looked hunted for a moment before he replied—

"Just around."

The girl raised her eyebrows; the skeptical expression on her face looked out of place on such a young thing, and made Sev grin. "Being 'just around' made you sad?"

Young Sime straightened up and folded his arms. The girl patted his head.

"I went down to the farm," said Young Sime after a moment. "They were killing a pig."

The girl nodded sympathetically, as though this was perfectly understandable, to be sobbing like your world was coming to an end over the death of a nearby farmer's pig. She resumed patting his head, slow soft pets on his thick black hair, and watched him with wide eyes.

"Is that all?" she asked eventually, and Young Sime nodded defiantly.

"That's all, Mary. What else would there be?"

"Well," she said hesitantly, "I thought maybe you had gone back to the Wood, and that giant had eaten your house."

Sev looked over at her own Sime, who was paying more attention to the people talking than to the words themselves and didn't seem to register this interesting statement.

"That's just a story, Mary," said Young Sime, rolling his eyes. "I wouldn't actually—" Words failed him when it came to admitting that he was crying, and he floundered for a minute. "Stories don't make me sad. Only things that actually happen make me sad."

"It made me sad when you told me about the princess losing her cat," confided Mary.

Young Sime looked down at her for a moment, and then relented.

"Alright, well, it made you sad because you're a girl. And because it was a sad story. I'm sorry I told it to you if it made you feel badly."

She shrugged her tiny shoulders. "It is alright. I like to hear the stories."

They sat side by side for a moment in companionable silence, before Mary ventured to ask anything else.

"Would you tell me another story, Simon?"

"Right now?"

"Yes, please, Simon. We're only visiting for tea. I'll have to go home soon."

"Alright," said Young Sime quickly, "but not here. Let's go into the house. I'll tell you about Maggot the Witch."

"Ew!" said Mary.

"No, no, it's very good! It's a good one, Mary, I promise."

"Yuck!"

"Come on." He stood up and gave her a hand,

reminding Sev so much of the Sime she knew that she gave an involuntary glance towards him. His eyes were fixed on his younger self and the girl named Mary, so set upon the couple that he didn't even blink as he watched the two of them meander out of the woods and cross the lawn towards the house on the hill.

"Can we move now?" she whispered to him, and he started in surprise. "Sorry." She patted him on the arm. "You looked kind of— mesmerized. In your own world. I didn't meant to startle you."

"It's alright," he said shortly, got up and started down the wooden steps towards the ground without waiting to see if she was following him. She did, though, as quickly as possible, although the fact that she had terrible balance didn't make it easy. Once back firmly-footed on the ground, she caught him up quickly and slid her arm through his. They walked on through the woods.

"Who was she?"

"Hmm?" He was deep in his thoughts, or pretending to be.

"You know who I'm asking about."

"She was my wife," he said shortly, "and did you see the clothes I was wearing? My uncle gave me those clothes. They'd belonged to his son, who died in a boating accident. Isn't that morbid? Uncle gave me his nightclothes as well, and every time I wore them I had nightmares about drowning. Why've you stopped?" He realized suddenly that her arm had slipped from his grasp and she was several steps behind him; turning, he raised his eyebrows quizzically at the expression on her face.

"Wife?" she repeated blankly.

He walked back towards her, hands in his pockets, head down like a chastised schoolboy.

"Wife," he agreed. "Not then, of course, because that wasn't legal even in that day and age. We weren't troglodytes. And it wasn't as though we were intended for each other, because this was right after they'd stopped making arranged marriages from birth— at least, they weren't as common then, though they certainly had their heyday and were fairly popular shortly before I was born. But later, after I'd grown up and she'd grown up. After I went into the RAF for five years—"

"RAF?"

"Royal Air Force. I was quite patriotic at one point."

She frowned and looked at him suspiciously. "I could be wrong about this, correct me if I am, but I'm reasonably certain they didn't have actual airplanes at this point."

"No, but they did in 1934," he agreed complacently. "Which is when I officially joined up. I only stuck it out for five years, though, instead of the six they wanted me to give. Something happened, snapped inside of me, and I could hear it clicking around at loose ends— I found a photograph of Mary and I had to get back."

She eyed him askance. He smiled tightly but his eyes were distant and clouded.

"So you went back and—"

"Married her. Yes."

"Oh." She wasn't sure what inflection to give this "Oh," and so ended up giving it as little as possible. Not that it mattered much, probably, because Sime was too deep into his own reminiscences in his head to notice even if she'd been screaming with a jealous rage. It wouldn't have been a jealous rage anyway, she told herself sternly, it wouldn't have been and it never would be. What on earth did she care if Sime had been married? Or if he still was, for that matter. It gave his habit of touching her so freely a disturbing tinge.

"And what happened after that?" *You can't have a thought like that and not ask. Just to satisfy your curiosity. That's all.*

"After that—" He breathed in deep, raised his shoulders from their slump. "I settled down. Stopped traveling."

"Why?"

"Because she couldn't come with me."

"Oh." This one slipped out before she had a chance to

choose which tone to couch it in; but that was alright, because all of a sudden the romance of his situation hit her and she was thinking longingly of a man who would voluntarily give up an eternal life of action and adventure just because he wanted to stay home with her. After a moment, the wrongness of this feeling as it applied to her own circumstances hit her and she shook the miasma of rose-colored feeling off and repeated it. "Oh."

He glanced up at her sharply.

"But what—"

"Matthew's not here, that much is certain," he said briskly, removing his hands from his pockets and taking her arm, stirring her unwilling feet to action. "We'd best be on our way and find out just where he's at."

Clearly her question would go unanswered. She settled for that and came up with a new one.

"What was it that you saw, that made you cry?"

For a moment the skin of his palms went cold, and she shivered. He tucked her tighter, closer to him and she interlaced their fingers, trying to give him some of her warmth.

"I went back, that first time. Not far enough— I saw the death of my mother," he said quietly. "When I was young, just a child, she caught cold, which turned into pneumonia within a week. We didn't have the tools to deal with things back then, not like your present. Something that should have been just a routine hospital stay and a few rounds of antibiotics turned into a rainy funeral. We buried her just over there." He pointed out across the grass to another, separate stand of trees that had a clearing in the middle of them. "It ends up being the family graveyard, years later on. There's even a stone for me, eventually."

She looked at him, shocked. "Really?"

"Well. The feeling is that there's one eventuality for us all— in 1902, on my hundredth birthday, my nieces and nephews pretty much assume that I've gone to it, and there's no possible way I can be alive. So they carve the stone, and lay it, and there I lie as far as they're concerned.

No matter where my body is actually at. One of those mysteries."

"What happened?" It finally came out, a simple question with what was undoubtedly a complex answer, but there it was with no consideration for tone or definition. She just wanted to know.

"Another time," said Sime, briefly. "I'll tell you, I promise, but— another time. Alright?"

"Alright," she agreed, and they walked on. She could see the chair standing forlorn and lonesome not too far in front of them. They walked forward, and very shortly were gone.

Chapter Eleven

"Need a rest?"

Sime's arms were folded on the kitchen table, his chin resting on them. He looked as though he needed to lie down for a bit, but he sat up at her question and belied it. "No, I'm fine. Could use something to eat though."

"Well, I'm working on it. Hold on."

Gas stoves were not the easiest thing for Sev to work with. She went through three matches before she succeeded in getting it lit, and then she singed her hair. Sime half-stood quickly when he saw the gout of flame, but she stopped screaming fairly quickly and waved him to sit back down. At last the gas was adjusted properly and she slid the pan on carefully as though afraid of waking a sleeping child.

"I do better in my own kitchen," she said.

"Well, you didn't blow up the house yet," said Sime, "so you're one up on me anyway."

There was so little in Matthew's refrigerator that she felt badly about going through it; but, telling herself firmly that most of it was bad anyway and she deserved a little something for doing him the favor of cleaning it out, she took the remaining five eggs and the wilted, twisted, sad little group of mushrooms and made them into an omelet. Not a very good one, she had to admit to herself, but given the vagaries of the flame and the limitations of the fridge it was the best she could do under the circumstances.

"Good," said Sime.

"Generous," said Sev.

She sat beside him and placed the list in between their plates. As they ate they scrutinized it. Sev had placed a check mark next to the few destinations they'd actually traveled to. Realizing how few they actually were, she sighed noisily.

Sime patted her shoulder.

"Don't get all depressed. We're working on it."

"We're never going to find him." She put her elbows on the table and put her hands over her face. "All of time, all of space, all those places he wants to go. We don't even know why, Sime! We don't even know what he was looking for."

"Probably something noble, I have no doubt."

"That's got to be sarcasm. Stop being sarcastic. For all we know, he was looking for the best wines in time. The quickest way to get drunk. Failing that, a good hangover remedy."

"Maybe he's looking for the perfect way to propose to you."

She drew her hands down her face, and turned an inimical stare on him. He grinned cheerfully at her.

"Well," she said, "not disappearing for weeks at a time would be a good start."

His hand stilled on her shoulder, near her neck, and he slid it slowly backwards, passing his thumb over her shoulder. She winced, and wondered if Sime's own shoulders could possibly as tense as hers. More than likely. Possibly much worse.

"You're all lumps and knots back here."

"I've had a hard couple of hundred years," she said, dropping her head so low her hair dangled in her plate. "Sime, please tell me where we're going next. I can't stand to make another decision that's going to turn out wrong."

"You'd rather have someone to blame it on?"

"You'd better believe it, buster."

He hummed to himself and looked the list over one more time.

"Well," he said eventually, "odd as it may seem, I'm going to say 1889, the United States of America— the Old West. Town called—" He squinted at it. "Pleaser?"

"Placer." She moved the paper towards her and looked at it. "Matthew's great great great great great grandparents were born there."

Sime nodded deeply. "Yes, that sounds about right. They try their best to hide it, but scientific types have a deep, secret yearning to be butch and macho. And, well, for Americans who aren't either super heroes, *Die Hard* sequels, or governors of state, that's all bound up in the Old West. Plus there's the element, if his family really does come from there like he thinks they do, of that certain— how should I put this?"

"Family feeling?" guessed Sev.

"Insane desire to mess up your own life by somehow influencing that of your forefathers," said Sime. "It's a type of suicidal urge. Most of us are at least somewhat susceptible to it." He looked at Sev sternly. "You don't have any family in this place, do you?"

She shrugged. "Not that I know of."

"Good. Good. It's no use, knowing too much about your family. You never learn anything to your benefit. Alright." He scraped the last bit of egg off his plate and downed the coffee as well, wincing as the free-floating grounds hit his teeth. Sev hadn't been able to locate any coffee filters and had ended up using a paper napkin from a fast food restaurant, to sad effect. Caffeine, she had decided was the main thing; Sime did not appear to agree. "Let's get going."

She glanced at the clock as she left the kitchen. She'd first arrived here to search for clues to Matthew's whereabouts at shortly after nine thirty. She'd made five trips, counting the first one, as well as two more little jaunts to All Saints. It was now nine forty-seven.

She reckoned she was doing okay on time.

"So why are you adept?"

Sime grunted as he wrestled with the large belt buckle. "Well, just look at me. Isn't it obvious?"

"No, I mean— why can you travel without a time machine? Why can you travel on your own when no one else can?" She put both hands out to stop him as he started to speak. "That's right. Tendence and Cavile can, I forgot. Why can only the three of you—"

"It's not only the three of us. There have been lots of Adepts over the years. Well, alright, not lots, but more than three."

"That's specific."

"Some, alright? It's something to do with something hidden in our genetic makeup— not sure just what, I'm sure you understand that none of us are keen on being poked at by scientists— and it only crops up once in a while, so only a few are born with the talent. Weaver is another one of them." He was quiet for a minute, smoothing and adjusting his costume, making all the fringes on his chaps lay flat. As soon as he stood up, they all fell haphazardly around again. "Man-aprons of the old west," he murmured to them, then looked up at her and said, candidly, "I'll tell you, I thought I discovered time travel on my own when I first started doing it. I had no idea that it was this big—" He spread his hands wordlessly.

"Wheel," said Sev. Then, tentatively, "Sime."

"Yes." He'd resumed the fight with his pants.

"Can you actually stop time?"

The pants yielded, and he stopped for a minute, hands on his knees, and considered.

"No."

"Oh. I thought it felt like you could." She sighed briskly

and brushed down her dress, adjusting her hat. "I look like a prairie dog."

"You look just like everyone else will," he assured her, and led her to the chair, carrying his hat. He sat on it before he put the hat on, and gestured to her to seat herself as well. She did.

"1889 it is, then," said Sime, and made it so on the YDI.

She made a mental note, as they were sitting suddenly at the outskirts of a town that was all the same dusty, windblown color, to ask him how exactly the Year/Destination Indicator worked, especially when it came to places. Nothing too technical, just anything other than, "It is, because it is," which was a little too Zen for her.

Arm in arm, they strolled up the street, nodding and bestowing an amateur, "Howdy, partner," on each presumable partner passing by. Sime paused in the middle of tipping his hat and said to her out of the corner of his mouth, "Stop doing that, Sev."

"Doing what?"

"Walking like that. You look sort of— jaunty."

She was in fact walking very jauntily. "I can't help it. It's the dress, it's the freest and least restrictive thing I've worn so far."

"Even though it makes you look like a prairie dog? A swaggering prairie dog?"

"Hey, prairie dogs are very comfortable with themselves." She was surprised and overcome by a sudden feeling of well-being, here in this ugly dress in this ugly town with a man wearing chaps and spurs. Six trips in, perhaps she was getting the hang of things. She grinned benevolently at Sime and he shook his head at her, smiling back.

"Sometimes I just don't—"

She leaned up and kissed him on the cheek.

"Don't get me?" she completed for him brightly. "I've got a good feeling about this one, Sime. I think this one will turn out well."

"You think we'll find him here?"

"Well, yeah. I guess."

"You guess?"

"Why?" She frowned suddenly. "Don't you?"

"We'll do our best."

She thought about this for a minute, contrasted her own enthusiasm with his more realistic attitude, and decided, despite everything, they complimented each other well. She nodded and held onto his arm more tightly. "Alright."

The time-honored place to start was the local saloon, which they located without difficulty at the end of the street, on the corner. It appeared to be the only such establishment in town, as the sign said simply "The Saloon". There was also a small set of lettering underneath that said "*J. A. Johnson, prop.*" Sev was faintly disappointed to discover that there were no swinging doors like she'd seen in all the Old West films. She'd always wanted to burst through both of them at once and mosey up to the bar; she wasn't sure how to mosey, exactly, but she figured she could get it after a few practice runs. Sadly, this dream was not to be. Sime did hold the door open for her, though.

"You'll have to be my sister or something," he said. "Again."

"Why? Think I'll get mistaken for a prostitute?"

"It's the Old West, Sev. No, strike that. It's *mankind*. A race where the males usually believe that 'woman' is synonymous with 'available.'"

"Sometimes it is," said Sev, shrugging lightly. "Sometimes it isn't. I'm a modern woman, Sime. *I* decide when I'm available."

"Yeah, sure," said Sime.

"It sounds like you're agreeing with me, but you're really not. That's such a guy thing. I hate that."

She tried to mosey but she tripped over her dress. Sime followed her, rolling his eyes.

They both made it up to the bar without further

incident, and after some miscellaneous difficulties involving hiking the dress out of her way, Sev even made it onto a bar stool. J. A. Johnson himself stood behind the bar, thus identified by some early version of a name tag. He put both hands fisted on the bar and leaned over towards them.

"Whaddyawant?"

"You're not from New York, are you?" said Sev involuntarily.

"Originally, yuh," said J. A. Johnson, nodding and agreeing after looking at her suspiciously for a second.

"Amazing," said Sev happily. Sime made a visible decision not to plumb the depths of this conversation's origin in her head, and ordered whiskey for himself.

"And water for the lady," he said, pointing at her with his thumb. "I promised our ma I wouldn't bring her home falling down drunk again, and it looks like it's going to be a difficult job."

Sev turned a glare on him. He smiled at her sweetly.

"You want to keep your head on straight, looking for your boyfriend," he advised her.

"Ya from England?" said J. A. Johnson, rapping a shot glass down in front of him and spilling half the contents across the bar and into Sime's lap. Sime held out his hands to let the liquid dripping off the bar pool in his palms, then licked it off.

"Have been, yes," he admitted, and shot the whiskey down his throat quickly, before any more of it could get away.

"But not the lady?" said J. A. Johnson, eyeing Sev with a look that said the honorific was doubtful in the extreme.

"But not the lady," agreed Sime. "She was raised here in the good ol' US of A. Confusing on the face of it, but two seconds of contemplation will clear it up admirably. Now, we're looking for a friend of ours, and perhaps you may have heard his name?" He turned to Sev expectantly. "What was his name again, sister of mine?"

"Adler," she said readily. "We're looking for a man

name of Adler. Pardner."

"Adler-Pardner?" murmured Sime. Sev jabbed at him with her elbow. J. A. Johnson, not letting up on the suspicious stare for a moment, nodded slowly and pointed to a dark corner of the saloon.

"Adler's over there."

Sev caught her breath so quickly she choked on it, smiling at the same time. Doing both at once, she ended up gasping like a fish out of water, and Sime gave a short laugh that didn't sound at all sure of its place in the world. She turned her head to look over her shoulder, but could make out nothing conclusive.

She slid unsteadily down from the stool and made her way with wavering steps towards the corner. She might have fallen halfway over there if Sime hadn't gotten down from his own chair and gone after her. She took one step back, out of rhythm and without sense, and he caught her by the elbows and murmured in her ear.

"It's alright, Sevannah. It's alright. I've got you."

She had to keep walking.

She wondered that she hadn't noticed him when she first walked in. Because, yes, there was the shape of Matthew's head, from the back, careful brown hair grown out a little now— which was only to be expected, because who knew how long he'd been here, really? Could have been months, by now. Could have been years. What if he was, like, eighty now? There was no telling; time was so relative, such a difficult concept to pin down. This made her giggle and Sime tightened his hold on her arm.

"Are you alright?" he whispered.

"Perfectly, perfectly, perfectly," said Sev, and strode forward the last few steps, and put a trembling hand out to Matthew's shoulder. She fisted his shirt in her hand, brought her body up behind his, and bent gasping over his head, clasping her hands around his neck despite the fact that Matthew always hated public displays of affection like this. In fact, it was one of the things they'd had an agreement about. Though, now that she thought about it, it wasn't so much an agreement as one of the Rules that Matthew had set for them both to follow, as though they'd get carried away and do something so out of place as to merit their exile from the country—

Not that this was the time for thinking of things like that. No. This was the time for embracing Matthew, rules or no rules. This was the time for letting him know she was glad he was alive even if she deeply and bitterly resented what he made her go through to find out that he was still alive; this was the time for hugging him hard and making him realize what he'd been missing all this time.

She hugged him hard.

"What in tarnation—"

The voice came from Matthew; she could feel it vibrate under her hands. But the voice wasn't Matthew's, and it took her so long to register that fact that she still had her arms around the man's neck when he turned to look at her. The face was so different from what she expected that she yelped and stumbled backwards. Sime caught her again.

The man was getting up from the poker table, looking bewildered and angry.

"Listen, woman!" he shouted. "When I want attention I'll pay for it. Do you get me?"

"*Well*," said Sime, and to Sev's deep embarrassment he was laughing.

"I'm sorry!" she told the man. "I thought you were someone else! The bartender said a man named Adler was over here."

"I *am* Adler!" the man, Adler apparently, yelled at her. His eyebrows were very bushy, like Mark Twain's, and drew together in an impenetrable shield over his eyes so she couldn't make out either shape or color. The ugly curve of his mouth and equally ugly tone of his voice made it quite clear that he wasn't at all happy. She cast a glance around the remainder of the poker table and reached the conclusion that either they were all related or no one had invented an eyebrow trimmer yet. Perhaps this was the fashion. Perhaps—

"*Matthew* Adler?" she clarified in a wilted, shaking voice.

Adler lowered his hand to what turned out to be his gun, ducking his head as well as he got into fighting mode. "*Donald* Adler," he gritted out irritably. "And if that Matthew so-called Adler comes my way again, I'll shoot him! You friends of his? Let me tell you what that young buck was doing. Claiming I'm his grandaddy! Claiming he's the son of my great great great granddaughter and would I like to shake his hand!" He hawked something in his throat harshly and spat it onto the poker table; the assembled poker players made small noises of disgust and moved their chips away. "As if I'd ever father children in this God-forsaken world! What kind of life would this be to bring an infant up in? I ask you!"

"Well," said Sev, though she knew she shouldn't say anything, really, not if she wanted to get out of there without a fight. Sime's hands on her elbows tightened unbearably to tell her he thought the same thing, so she had to fight him off as subtly as possible. "Maybe you did it on accident?"

There was the pause of no one breathing, everyone listening, everyone waiting.

"What exactly, little lady, are you trying to say?" said Donald Adler, Sev's potential great great great great grandfather in law, in a slow series of careful words that would have alerted anyone, regardless of their year of origin, to the danger of treading on thin conversational ice. Sev squared her shoulders and smoothed her dress.

"I— never mind," she said.

"No, really," said Donald Alder, and his voice was smooth now. "I want to know."

"No, really, never mind. Forget I said anything."

He watched her for a moment, and grunted. "You're looking for this Matthew so-called Adler? This strange man in a strange land, and getting stranger by the minute?" He waited for her to nod, then echoed it, gritting his teeth and turning his eyes to the stairs nearby them.

"Looking for him for a reason, are you?"

"Well," said Sev, and briefly weighed the pros and cons of telling the truth. She reached the conclusion that it couldn't get them in any worse a spot than they already were, and said, "We're supposed to get married. He's my fiancé."

"Aha," said Donald Adler quietly, and nodded again. He rubbed his hand over the scruffy beard on his chin. "Well, perhaps I'd be doing you both a service by showing you something, then." He tossed his head back and boomed, "*Matthew So-Called Adler!*" at the ceiling.

Sev glanced upwards involuntarily, half expecting to see Matthew lurking in the rafters. But there were no rafters visible here. There was only the ceiling, the floor of the second storey.

There was also a commotion, a disturbance, something of a ruckus. A moment later a figure rushed out on the top landing of the stairs, tucking things in, tightening his belt, standing barefoot and with hair rumpled; he stopped dead at the sight of Sev, and dropped his hands to his sides.

"Matthew," she said.

He cleared his throat. "Sevannah."

The blond girl who followed him out put her hand on his shoulder, adjusted a strap, and said in a charming Southern drawl, "Oh, hon, is this a friend of yours? Can I meet her? I've just been dying to meet some more of your family, after—" She caught sight of Donald Adler at the foot of the stairs, and started to rush down them, cooing all the while. "Why, there's the man himself, and such a lucky man too! Would you believe that you're this man's great great great great grandaddy? And you lookin' so young, too!"

Sev took a step forwards, and Matthew took a step back. The look on his face was one of pure fear, nothing to temper or alter it, and Sev folded her arms.

"Let me get this straight," she started, but Donald Adler was louder.

"That's *it*!" he roared, and pulled out his gun. "I've just about had it up to here with all this runaround about me bein' family to that cross-eyed son of a cuss up there with his trousers round his ankles! Say it ain't so, Matthew So-Called Adler!"

There was another moment of waiting with bated breath; there seemed to be a lot of them in the Old West. Sime put his head in his hands.

Matthew cleared his throat.

"I'm not a liar by nature," he said. "And I don't think I can do it now. You, sir, are in fact—"

That was all Donald Adler needed to hear. The gun was out, his finger was on the trigger, and all it took was a squeeze. Before the shot was even heard, Matthew was stumbling towards the railing. There was a protocol to these things, Sev thought numbly. Railing kills. There went Matthew, falling over the railing, landing on the tables and the poker-players below. Not moving, now. Very still.

"God in heaven!" cried the blond prostitute. "He's been shot by his great great great great grandaddy!"

"Shut up!" roared Donald Adler, and shot her too. There wasn't much to do after that except fight; which, after another second of bated-breath-holding, the inhabitants of the bar did. Sev ducked and weaved through them all and found her way to Matthew's side, crouching over him in the remnants of the shattered table and getting to her knees beside him.

"Matthew—"

"Sevannah," Matthew didn't say. He didn't say anything. Sime said it. He stood above her like a guardian angel, standing tall and dark and brooding. Less like an angel, she revised in her mind hastily, more like a gargoyle. The grimace on his face, the bad lighting—

She thought she might possibly be out of her mind

"Sevannah. We have to go."

"But. Matthew. He's."

"He's dead, Sev. We have to go."

She was crying jerkily now, and moving her hands up and down from her face to Matthew's like a marionette with a hopelessly drunk puppeteer.

"How can he be dead? He hasn't even been born yet!"

"I explained it to you, Sev, the MWI, and the— with the— we're in a different sequence of events and— look, can we talk about this outside? I hate to rush you but we really need to— urgh!"

Someone had hit him over the head with a chair. He collapsed, partially on Sev, partially on Matthew, or what was Matthew, or what would be Matthew.

She ended up dragging both men outside, and standing forlornly alone in the sunlight and the dust as she thought about how hard it would be to dig a grave with your bare hands.

Chapter Twelve

The hardest thing was for Sime to convince her to leave the body where it was. There wasn't anything they could do about him, he told her, and when she looked up at him with tear-filled eyes, he softened visibly and clarified it: there was nothing they could do for this version, in this universe. For the Matthew lying right at their feet, the hunt was ended, the mission failed. All they could do was go home, and get ready, and try again.

Sev really wasn't operating on all six cylinders, sitting there next to what had been Matthew, so Sime explained this a little more fully when they got back to the basement

"You know what we can do about this, right?"

"No. No, I don't know what we can do about this. I don't have any idea what we can do about this." She lifted her hands to indicate the situation and her bafflement as to how it should be handled, and then let them fall by her sides once more. "What can we do about this?"

"I've told you about Okasina's Theory."

"Changing universes," she murmured. She felt the stirring, the slightest flicker, of hope. "Can we do that? I though you said they'd implode or something."

"We *can* do that. And they do. It's not easy." He

thought for a minute. "We'd have to go back to before we'd been there, and prevent it from happening. Maybe catch Matthew as he comes in for the day. Prevent all that from ever happening."

"Prevent all what, exactly? Maybe we can catch him in the act." Sev's voice lowered into a growl and her eyebrows beetled over her nose. "You're right, Sime. We have to save him. We have to save him so I can kill him."

Sime watched her for a moment, smiling faintly. "Maybe that's it. Maybe that's what I didn't do, and told myself about, beat myself up about. Maybe I didn't let us go back and save him, maybe I told you that was all there was to it and nothing could be done—"

"We have to save him," repeated Sev grimly, "so I can kill him." She gave a puzzled version of her set frown to Sime. "Why would you do that? Or, why wouldn't you do that? I don't understand."

He shrugged lightly, and brought his gaze up to look at her finally, and with all the honesty he could manage. "Maybe I thought I'd save you from him. From wasting your life with someone you don't love."

She let that sit in the air between them for a minute, let it sink in to her skin. "You'd— don't be ridiculous."

"I mean it." And he looked like he did.

"Sime, I really don't think this is the time to talk about this."

"Sev, your fiancé is dead, for the moment. I can't think of a better one."

The logic of this was undeniable, but she denied it anyway.

"You're just emotional," she told him. "From that bump on your head. There is no reason for this to happen; this doesn't happen, not to me. Sime, I was so lucky to find Matthew. So lucky. It came late, in my opinion, and boy was I ever glad—" She stepped away from him, turned to look at the room, Matthew's basement room, cluttered with his things and rich with his impression in a way that she never had been and never would be.

"You settled," said Sime.

"So what?" She didn't bother to argue. "I don't like being lonely. There's so few decent guys left, Sime— you don't know. Back in your time they're probably all over the place, probably it's crawling with guys who open the door for you, say please and thank you, don't trash your cooking and don't leave you for an aerobics instructor." She pressed the heels of her palms to her eyes. "An aerobics instructor, Sime! Can you get any more '90s than that?"

"Well," said Sime, then hesitated for a moment. "We didn't have aerobics instructors in the early 1800s, but I get your point. Terrible things happen to humankind over a long and bloody history, and as a result the quality of everything goes down, including your average guy. That's only to be expected, Sevannah. I'm sorry, but that's just—"

"Not good enough," she said stoutly, shaking her head. "I'm a good person. I am a good person, Sime, and I demand other good people to fraternize with."

He smiled at her gently. "I wish that was the way it works, but— well, you found Matthew, for what it's worth."

"Yes."

"And you found me."

She took a deep breath, let it out slowly. "Yes."

He stood very still when she put her arms around him, nestled her face in the crook of his neck, and it was only after a few times feeling her breathe and hearing her heartbeat that he relaxed enough to respond, looping his arms around her back and holding her close.

"What's this for?" he murmured in her ear.

"It's called a hug," she whispered back. "It makes you feel better when you're feeling bad. Or at least it's supposed to."

"Well, is it working properly?"

It was, in point of fact. Sime was warm and getting warmer, and he smelled like leaves in the autumn. Matthew hadn't been much of a hugger, though Sev was— she wanted to hug people all the time, chaste full-body contact that was all about reassurance, and she often indulged in what she considered as necessary though peculiar behavior: hugging total strangers on the street. Striking, then running away. Leaving baffled but undoubtedly obscurely comforted unknowns liberally littered behind her.

"I haven't done this since—" said Sime, and stopped.

"Since when?"

"Just since."

She held him tighter for a moment— he dropped his head onto her shoulder, tilted sideways and breathed on her neck— and then put him away at arms length. His hands dropped to rest on her waist, as he looked at her quizzically.

"Why did we stop? It seemed to be going so well."

"Sime, I know you said you're married. I don't think it's fair to you, to me, to her, to anyone, for you to leave her in your own time and come to mine and— whatever. You know?"

He opened his mouth as if to say something, then closed it again and nodded. "Yes."

"Weren't you happy with her? Didn't you love her?"

"I was very happy and, yes, I loved her very much." He stepped away from her, removing his hands from her waist and raising them to cover his face, to blot out the light and Sev's concerned expression. "I have a headache. I'd rather we didn't talk about it."

"So it's okay to discuss what you see as me 'settling' for Matthew, but not okay to talk about you leaving your wife in another century and coming on to a girl from the future."

"Exactly."

She sighed deeply. "Well, I must say I'm disappointed." She waited till he looked at her before going on. "I'd thought they were all nice, good guys in your time. I must have been wrong a little."

"There's always one glaring exception to the rule." He wasn't joking; she knew his joking voice by now and this wasn't it. He was deadly serious, that much was obvious, but there was something else in his set, immovable face that hinted at there being more to this story. Sev shrugged mentally. If he wasn't willing to share with her, there wasn't really any way to get it out of him. She just had to direct her mental energies elsewhere, on a more worthwhile project.

Saving Matthew, for instance. She stepped away from Sime.

"So how do we handle this?"

"It's really very simple," he told her, fiddling with the YDI.

"Really?"

He paused for a moment, looked up and gave her the first grin she'd seen from him in a while. "No. Not really. It is insanely complicated. But that's," he added, sitting on the machine and gesturing for her to join him, "what I like about it. Now. We're going to show up same place and roughly the same time, only a few hours before. All we have to do is go to the saloon, ask for Matthew Adler very specifically by name, find out where he is, shock him, beat him into submission and drag him by the hair back to the machine where we can take him home, interrogate him, and demand an explanation for his behavior." He paused for a moment, looked sideways at Sev. "At least, if you want to. If you're confused. Myself I pretty much get where he's coming from, I just don't happen to agree with it."

"Are you going to tell me it's like a bachelor party? One last fling in the Old West, before he ties himself down with the ball and chain?" she said dryly.

"I'm not, but he probably is," Sime told her candidly. "Now just hold on a minute."

She held on the required length of time and they were back in the town in the Old West, true to Sime's word, just where they had been before. The trip into town went more quickly, this time, and Sime carted the chair along over one arm. He also reached down as they started out and grasped hold of Sev's hand. She thought about this off and on along the walk, debating as to whether it was allowed or not. As she never reached a decision one way or another, apparently it was. He didn't let go of her till they reached the door to the saloon of J. A. Johnson.

He held the door open for her.

She strode up to the bar with a great deal more confidence than the last time they were here, and demanded of J. A. Johnson the whereabouts of one Matthew Adler, stressing the Matthew. After some nervous hemming and hawing on his part, possibly because she looked exactly like what she was— a jilted fiancée out for revenge— she was directed up the stairs and to the second room on the left. She took a moment to note the poker game just getting started by a gang of men with bushy eyebrows and then forced that out of her mind. It felt like walking through ghosts, this chronologically-challenged version of deja vu, but there wasn't anything she could do about it now.

"We could have just knocked and found out for ourselves," observed Sime, climbing the stairs behind her, trying not to trip, and adjusting his grip on the chair. "It's not like a motel. There aren't that many rooms."

"I'd prefer to do this as quickly as possible."

"Suit yourself."

"I will. Thanks."

She reached the recommended door and hammered on it with both fists.

Sime rolled his eyes. "He'll think it's some irritated husband or father, you know, if you go at it like that. He's probably crawling out the back window right now, the worm."

"Probably," Sev agreed, and banged on the door harder. She hesitated for a moment, pausing so see if there was any response, and not finding any. She knew she really wasn't allowing enough time for Matthew to find and put his pants on. This thought made her angrier and she unleashed a furious fusillade of knocks on the door, as well as a few kicks. The door opened suddenly and she bashed an unsuspecting Matthew on the nose. It was the most satisfying ending to knocking on the door she'd ever experienced, and she wasn't about to apologize.

He stared at her, eyes wide, hands going up to cover his wounded nose.

"Sev!" His voice was nasal and squeaky with disbelief and pain.

"Matthew," she said, "we've come to—"

"Not a lot of time for this," said Sime. "It's not all that necessary." He set the chair down, pushed Sev into it, yanked Matthew over and pushed him onto Sev, then leaned over and threw his arms around both of them, kicking at the YDI with his foot. The recall button worked admirably, and they were in the basement once more.

"Get *off* me!" said Sev, who wasn't used to taking this much weight all at once and was having issues. Sime sent a wry glance into the midst of the huddle, presumably aimed in her direction, and straightened up, letting them go. Matthew got up more slowly, looking distinctly woozy.

"Well, this is— unexpected." He took a few steps away from Sev, turned around, put his hand up to his careful hair and let his mouth hang open for a few seconds before anything came out of it. "I just— I'm not sure what to say."

Sev just glared at him, so finally Sime prompted, "I would imagine an apology is in order."

"An apology, yes," said Matthew, "of course, an apology would be— Sevannah, I'm very very sorry, but somehow the recall got pushed on the machine and it came home without me. I wasn't expecting anything to happen— I really thought nothing would happen, time travel had always been perfectly safe up till then, but. I should have left you a note. I should have left a letter in the event of my unexpected and unexplained disappearance. I apologize most deeply."

"Are you going to bow?" asked Sime. "You look like you're about to bow."

Matthew's back was in fact crooked in a downward direction, but at this he straightened up and said, "No, no, of course I'm not going to bow. That would be pointless."

"I don't know," said Sime, eyeing him. He appeared to have taken a deep dislike to the actual man Matthew; nearly as deep, or possibly even deeper, than the one he'd had for the concept of the man Matthew. "It might be funny to watch."

"Who are you, again?" asked Matthew, baffled.

Sev stood up then, and both men turned to look at her. She advanced on Matthew, and poked him in the shoulder. In the interview that was to come, she sensed she would do a lot of this.

"I looked for you for two weeks. I went to the police. I called your father. He said you'd done this before. Is that true?"

"Time traveled?" Matthew guessed.

"*Disappeared*, you doorknob," said Sev, with a punctuating poke.

"I—" Matthew, caught out in his own lie, had to face it or be impolite. He swallowed several times. "I'm not a doorknob. I, yes, it has been a problem a few times now, getting back home at the right time. I believe there was a fault in the machine. I didn't realize that my father would notice I was gone; we speak so rarely." He looked at her helplessly. "I'm really not a doorknob. I am, however, sorry, Sev. So sorry. I'm apologetically sorry."

"Oh, for God's sake," said Sime, rubbing at his eyes with his fingertips.

"And after I go to the police, and your father, and after I break into your house to look for clues, I discover to my amazement that my boyfriend's babble about time travel was in fact true— even though he never bothered to take me with him!" Poke, poke.

"Babble?" said Matthew, vaguely affronted. "Your boyfriend's *babble*? Sevannah, that... that was highly sophisticated science I was explaining to you all that time!"

"Right, and you expect a layperson to understand all that? Listen, Matthew," she poked him, "every time you opened your mouth about science and fairy tales I pretty much shut off, okay? I got to where I would build and decorate an entire house in my head just so I could look intrigued for long periods."

Matthew looked shocked.

"You mean you weren't paying attention?"

"That's right," said Sev ruthlessly, poking away. "Not paying attention to *anything* you told me if the words were more than four syllables long, and even some of the shorter ones were a little iffy. You could have *demonstrated*, Matthew. Could have brought me here and showed me how it worked. Could have used some metaphor I would understand, like, like—" She floundered briefly and was enlivened by the sight of Sime, who was watching the proceedings with an unholy mix of gravity and amusement. "Like a river! Time, Matthew, is like a river."

"That's a song, isn't it?" muttered Matthew.

Sev perceived that he was utterly distracted by this and stopped, dropping her hands down to her sides. She steeled herself, took a deep breath.

"Do you know," she said slowly, "that we had to go back?" Matthew glanced up, brow furrowed in puzzlement. "We had to go back to a time we'd already been to, and change things, in order to save your life."

"Sev," said Sime, looking up.

"*Sev?*" said Matthew, squinting at him.

"Shut up," said Sev. She sat back down on the kitchen chair and put her hands over her eyes. "You were dead, Matthew. You got shot. All that time looking for you, and we finally find you, and you're cheating on me with a girl in some bar, and then you have the all-fired arrogance to get shot before I can properly guilt-trip you. Before I can even hit you. Before I can even scream at you or throw things at you." She paused for a minute. "Before I could tell you goodbye."

"I was dead?" said Matthew.

"Are you familiar with Okasina's Theory?" asked Sime, raising his eyebrows. Matthew hesitated, then nodded.

"I've read the literature."

"Well, now you've seen it in action."

Matthew stared at him, and Sime could see little beads of sweat breaking out on his brow. He looked decidedly ill.

"I was— dead? I was actually dead? And now I'm not anymore?"

"Basically, yes," said Sime.

Matthew looked back at Sev, bewildered. "I don't get it. Why— why aren't you glad to see me, then?"

She dropped her hands into her lap, looked up at him.

"Oh, Matthew. I am. I am glad to see you. I am glad you're not dead." She stood and walked towards him, put her arms around him very carefully, leaned her face in to rest against his, holding the rest of her body back so he wouldn't feel threatened by physical proximity. She kept all her movements slow, her touches gentle. She sighed quietly on him, and waited till she felt him relax before she punched him solidly in the gut. "Dead people can't feel pain, you see," she tossed over her shoulder as she strode back to the chair and sat down, folding her arms, crossing her legs, and narrowing her eyes. Sime watched her admiringly.

"It's like seeing one of those old-fashioned gates at a castle come crashing down," he said, flapping a hand at her. "I've never seen someone so completely unapproachable in my life. When you shut it down, you really shut it *down*."

"Urghk," said Matthew, doubled over, and did a slow crashing dive into the basement floor.

"See, I told you you should bow," Sime observed.

Here are Tendence and Cavile. They have ways. They get into places no one else has ever been, and they tour through all times as easily as you please, looking for unlicensed travelers. They're on no lists, but in every club ever created. They never even have to pay a cover charge.

They've caught a man named Haze, Jonathon Haze. In the world of time-travel— not that different from the internet, Tendence reckons— he goes by the handle "Purple Haze," but this is, they decide jointly, likely a youthful aberration. His decision to hack the Corporation's signal and go on a free ride through the eighteenth century, however, will have much more grievous consequences. Tendence doesn't even pretend to understand it.

"Eighteenth century," he says, and he shakes his head. "Oh, why, man?"

"Why not?" rumbles Cavile.

"Hardly seems worth it," Tendence murmurs, raising one eyebrow with the utmost delicacy. He takes Jonathon Haze by the wrist, breaking it only slightly, then recalibrates and hauls him upwards till the delirious young man is more or less upright. "And then not to even bother trying to run. One wonders what sort of death wish you had."

"Perhaps he's been feeling low," his colleague suggests. He is ignored.

"When we get to the end," Tendence tells Jonathon Haze, almost kindly, "keep in mind that that's it. There is no more. The large lady has warbled. Your number is up. That's all she wrote. And any other cliches along the same line you should care to remember."

"Okasina's," murmurs Jonathon Haze, likely meant to be followed by, "—Theorem," but he's drifting in and out of consciousness.

Cavile clears his throat. "Ain't no bender like an eighteenth-century bender," he says, and earns a glare from his colleague. Tendence gets in the young man's face, hunts around till he's secured his gaze. The young man's eyes are bleary, and also brown.

"Okasina was wrong," he says. "We are right. Listen to me. This is all."

Millions of universes fold in on themselves with the sound of paper tearing. The sound of the ticket, tearing from the pad, folded into Jonathon Haze's fudging fingers. The young man looks at it for a moment, and then he *laughs at his left shoulder. Cavile steps close to take a look himself, frowning slightly.*

"It isn't that funny, really," he says.

"They keep deluding themselves." Tendence's voice is so quiet as to be nearly silent, and his well-cut lips scarcely move. But when his eyes flash up to Cavile, they are darkened with anger. "Fools."

Okasina's Theorem states that there is a universe for all decisions; that if one has the required tools of a time machine, foreknowledge, and more than rudimentary intelligence, one can bypass the accepted ways of things and change one's future, and one's past, and one's present, in manners that are not only previously unheard of, but frankly ridiculous; that, in knowing one's end, one can circumvent it and somehow conspire with the universe to live forever; that there are no fixed points in time, and everything is relative.

Okasina's Theorem fails to take into account Tendence and Cavile.

The ticket is delivered, and the punishment kicks in. Universes down the line seal themselves up neatly, closed-loop, and in every one, Jonathon Haze is just a memory.

Sime slid into the seat next to a rueful-looking Sevannah, who was drinking coffee with grounds floating merrily in it like drowned fleas.

"It looks like you used your coffee to drown fleas," he told her.

She glanced down into it and sighed. "I know. Turns out the reason I couldn't find any filters was that Matthew was out of them. Had to use another paper napkin." She took a sip, shrugged, and wiped at her teeth. "Not too bad anyway."

"You've got another one, there." Sime wiped it away off her lower lip with a careful thumb. He folded his arms in front of him on the table, put his chin down on them and looked up at her like a child.

"So I was thinking I would love a thank you, if you didn't mind."

She shook herself, and managed to relax into a smile. "Of course. I should have thought— I didn't mean—" He raised his eyebrows at her and she leaned over and kissed him on the forehead. "Thank you, Sime. I really mean it. All that help you gave me, all those times we had— all those times we had to visit—"

He nodded and smiled at her crookedly. "It was fun, actually. I hadn't been to some of those places for a long time. It was nice to see them again before—"

"Before what?"

"Nothing."

She thumped him on the arm. "Before what, Sime? Obviously you wanted me to ask or you wouldn't have used such a provocative manner of speaking."

"Provocative? Me? Are you kidding?"

She thumped him again. "That was a highly auspicious time to break off talking, Sime." She paused. "Or do I mean suspicious?"

"Possibly both."

"Come on. What's going on?"

He glanced around them at the otherwise-empty kitchen. "Where's the boyfriend?"

"Getting some rest, I think." She snorted. "Making a time-travelling tour of bars of the ages really takes it out of you, I should imagine."

He nodded, smiled at her, leaned closer. "Can you keep an eye on him while I vanish for a little while?"

"Do you need to sleep too?" She rotated the coffee cup in the wet ring it had created on the table. "That's fine, I'll be up. I don't think I could sleep, without artificial assistance."

"Like someone bashing you over the head?"

"Or drugs. Jeez, you're violent."

"You bring out the best in me. No, I'm not tired. I just have something I need to do." He paused for a minute and looked at her curiously before coming to a decision. "You remember Weaver."

"Man who lives backwards and travels with himself? Yeah."

"I'm going to find him."

"So soon after finding Matthew? Are you trying to break a record or something?"

"No, no no." He shook his head. "It won't be like that. Weaver always leaves clues as to where he can be found. Sometimes you get there and there's just another clue, that's all. I can deal with that. I have a few things I need to ask him— can you manage by yourself? I ask because I won't be gone long but I might not show back up at the exact time I left." He grinned. "Time travel without a machine is not an exact science."

She grinned wryly. "Yeah, well, time travel with one isn't an exact science either. I don't mind. Just— be careful."

He nodded slowly, watching her. "Yes. You too."

"Okay."

"Okay." The disappearance was slower than she expected, but he looked like he was controlling it, his eyes fixed on her, his jaw set, as he slid into the stream of Time, struck out for the opposite bank, and melted into nothing, just there in front of her.

Sev decided it was really fantastic, the way things didn't surprise her any more.

Chapter Thirteen

Matthew approached her slowly, carefully, tentatively, like a lion tamer that was very new at his job.

"Can I explain a few things?"

She glanced up at him. "I wish you would."

He, very carefully, pulled out a chair for himself and, even more carefully, sat in it. He folded his hands on the table neatly before him and arranged a look of earnestness on his face.

"Sev, I did not mean to leave you in the lurch. I did not mean to go without letting you know I was going. Old habits die hard, you know."

"I'm aware."

He paused before going on. "I also did not intend to cheat on you. Please understand I was there for two and a half months and it didn't look like I was ever going to get back. I was distraught. I was missing you very much. I was also down to my last two dollars and it was kind of now-or-never. Kind of sink-or-swim. Kind of eat-or-be-eaten."

"Please stop talking," said Sev.

He nodded, looked at the table. "But I didn't mean to hurt you. That's all."

She heaved a gusty sigh which stirred his hair, though

not much. "Alright. I get it. I understand. I do. Let's change the subject. Tell me about time travel."

"Well," he shrugged lightly. "Something I was always interested in, even as a boy. Especially as a boy. My parents encouraged me to think about things, consider possibilities that most people wouldn't entertain for a moment. I did. I was very good at it. I always wanted to visit times in history and get the real stories of what was going on. Everything you learn in school, in the history books, it is all so subjective, you know." He looked pleased and proud as a new father for a moment. "That's what I was doing, you know. Going back to interview people for their sides of the story."

She looked at him incredulously. "Are you serious?"

"Yes!" He smiled at her, and it was as close to an honest, outright grin she'd ever seen him come. The subject gave him life and enthusiasm. She wished it gave him euthanasia. "And best of all, along with this noble desire to educate the common man about the real story of history, it was a way to make a better living so I could keep you in the manner to which someday you will become accustomed."

She shook her head. "Wait. Wait. This is your get-rich-quick scheme? This is your way of making monetary use of time travel?"

"Yes!" He beamed at her. "Imagine a book told from Merlin's point of view. It would be a guaranteed best-seller!"

"On the fiction lists, maybe," she amended. "You know, Matthew, some people go back in time and place bets. Some people go forward in time and get tips on the stock market. You're the only person I've ever heard of to travel around in time and conduct interviews like some chronologically-displaced Ken Burns."

"Thank you, Sev." He looked immensely pleased.

"Well, it wasn't really a compliment."

But he wasn't paying attention; he was talking on and on. "It took a while to get the machine to work, I must admit, even though I got the plans off the internet. For the longest time," he confessed, "I couldn't get it to travel in space at all. The YDI was malfunctioning. I kept visiting different eras in the history of my basement. Kind of boring."

"Why did you go to the future? You can't write a biography of something that hasn't happened yet," she pointed out reasonably.

"Oh, that." He waved a hand in a calculated imitation of carelessness. "I just wanted to see the aliens, that's all."

"You are such a geek," she told him.

He beamed again. "Yes! You're absolutely right. I am, aren't I!"

She shook her head wordlessly and he sobered after a moment.

"Perhaps we should talk about our relationship, Sevannah. I mean— it's obviously very important. To you and to me, I mean, to both of us. I can see why, now."

"What do you mean?"

"I mean—" He flailed for a moment. She'd heard about flailing, but wasn't sure she'd ever seen it done; she watched avidly. "I don't think many people would have saved me, is all. That took something extraordinary. That took Sevannah Carlson." He gave her a look of doe-eyed devotion that was so overdone she wanted to hit it. Yet she refrained; somewhere in the shallows of his counterfeit emotion was a spark of something real— he was, at least, not ungrateful. He appeared gratified by something, but she wasn't sure what it was. "I owe my life to you, Sev. I hope I won't forget it."

This seemed like such a strange thing to say that she wrinkled her nose at him.

"Well, I hope not too, Matthew."

"Why are you making faces at me?" he asked, somewhat petulantly. "I really don't like it when people make faces, Sev. Did you forget?"

She hadn't forgotten.

"I'm making faces at you, Matthew, because I am tired

of this conversation. I am tired of waiting around. I am tired of— " She broke off, suddenly, and looked at the clock on the oven. Unless her timing was very off, though, it was mistaken. "I wonder where Sime is, right now?"

Matthew shrugged. "Somewhere in time, no doubt."

"No doubt," she agreed, "but where?"

Locating Weaver took Sime longer tan expected, despite of the proliferation of clues provided. As a matter of fact, the almost lavish abundance was part of the problem. Many of them contradicted each other, and nearly all of them led to dead ends. Some of the dead ends were nearly Sime's own. Making a narrow escape from a Mongolian horde, he swore under his breath. The next time that happened, he was going to accept the challenge to fight, just to take out the pent-up aggression. He hated running away from things, and these days it seemed like that was all he did.

The shift in time and place from the wretched reaches of Mongolia to Scotland was sudden as a step. Sime didn't even stumble.

Crouched in the shadows cast by the moonlight against the vast stones, Weaver was no more than a formless mass with eyes glinting from the depths. Sime had always found Stonehenge a little too creepy for his taste, had heard a few too many stories about ghosties and ghoulies and entrapped souls to feel comfortable now, here in the dark.

"This is a strange place to hide," he told Weaver, who refused to come into the light.

"It is a place they will no longer go," said Weaver, and his voice was raspy, raspier than Sime remembered at least. It was the younger man, in the older body, speaking; the later version of himself was apparently asleep, tucked in a ball alongside him in the shadows. "They've been here. They didn't like it."

"Who didn't?"

All the answer he got was a dry laugh, and then, "Who do you think?"

"Alright," said Sime, clasping his arms around himself in a futile attempt to warm himself from his own body heat. "Alright. I get that, and believe me, I really get it. I wouldn't come here for a pleasure cruise myself. I come here because I have to, Weaver. Because it seems that no one else can answer my questions. It's gone on long enough. I need to end it."

There was a pause in the night, an empty space, like the wait for a heartbeat by a hospital bed.

"Why you?" said Weaver at last, in his dusty, pale voice.

"Because I'm the only one left," Sime managed at last. "They reached Oedipus, and both Ares and Dominus haven't been seen in years. Never mind Fred. I'm the only known Adept left, and you know they travel too fast to be caught up by a machine. I need to do it now, while I can, or it's all over. For everyone."

"What makes you think that you—"

"I don't think," interrupted Sime harshly. "I *don't* think I can do it. I don't have a plan, I don't have a thought, I don't have a hunch, I don't have a clue. All I have is a need, and an apparent suicide wish. That's all."

"Ah. Obligation. Your duty. Admirable." There was a dry chuckle from the shadows. "Do you know how this all started, Sime in Time? How Tendence and Cavile came to be? How I ended up here in the shadows of these ghostly stones, tainted by long-ago evil and visited only by the foolhardy and brave?"

"I have a feeling," said Sime, "that you are going to tell me."

"They were but as children in time when it began. Perhaps they didn't understand at first." Weaver's words crept out slowly as though they had to be untangled first.

"But they began to comprehend, oh yes— such power as they discovered, time at their fingertips and the world as their bow to bend and break; as everything around them altered to their liking, times changing and flowing and shifting, clockwise the turn of the earth, as they set invisible boundaries and unsuspecting people *died* from running up against them— their mothers died, and their sisters, their wives and their kinsmen— universes melted into nothing, into slag, into refuse, into memories. Do you know what happened to me? Do you, Sime, Sime and his obligation, Sime and his duty? *I* realized too late what was going on, and I attempted to stop them. *I* gave it my all." A dry chuckle escaped the old man like a snake slithering over dried leaves. "And they caught me. They caught me, they said— they liked a man who thought the way they did. Altering time. Catching them up. They wouldn't kill me because I was like them, they said, and that was worse than death— oh, but I learned— oh I *learned*— the woes of messing with reality. *This*, my lad—"

This was the time. He moved dramatically into the light, his face horrific, the flesh half melted, his teeth rotted and black, his age a mockery of itself, the life in his eyes turned cold and pale. His breath alone was silent, dramatic. He chose instead to hiss.

"*This* is what you get from *screwing with the universe!*"

There was a pause. Sime swallowed hard in the silence.

"What? Italics?" he asked.

Weaver sank back into the shadows and was quiet for a moment.

"You think you're clever."

"No, I know I'm clever. I know I'm very clever. I am also very stupid. It's a sort of paradox, you see." He sighed and scrubbed his hands over his face. "Always running into those buggers, paradoxes. Paradoxi. Multiples. Many."

"That is the reality of the situation," said Weaver, almost sullenly. "Paradox."

"But I'm not sure I get it. You've already been punished by Tendence and Cavile, and I agree, it's bad— but as bad as it is, it's not death. They didn't kill you. You could be a pile of dust somewhere now, wherever you'd been born, wherever you belonged, but you're not. That's got to be better, right? But if you've already been found by them— why are you here? Why are you hiding?"

There was another pause, as the old man thought this through, and gave a dry chuckle. "Someday, Sime, if the odds are lean and days are against it, you'll find out for yourself what its like, to be caught up by those worthy, unholy personages. They won't do to you what they did to me. They don't know you. They have no reason to like you. What do they do to people they like? They age half their body, and leave the other half intact. They find the version of their prey that is nearest to the end, and they bring them together so they can see how long it will last; and it will last forever, you see, because time travelers cannot die. They cannot die at all. Not on their own."

Sime got to his knees, feeling a little urgency now, wanting Weaver's help and fearing the verbal sea he had to wade through in order to get it.

"What are you saying?"

"He is very close to the end, now. I cannot die unless I am given a way for my suicide. I think."

"What do you mean?"

Weaver lifted his wrist and shook it feebly. The iron caught the light, clanked dimly as it hit together. "It is unbreakable."

Sime reached out and caught the chain, pulling it slowly towards him till it caught somewhere else— on the hand of the sleeping man. More accurately, around the wrist of the sleeping man. Weaver was chained to him.

Weaver was chained to himself.

"He's very near the end," Weaver repeated. "They couldn't figure out if he was going to die or not, so they brought him here for me to watch over and soon I will find out for myself. If he does, I will be the first."

Sime put one arm under the man's neck, the other under his knees, lifted him carefully and smoothly into the light. He was much lighter than he'd expected. Weaver gave a cry of consternation but Sime shushed him and examined the other.

It wasn't a man, after all; it was a boy. Probably about fourteen, and not really sleeping, Sime thought, but in a coma. His face bore the same injuries as his other self, but it was far worse this many years into the future of his life, and at this point dust was coating all the uneven, long-dead surfaces. Sime swallowed hard, and put his hand to the boy's pulse. It was very slow.

"You'll find out soon," he told Weaver.

"Or never," said Weaver heavily.

"No answer is still an answer." Sime glanced up and down the boy's body, frantically. "Can we wake him up? I need to ask him something."

"What is it?"

"How to deal with Tendence and Cavile. He's got to know; he's lived through all this time, all the time you have, and he's the only one who's seen their birthplace, the only one who had them trapped for any length of time at all." He glanced up at the older Weaver, who was staring at him out of the darkness impassively. "The last time I asked you, you couldn't remember. You said you must not have gone through it yet."

"That was before I had my brain opened to the world," said Weaver. "Now I know everything he does." He gestured towards his older self in what could only be called contempt. Sime understood it: he was sitting here chained to the death of himself, and all he could do was wait till he turned into it. Then there would be two of them, the same, a paradox in all terms, cadavers in the moonlight.

Sime placed the boy back in the shadows, and straightened up.

"I need to know how to catch them," he told Weaver. "I need to know now."

Weaver mumbled nearly-silent words to himself for a moment before he answered. "The same way you catch any fish. With bait."

"Was that your idea?"

"Yes."

"But it didn't work."

"I didn't have the right kind of bait."

Sime sighed. "What kind should you have had?"

Weaver lifted his hands and stretched them one to either side, expanding to include the landscape around them.

"Someone of the earth," he whispered. "Someone not me. Someone to stand and look easy as they crept crept crept on, so I could dash behind their backs and say my words of power."

Sime dropped back to his knees, hunched over, leaned towards the old man in anticipation.

"What words of power?"

"Lobotomy," whispered Weaver. "Anaesthesia. Scalpel." He looked at Sime, eyes milky in the moonlight. "That is why they never sleep. They would become one. They would be in one time and one place and in sleep lose all control."

Sime nodded, slowly, trying to assimilate all this and hoping it would make more sense in his head later on. "Thank you, Weaver. I'm going to try. I'm going to—" He smiled weakly. "I'll give it my best, alright? For you, and for Oedipus and all the rest."

"For all of us," croaked Weaver. Sime nodded more deeply.

"For all of us. Tell me. If you know what he knows," and he gestured towards the dying man in the shadows, "even though you are so much younger than him and have not gone through his experiences— what is the point of living backwards?"

"Point? There is no point," said Weaver, sinking back against a stone. "Did you think I chose this for myself? It was a cruel trick played on me by the universe. So cruel, I wonder if perhaps Tendence and Cavile themselves did not think of it."

Sime nodded once more, and turned to leave. Weaver did not speak as he moved away from the stones, not even to say goodbye. He faced his future silently, lying there beside him, struggling for breath.

Sime left Stonehenge and Weaver behind as quickly as he decently could, and returned to the kitchen to find Matthew and Sev arguing over their relationship.

Sev was in the middle of pointing her finger at Matthew and railing at him, and Sime reflected that if her finger was a gun Matthew would be in sore straights.

"And then there's the issue of your mother!"

"My mother?"

"All those telephone calls? Three times a day, you're calling her! You call her more than you call me! She comes over and makes your food, cleans your house sometimes. Don't you see something a little strange there?"

"That's an irrelevant contribution to the conversation," said Matthew, going crimson.

"I think this completely comes as no surprise to anyone whatsoever," put in Sime. Sev looked up at him and was out of her seat in a split second, throwing her arms around him.

"God!"

"Nope. Sime," he corrected her, and gave a smile so brief it looked like a nervous tic. "Close, though."

"You're back! You left me here with him for half an hour! How could you do that?"

"Trying to save the world, is all," said Sime, and shrugged. "Sorry. Wouldn't have left you alone with your boyfriend if I'd known it would bother you so much— which, think about it, may indicate something worrying and doubtful about your relationship," he whispered in her ear. She patted him on the cheek and took his hand, drew him towards the table.

"So did you figure out how to save the universe?" she asked, seating herself once more and letting go of his hand. "He's great at saving the universe," she told Matthew.

"Does it all the time, it's like a hobby with him."

"I think I've got a clue how to go about it," allowed Sime.

"Oh, don't be so modest. You know just what to do, don't you?"

"Not really, no."

"Oh." She lapsed into silence, looking disappointed. Sime smiled at her, reached over and smoothed his hand down her arm to reach her own hand, lacing his fingers with hers and squeezing briefly before letting go.

"I don't think," began Matthew, sitting up straighter.

"We know," said Sime.

Sev laughed, and Matthew looked sorely wounded. His erstwhile fiancée sat forward, reached for his hand comfortingly, smiled at him for a moment. He smiled back and she turned away.

"So what's the first step? You do at least have a first step?"

"Yes," Sime acknowledged. "I do have a first step. And it's a good first step, a great one. It's the rest of the plan that lacks finesse. Are you familiar with fishing? The basics of it at least?"

"Yes," said Sev.

"Not really," said Matthew. They both glanced at him for a minute.

"Are you serious?"

"Fishing," prompted Sevannah. "You'll have to ignore him."

"Fishing," agreed Sime, and did so. "Well, we're setting out to catch the biggest swordfish of them all. First we need a little—"

"Bait?" suggested Sev.

Sime nodded. "Hook, line, and sinker. First, of course, we need someone who's been chased by Tendence and Cavile in the first place. Someone whose presence is known."

They both turned, very slowly, to look at Matthew, who looked immediately guilty in the manner of men who

don't know why they're being stared at.
  "Who, me?" he said.

Chapter Fourteen

"We're going to do this quickly," Sime directed, spreading the papers out over the kitchen table. The three of them leaned over them like architects quarreling over a blueprint, trying to decipher the original motive for having the kitchen upstairs and with a toilet in it. "You'll have to keep your focus. This is not a series of pleasure trips. You are not going to be sightseeing. Do we understand?"

"Yes, sir," said Sev, and saluted neatly. Matthew mumbled something and Sime glared at him.

"I'm serious, Mr. Adler. If you thought narrowly escaping your own death was a hat trick, and I'm sure you did, you have no concept of what you're going to be narrowly escaping this time. And if you *don't* narrowly escape it— if in fact you don't escape it at all— I will not be able to collapse universes in order to save you. I won't be able to do anything to save you. Do you understand?"

"Yes," said Matthew, who looked like he was having a panic attack and was having trouble breathing. "I get it, I get it."

Sev put her arm around him, and he eyed her narrowly as though she was planning something dastardly, like a face-making competition. She made a wry face at him and rubbed his shoulder vigorously for a moment before leaving him alone. His head sagged downwards and he sighed with something like relief.

"Very well," said Sime, turning back to the lists and tapping one finger against his lips. He looked pensively up and down the scrawled, illegible handwriting and shook his head. "We have got to teach you to write, Matthew—"

"I wrote those ones," said Sev, pointing to the ones on the left.

Sime eyed her balefully. "Clearly you two are meant to be together. Equally clearly, your children are doomed. Come on, now. You're going to skip through the Middle Ages, over to the birth of Christ, forward to the sinking of the Titanic, over to the inauguration of one of our first presidents, forward again to the San Francisco earthquake—"

"Which one?"

"Take your pick," said Sime, waving a hand irritably. "Take several picks. Skip around at random, it doesn't matter. The point is you two go everywhere you can think of, as quickly as you can, and make your presence felt. Don't put on costumes, use early-nineties slang, insult everyone, snap pictures, be tourists but don't actually tour. Time is of the essence here. Time is everything."

"Can we go see Elvis?" asked Matthew. Sev turned to look at him, incredulous.

"You like Elvis? I thought you didn't listen to anything that had been written after the 1700s."

"I like Elvis as a historic personage," said Matthew defensively. "He had some very interesting things to say."

"Like 'you ain't nothing but a hound dog'?"

"Well, you see, that's taking it out of context, Sevannah, what that song was really about was—"

"Cryin' all the time?"

"*People!*" bellowed Sime, and a hush fell briefly over the room. "*Really*, we need to move quickly. I'm counting on the two of you, and I'll be waiting at the rendezvous."

"You rhymed," said Sev, mirthfully.

He glared at her and she grinned back at him. He shook his head.

"Go," he said. "Go, go, go, go, go."

"There is no time for that."

"I've always wanted to see if it really was as heavy as I read."

"You're going to be clanking everywhere. Suppose it rains. You'll rust."

"I'll take that chance. It's only for a moment."

"Sev, take off the suit of armor, it's too big for you, you're going to—"

It was quite loud. Matthew had to help her up.

"I told you so," he said grimly.

"This," said Sev definitely, "is not December."

"You're right," Matthew agreed. "It is a little chilly though."

"The thing is," said Sev, brow furrowed, "there's something I don't really get about the whole thing. Think about it. If they actually believe Jesus was born on Christmas Day, and if they actually think that he died on a cross, instead of X-mas shouldn't it be shortened to, you know—" She sketched a T in the air. "—mas?"

Matthew's brow furrowed. "Plus-mas?"

"Well—"

"Look! Sheep!"

"Oh, God! *Run!*"

"This," said Matthew, gasping, "is not fun."

"It's called a revolution, Matthew, not a funvolution.

Get back on the chair."

"Right."

"What on earth are you talking about? There's nothing to indicate William Shakespeare was a thief!"

"There's nothing to indicate that he wasn't."

"Do you not read history books?"

"Not if I can help it, Matthew. Look, the speculation going around is that at least most of them were penned by someone else."

"The history books?"

A pause.

"I think you should shut up now."

"Well, we could go and ask him if it's that big a deal—"

"I don't care to be lied to by William Shakespeare, thank you very much." Honestly, his ruff was terrifying in person. "Anyway, we haven't the time. We've made our presence felt by having screaming matches in the town square, that's good enough. Let's go."

"That is not Leonardo Di Caprio!"

"I swear it is, Sevannah. I swear I just saw him. He went into that stateroom carrying a pen and a pad of paper."

"You're lying, Matthew. I can tell by the way your eye is twitching."

"No, no, that's just a nervous tic. It's brought on by the stress of time travel."

"Fine, then. Go get his autograph."

"I don't want it. I though you might, though. He's just in there. Just—" He gestured her forward with little shooing motions of his hands. She regarded him stoically.

"Matthew, you choose the oddest moments to try and demonstrate that you have a sense of humor."

"Stop, stop right here for a minute."
"What are you doing?"
"I thought I saw someone I knew."
"What are you— Matthew!" He'd leaped off the chair as soon as she stood up, though, and hurried off through the crowd. She crossed her arms, tapped her foot, glanced at the YDI. The present? Her own year, only earlier. Home territory. Boring. She supposed it meant she was out there somewhere, in this city. She wondered what she was doing. Nothing important, probably. Getting her hair done. Fielding phone calls on when she was going to provide her parents with grandchildren.

Matthew came hurrying back, looking pleased and gratified and rather self-important.

"Done and done," he announced, sitting back on the chair and opening his arms for her to seat herself. She toed the ground and eyed him.

"What, exactly, did you do and do?"

He hesitated for a moment, gave her an indulgent smile. "I just made sure everything was going to be okay."

She raised her eyebrows. "You captured Tendence and Cavile and took the Corporation down, meaning free time for all?"

"No," he admitted. "I meant, everything's going to be okay for me, specifically. At least, as far as it depended on me, you see— I sort of—"

"*What*, Matthew? What did you do?"

"I ran into that bookstore over there, found myself where I always am in the science fiction section, and told myself about you." He beamed at her. "I told him, when he finds a girl named Sev, he should latch onto her and not let her get away. Because she's the one who will save his life."

"And you believed you?"

"Sev, it was the *science fiction* section. I was virtually surrounded with circumstantial proof of time travel anyway." He crossed his legs. "I must have, at any rate. Otherwise, I wouldn't be here, would I?"

She paused for a moment, time and space running through her head, remembering very carefully, very cautiously, the first time she met Matthew. His eagerness. His enthusiasm. His insistence. The day they met, they had gone on their first date.

"Oh," she said.

"Uh-huh!" said Matthew, jiggling his foot. "I know, right?"

He patted his lap, and she sank into it.

She was very quiet for the rest of the trips, not even stirring when they showed up in Elvis' kitchen and surprised him halfway through his fifth peanut-butter-and-banana sandwich of the day. When they arrived at the rendezvous, she regained a little of her spark at the sight of Sime, who was dressed in a pair of jeans and a white pinstriped sport jacket, a carnation in his buttonhole, looking strange and suave at the same time in a way that was inexpressibly, incontrovertibly *him*. She threw her arms around him and held him close.

He looked over her shoulder at Matthew, who was frowning slightly but looked as though he wasn't quite sure what to do about this sudden outpouring of affection.

"Have a nice trip?" he asked brightly.

The rendezvous they'd chosen was a restaurant in Portland, Oregon. The timing was cautious, quite close to Sev's own time, but enough before that she wouldn't rejoin her proper timeline. Sev glanced around.

"I used to love to eat here, when I lived in Oregon," she said conversationally, swinging her arms and eyeing the menu tacked to a wall. "Of course, now that I'm here, that sad little omelet seems like a very, very long time ago."

"It *was* a very, very long time ago," Sime told her. "There probably won't be time to eat till later. Till— after." He turned to Matthew, since Sev still seemed unaccountably intrigued with the menu. "Did you notice any signs that they were after you?"

"Here and there, maybe," said Matthew nervously. "I thought I saw them a few times, out of the corner of my eye. Usually arriving just as we were leaving."

"Fine. Great. A public setting like this, they won't move in immediately. They prefer to get their prey on their own if they can, otherwise attention gets drawn to their employers, and that's exactly what the Corporation doesn't want. Don't leave the main room, though. Don't leave each other's sides, on any account." He walked forwards, past the hostess' desk, nodding at her pleasantly, and scanned the room anxiously.

"Table for three, sir?" asked the hostess cheerfully.

Sime reflected that nodding at people pleasantly only brought unwanted attention to the nodder, and decided not to do it any more.

"Table for two," he said, "the two of them. I'm just—I'll accompany them for a moment."

"Are you sure you wouldn't like a chair, sir? I'd be happy to—"

"No, no, that's fine. Just go ahead and seat them."

"But, really."

"I promise I won't complain to the manager."

The hostess nodded despite her obvious bafflement, and said, "Just as you like, sir," which was something Sime liked to hear every now and then. She led them out of the entryway and into the main room. Sev looked like she was trying to perform complex mathematic variations in her head, and Sime hoped she wasn't trying to figure out how they'd divide up the bill.

"I think," she said carefully, and then dove underneath a table that they were passing at the moment.

"What on earth—" started Matthew. Sime glanced around and gestured to him frantically to follow the waitress, to make less noise and be as unobtrusive as possible. It was a futzy and complex message to put into silent gestures, and Sime doubted that Matthew got the full import; but he got the gist, at any rate, which was the important part. Sime got down on his knees at the table, grinned cheerfully up at the people who were eating there, and said to Sev through his teeth,

"What's the issue, sweetheart?"

"My sister's over there!" she whispered. "The woman with the bleached-blond hair, trying to hide forty years of tanning wrinkles under fifty pounds of makeup."

Sime stuck his head up and observed.

"You don't want her to know you're here?"

"She's a talker," hissed Sev. "She'd come over and talk to me and want to know every detail that's been going on and tell me every detail that's been happening to her, and I wouldn't be able to concentrate on the matter in hand. You know. Saving the universe?"

Sime put his head up again and observed once more.

"She's on the phone," he advised her.

Sev looked confused for a moment. "What day is this?"

"Thursday. The 18th I think."

"Of—"

"March. Why?"

Sev got that look again, the one that indicated the gears were turning and smoke was about to start coming out of her ears any moment now. "I think she's talking to me."

"What?"

"I think that's me on the phone. Hold on. I need to get closer. If I can hear her, I'll know for sure."

Without waiting to see if Sime was following her, she scuttled out from under the table and towards another one, zigzagging between table legs and diners' feet till she finally reached the one where Matthew had been seated. She ducked underneath the tablecloth and tried to hear something over the pounding of her heartbeat. It startled her momentarily when Sime's feet and legs stepped carefully by her and he sat down just behind her. She gasped for breath, got it back, settled herself back against his legs and listened carefully.

"Can you stop shouting? I'm in a restaurant. People are taking an interest. This one guy keeps leaning over in my direction. But that could just be the cut of my shirt." Taylor gave a merry laugh, one which Sev remembered clearly and which made her cringe. "Sevannah, what's your opinion on dark-haired guys? Because this guy has a friend. If you wanted to come up this weekend, I'll go ahead and wrangle us a double date. No problem. Easy. Pushover. Sound good?"

Sev tugged on Sime's pant leg and after a moment he bent down and stuck his head under the tablecloth.

"I've definitely heard this conversation before," she whispered to him. "I'm on the other end of the line and—ha!" She started to laugh, had to stuff her hand in her mouth to quiet herself.

"What?" said Sime, concerned.

"It's you! She's talking about Matthew and you! She's saying he's the one who's—" She sobered abruptly. "Sime, tell me that Matthew is not trying to look down my sister's shirt."

"Okay," said Sime without checking, "he's not trying to look down your sister's shirt."

She glared at him.

"Really," he said. "Can we focus?"

"She's talking about the two of you, asking if I'd be interested in you, because she's interested in Matthew and wants to know if we'll double date." Sev shook her head. "It's really not that funny. But it sort of is, too."

"Focus," Sime reminded her.

"Oh. Right. Has she hung up the phone yet?"

Sime put his head up and checked. "Just now."

"Alright, that means she's going to come over here and flirt with you. Consider yourself warned."

Sime looked alarmed. "What do we do about it?"

"What can you do about it? My sister is a force of nature when she's on the prowl. She's like a bloodhound. She'd tree you no matter how far you run. Oh my god, she's Tendence and Cavile wrapped into one. Okay, look." Sev pulled off her platinum engagement ring and the silver-and-onyx ring she'd been given years ago, and pressed them into Sime's hand. "They're going to be small," she warned.

"Here, here," whispered Sime to Matthew, picking up some of Sev's urgency. He passed him the engagement ring. The silver one he put on himself. It wouldn't slide down over his knuckle— in fact, he had to force it to make it to his knuckle— but it was on his ring finger for what it was worth.

Matthew's hands, strangely for a fairly delicate man, were much larger, and he couldn't get the engagement ring much past his fingernail. He palmed it decorously as Taylor arrived, simpering, grinning, wheedling and pretending to be a kitten.

"Hello, boys."

"Men," said Sime, glancing up at her. "I worked very hard to get all this gray hair, thank you very much, and I'd rather you didn't ignore it." He tipped his head to one side. "What did you do to get yours?"

The conversation didn't last much longer than that. Taylor marched off in a huff, to search out more viable prey. Sev was giggling when she came out from underneath the table and stood, stretched, put her hands on the table and grinned at them both.

"Good start. Sime, I had no idea you were so rude. I mean, I should have suspected, but really." She glanced down at Matthew. "Hon."

"Yes?" said Matthew, looking exhausted all of a sudden.

"You were trying to put the ring on your pointer finger."

He glanced down at his hands in some confusion.

"I was?"

"Yes," said Sev delicately, teeth very sharp, "you were." She grabbed the ring back from him. "If you don't even know which finger to put the ring on, how do you expect us to get married?"

"Hey, give him a break," said Sime. "He's the original absent-minded professor. He could be, actually. That's not necessarily a joke. But if it is, it's a funny one."

"Everybody's ganging up on me," muttered Matthew, sinking into his seat.

"My sister'd like to gang up on you," said Sev fiercely, "and if you ask me, you two deserve each other." She turned to Sime. "Can we get on with it? I feel like we've been wasting time."

"Good point." He got up and directed her to the chair, pulling it out for her in a thoroughly gentleman-like way. Sev thought about how his politeness underscored how miserably caddish Matthew was looking, sitting there feeling sorry for himself, and wondered if he'd done it on purpose. "There's no being sure when exactly they'll show up. I'm sure they know you're here, but they're probably waiting for you to come back out. I'll be keeping an eye out from a few minutes ahead. Keep them talking."

"Keep them talking?" repeated Sev.

He bent and brushed a quick kiss on her forehead. "Keep them talking." He disappeared faster this time, fading into thin air like mist like the sun breaking through clouds. Nothing left. He was only a few minutes away from them and Sev missed him terribly.

She took a deep breath.

"Keep them—"

"Keep us whatting?" came the decorous tones of Tendence, who stood at their table as though he'd grown there but had in fact walked quickly and silently over from the entryway. He gestured to Cavile, who was still complimenting the waitress on her hairstyle, for him to hurry it up and join him, then turned back to Sev and smiled benignly. It would have been benign, at least, if it hadn't been for the disconcerting effect of his double rows of white teeth. As it was, it was like being smiled at by a friendly shark. People who were on a level with him probably didn't even notice, she thought; it was just when you were looking up like this—

She gulped, and stood up, tugging at Matthew's sleeve for him to do the same. He did, rather less gracefully, stumbling over the table leg and his shoelaces. The two of them backed away from Tendence and Cavile, who advanced on them with slow-but-sure purpose, like a tortoise getting monumentally fed up and murdering the hare.

"We've been looking for you, Mr. Adler," said Tendence. "You've managed very well for someone doing it all by your lonesome."

"I— I, uh—" said Matthew. Sev glanced up at him.

"Yeah, he's good like that," she said. "Very intelligent. Able to leap tall buildings in a single bound. Stops trains with his face."

Tendence grinned widely.

"I like that one. 'Stops trains with his face.' We'll have to try that one sometime, eh, Cavile?"

"I already have," said Cavile.

"Tell me, Mr. Adler, how did you manage it? Is time travel really getting so easy that any layman with a hobbying bent can do it? Is it going to replace ham radio as the technical favorite of balding fat guys everywhere? Will they sell it in kits like model airplanes? Tab A into Slot B, enjoy your flight?"

"Er," said Matthew. This was too many questions at once. His brain was shutting down in self-defense. Sev rolled her eyes.

"They already sell it in kits," she informed them. "Makes things easier, except the instructions are in Latin. Did you get all this from some sort of murderous bully handbook? 'Sinister Banter for Dummies'?"

Tendence paused, his eyes veiled suddenly with his lashes.

"Now, I'm rather certain," he said, voice silky smooth, "that your companion told you about us. About our work, and who we work for. About our reputation. You must realize that we will fight to uphold that valuable reputation, and that nothing you can do can stop us from winning. No matter what steps you take, no matter what moves you make—"

"Every vow I break, every smile I fake, you'll be watching me?" finished Sev.

Tendence's eyes were green, and they smiled as dangerously as his mouth.

"You have already lost," he said softly. "You are already dead, you have just not stopped moving yet."

Sev swallowed hard. Where was Sime? It had been a few minutes, and he was supposed to be here— 'a few minutes' being exactly what he said. And he'd promised, too. She nudged Matthew as surreptitiously as possible.

"Will you come out of your trance? I'm sick of bantering for you!"

"Urgh," said Matthew.

Sev shook her head. Clearly, it was up to her. She'd suspected as much from the start.

"So you two are more than cold-blooded killers, is that what you're trying to tell me?"

"Even that would be assuming we have blood," corrected Tendence gently.

"And here's a question," she said, brightly. "What are the two of you— full-grown men, time travelers, adepts and all, snappy dressers— what are you doing working for someone else? Shouldn't *you* be in charge? The way I heard it, you're the first ones that started to time travel anyway. Why isn't it *your* Corporation?"

Tendence spread his arms. "We are humble men, madam, though we know our own worth. We have never sought to be in positions of power. We exist merely to follow the rules, and the Corporation sets those rules. It's no more than our duty to enforce them."

"So there's nothing I could do to convince you to abandon the Corporation and follow your own rules? Or mine, even?" she suggested.

"Nothing," said Cavile solidly.

"That's right," said Tendence. "As long as the Corporation is in power, we're obligated to work towards its ends. Not our own."

Sev sighed deeply.

"Nothing I could do?" she repeated, softly this time. "Nothing I could— *persuade* you with? Nothing I could— *offer* to you?" She hadn't actively tried to seduce someone in nearly a decade. It made her hips hurt. Her shoulders didn't feel so hot either. That was probably a problem. Tendence and Cavile looked on in detached interest.

"Are you kidding?" said Tendence.

"I've got a wife waiting for me in 1409," said Cavile kindly, "otherwise I'd be glad to take you to a movie."

"You have a *wife*?"

"Ow," said Tendence.

Cavile didn't say anything; he merely toppled over forwards, crash-landing on the dessert tray.

"Like felling a tree," said Sime, cheerfully, and put the poker down.

Sev screamed at him for a few minutes, while he waited patiently.

Chapter Fifteen

"Sorry," he said when she had stopped. "You were doing so well, I wanted to see where that was going. Usually when they tell you about their wives, it's time to go into action. They don't share personal information with people in general. Just those who are going to die immediately afterwards."

"Wives," repeated Sev blankly. "As in *harems* or to each his own?"

Sime frowned thoughtfully, rubbing his chin with the hand that wasn't holding the poker; he'd tried to do it with the other one earlier and had nearly put his eye out. "Definitely the latter, I think. These two are romantics. They believe in one love for the ages." He glanced up, eyes darting from Sev to Matthew. "I never could understand romanticism, myself."

"Me neither," said Matthew candidly. Sev snorted and Sime dropped the poker to cough violently.

"Well," he said, when he'd finished and wiped his hands on his pants, surreptitiously, "now to the second step. We've got them prone, prostrate, unconscious— all we've got to do is ensure they remain that way." He pulled a small white box from his pocket and opened it, revealing a two-part syringe and a small plastic vial with a rubber top, something like a portable insulin kit. He assembled the syringe with ease that suggested he'd done this before.

"You're not a user, are you?" said Sev suspiciously.

"No, no. I practiced a few times when I picked this up. If there's one thing I hate," he announced, "it's getting to the big action sequences that decide the whole story and then the whole thing is brought to a crashing halt by the ineptness of the hero when faced with something small that requires assemblage. It just *bugs* me. Here we are." He pulled some of the liquid in the vial into the shooter, as quickly as efficiently as a nurse, injected it first into Tendence's arm and then the rest of it into Cavile's. On second thought, he added another half measure to Cavile. "Got to keep the big bugger down."

"What is it?" asked Matthew.

"Sedative," said Sime briefly. "The most sedating of sedatives I could find." He glanced at Sev, who was crouched down next to him. "You going to be alright to keep an eye on them while I head off?"

"They're sedated," she said, and shrugged. "How hard can it be? Sime—" She took his arm as he turned to go. "What is it that you're going to do? You wouldn't tell me."

"And you think I'll tell you now?"

"I want you to." She paused for a moment, then smirked at him and the expression on his face: open, heartfelt. "I want to know where to go if you don't come back, to look for your body or your ashes or whatever. To find you."

"You're going to come after me?"

"If you don't come back as soon as possible, yeah."

"You'll have to give me half an hour at least, to allow for any discrepancies in my internal clock."

"You swallowed a clock?" said Matthew. They turned to look at him for a moment, and he stared back with his native intelligence successfully hidden. Exhaustion-induced stupidity was evident on his face. Sev sighed and managed to tell him quite kindly that Sime was referring to his ability as an Adept, to travel without a machine. "Oh," said Matthew, and tried to go to sleep without shutting his eyes.

"You're not really going to marry him, are you?" said Sime quietly. Sev looked at him impassively.

"It's all in the future," she said. "At the moment, who knows?"

"I see."

"Tell me what you're going to do."

What Sime was going to do was this. He knew that, guarding all the pivotal moments of the birth of the Corporation, were variations of Tendence and Cavile all along their time line. There were six members of the board, and their histories had been analyzed to discover what exactly had led to them forming the Corporation and taking over control of time travel. But it was a difficult thing, deciding what exactly makes us what we are, makes our lives what they are; it was as tricky as figuring out which option to take in a universe of options; as determining if we're still *us,* fundamentally, no matter which universe you go to. It was as elusive a question to answer as "Where does the mind go when we're in a coma?" or "Why does one sibling inherit their father's eyes while the other looks exactly like their great-great-grandmother?"

And if there was one multi-universal, incontrovertible fact, it was that everyone needed to be born. And if you weren't, then all the decisions and figuring things out and determinations wouldn't be the slightest bit of use to you. Not even if you were a brain in a vat. Especially if you were a brain in a vat.

Sime himself had a few options. Kidnapping was one of them, of course: baby-switching. Ensuring that they were sent to private boarding schools where they'd be bullied into submission. Murder was pretty much out of the equation; despite his drastic feelings about the Corporation now as a group of adults, infanticide was a little too much for him to stomach. The best way, of course, though it would require pinpoint precision and timing, was to prevent them from being conceived. Fathers being called away on business trips, older children protesting their bedtimes, mothers having headaches. Lovely, Sime congratulated himself, absolutely brilliant. A series of being in the right place, at the right time, hopefully avoiding any further Tendence and Cavile future-selves, and not getting caught by anyone else. It took a little more calculation than otherwise, but he felt more or less up to the challenge.

He didn't want to tell Sev, because it would have taken too long and lead to explanations and protestations that wouldn't have gotten them anywhere much. So he lunged forward and kissed her on the side of the mouth, smiled slightly, and disappeared.

He was reasonably sure that she cursed him thoroughly afterwards, and as a matter of fact he was right.

But Sime was floating through time and space, carrying names and dates in his head, and as he steeled himself on the banks of Time for that first dive into the freezing water, he felt nothing beneath his feet; only felt, clockwise, the turn of the earth.

Here are Tendence and Cavile, eyes glazed with lack of sleep, eternally shouldering the responsibility of the Corporation's protection. On either side of them, forward and back, left and right, the long line of their other selves is busied with the everyday (every day, ever) duties of the Corporation's enforcers. The Knights Templar of time, although that suggests rather too much shining armor. No one can sustain shining armor when they have the dust of ages whirling past them at every turn.

Here are Tendence and Cavile, lying full-out and flat,

eyes closed with lack of sleep, sudden as a flicked switch, as a burst of light in a pitch black room. On both skulls, some dramatic welts are rising, worthy of investigation by a dauntless phrenologist. Their hearts tick over like a watched clock, as in the distance the knowledge of themselves, their other selves, recedes. Here, and only here, are Tendence and Cavile.

They begin seriously to dream.

"We need to talk about this, don't we?" said Matthew forlornly.

Sev looked at him, glanced around at their surroundings: the tattered, seriously disrupted restaurant, nearly empty as most of the diners had fled in terror, the frightened staff frantically hanging all the "Closed" signs they could and scrabbling for their tips, the time-traveling psychopaths lying unconscious at their feet. She raised her eyebrows at him.

"There's no time like the present," he told her, ruthlessly sticking to clichés despite their having been disproved conclusively on a number of occasions.

"Fine. Talk." She got up and wandered over to one of the other tables, where the waiter had just delivered the order before all this happened. It included spaghetti, and she swept the plate up, cradling it like a child. She hummed happily to herself for a moment, then started the search for a fork. The silverware seemed to have hid itself under the table. On the whole, though, dirty silverware was less likely to kill her than other things, so she decided she didn't really care.

Matthew made himself more comfortable, sitting cross-legged as far away as he could get from Tendence and Cavile while still pretending to be watching over them. Sev wandered back over and plopped herself down between the two of them, twirling strands of pasta around the liberated silverware and still humming.

"You seem awfully happy."

"Oh, I'm not," she assured him. "This is a defense mechanism. I always hum when I'm upset or nervous."

"You used to hum on our dates all the time," said Matthew, disconcerted.

"Oh, really? Huh. You said there was something we needed to talk about?"

"This." He gestured at the space between them emphatically. Sev's eyes followed his wagging hand till she felt dizzy, then she ate another bite to make her feel better. "This— whatever this is."

She swallowed. "How can you talk about something if you don't even know what it is?"

"Sev."

"I mean, I guess we can manage, but it'll be like playing Twenty Questions. Animal, vegetable, mineral, bigger than a breadbox, smaller than a Volkswagen Bug."

"Sev!" He banged his fists down and broke a plate. "Ow!"

"Careful," she said, and took another bite. "I understand, Matthew, I do, and believe me I take this every bit as seriously as you do. Possibly more so since I wasn't able to go back in time and tell myself to avoid you like the plague. Flippancy is another defense mechanism. If I don't get some relief from stress soon I'll start throwing cutlery."

"At me?" He looked betrayed.

She shrugged. "At whoever presents themselves. You know how you can tell a victim? The target painted on his back. Or the top of his head, if he's bald. Bald people were created to help the rest of us improve our aim, that's all I can say."

"Sev, you don't know what you're saying."

"On the contrary. I know exactly what I'm saying, I just don't know why I'm saying it." She laughed, and spaghetti sauce was briefly turned into a projectile weapon. "I always get like this in life-or-death situations. You should have seen me the last time I visited my aunt. I ended up with a lampshade on my head singing 'Here

Comes the Sun.' I was singing it. Not the lampshade." She shook herself slightly. "I'm sorry, Matthew. Part of it is that I don't really want to talk all serious-like with you. It's not that I don't trust you— at least, it's not *just* that— it's that I don't like you. I mean, I wouldn't shout insults at you if I passed you on the street, but I'd rather marry one of these fellas than you." She gestured to Tendence and Cavile, who in the manner of all well-sedated persons, lay there unmoving. "And considering that I now know that would be bigamy, that's saying something." She considered. "That's saying a lot. Did you ever realize that 'bigamy' is really just 'Big Amy' without a space in between? That's pretty bad. I mean, poor Amy."

Matthew put his hands over his face and squeezed. "So you think we should break up."

"I think we're already broken up, Matthew. I've sort of thought that since I realized that the only reason we were together was in the event that you needed someone to save your sorry self. Actually, I take that back. I've sort of thought that since I came across you in a bar with a hooker." She paused for a moment. "I take that back again. I've sort of thought that since our second date, when I discovered that despite your gentlemanlike exterior, your favorite movie is Rocky III and you think only men should be helicopter pilots. I refuse to marry a male chauvinist pig, Matthew, and even though you hide it well—"

"Since our second date?" whispered Matthew.

"Yup." She nodded emphatically. "So you'd better be glad that I was desperate enough to let it continue. Otherwise who would have saved you? No one, that's who."

Matthew folded in on himself like a mis-mixed cake, sagging at the middle and drawing all the extremities in to cover the void. "Why did you let it go on, then?" he asked dully. "All that time we spent together, and here I thought we had something really special."

Sev considered him for a moment, and softened somewhat. "We did have something really special. We had a relationship that wasn't ugly." She repeated the word 'ugly' to herself, nodded. It was exactly right. "It was the first relationship I'd ever had that wasn't that way, Matthew. It was a kinder and gentler relationship. It was the kind you put a bow-tie on and bring home to your parents. It was having a date for any important office parties, having someone to take care of you if you were really sick, having someone to put on your In Case of Emergency Please Contact information. It was all those things and more, and for that, I'm grateful." She paused for a moment, then ventured quietly, "It just wasn't real."

"Oh," said Matthew, as though he understood now. "I get that. I get not-real. Yeah," he sounded relieved, "not-real happens to me all the time. What do you think this is?" He gestured around the restaurant, at Tendence and Cavile, at his left hand which was bleeding slightly where he'd inadvertently broken the plate with it. "None of this is real. All of this is exactly not-real. See?"

Sev yawned and played with her food. "Suit yourself, Matthew. You're the scientist. Has it been half an hour yet?"

"How can you tell time at this juncture without getting depressed?" Matthew murmured listlessly, leaning over to sag against the wall.

"Good question." She stood up and started to go in search of a clock. Sime materialized directly in front of her and she walked into him. "Oof!"

"Well, if nothing else, I've got timing," said Sime, with a certain amount of dazedness. He caught her by the arms, and Sev smiled at this gallant gesture, until it turned out he was using her to support himself and not the other way around. She helped him to sit down, and hovered over him anxiously.

"Are you alright?"

"A little tired," he admitted. "I don't think I've ever traveled through time quite that fast. At least, not since I was a rookie and did it to show off."

"And this isn't showing off?"

"No. No, this is necessity speaking, here." He put his

elbows on his knees, rested his head in his hands. "How long has it been, for you?"

"It's hard to tell— somewhere around twenty minutes, I'd say. How long has it been for you?"

"Much longer." He eyed the empty spaghetti plate she'd left behind. "I haven't eaten since I stole a pretzel in 1923 New York. It's almost done, Sevannah."

"How almost? I mean, how close are you?"

His eyes appeared over the edge of his fingers, shining like stars in the dim light. His breathing, slow and steady, was given a deep, almost musty sound by the cupping curve of his hands.

"One more," he said, so quietly she almost didn't hear it.

"One— well, that's wonderful, Sime! One more and you've done it! Do you need help? Can we do anything to help you?"

He shook his head. "No. I just came back so that you wouldn't worry. This one is going to take a bit more time." He dropped his head, took a deep breath that moved and shuddered his shoulders like mountains.

She put one hand on his head, fingers in his thick dark hair.

"What is it?"

"Do you remember," he said, and had to stop and clear his throat. When he started again the hitch was gone, his voice was stronger, and he got through all of it without stopping again. "Do you remember when I told you that one of the Board members was born about forty years after I was? Well. It turns out there was something I didn't know. And— there's something you should know, Sev, that you don't. I didn't tell you. Don't ask me why I didn't, I just— didn't."

"It's about your wife, isn't it?" said Sev quietly.

"What?" said Matthew.

They ignored him.

"We were in an accident," Sime said. "We were on our way to church. Sunday morning, eight o'clock. There was another coach, going much faster than it should have been, thundering by. It startled our horse and she began to run. She ran much too fast. The coach overturned as she was running and the lanterns caught it on fire. And I couldn't stay; I had to get out; because I couldn't take them with me."

"Take who with you?" Sev asked, gently.

"Mary and my son," said Sime. "Andrew. My son."

She breathed in, tried to focus on a way to make all this better. "Couldn't you go back and change it? Make it so it didn't happen, so you never got in the coach that morning?"

"I tried." His voice was bitter, admitting his own failure. "The streets are littered with versions of me, for anyone who cares to look; I'm watching from all angles, I'm trying to prevent it. No matter what I do, it happens. Sevannah— it's the defining thing. In all those universes, this happens; this is what makes me, me."

"That's horrible," said Sev, who was starting to cry. "And I don't believe it."

"The other coach," he went on, "contained a woman who couldn't get the medical attention she needed, at least not fast enough. She was being taken to the hospital, just one street over. She was going to die. She did die. But the baby lived." He turned to Sev suddenly, a strange and sudden determination in his eyes. "I don't want to go back. I've been there so many times, over and over, and I don't want to go back."

"The baby?" she said, wiping her eyes. "Is the baby the last—"

"Every time I go back," he said, ruthlessly, "I hit the moment I left and I'm me, living again, in my own time again, feeling cells pass on and heartbeats disappear and watching my wife and my son die because I can't do anything to save them."

"Is the baby the last one?" She spoke quite calmly, she thought.

"Yes," acknowledged Sime.

"Then you need to. One last time."

"*But I don't want to.*"

"And this is you," she pointed out, "given a choice to be self-indulgent or self-sacrificing, to be selfish or to be giving. To alter universes for better or worse. This is the choice. *This* is your defining moment. And I will come with you."

She put her arms around him, tried to comfort him, to convince him, but he stood still and ramrod straight. She was reminded that it was as impossible to hug an unwilling person as it was to hug a cat. She tried anyway, hung on, pulled him down into her and tighter, and something about her weight, warmth, gravity culled a response from him and he slowly put his arms around her back, bent his head to her shoulder. For the time being, they held on.

Chapter Sixteen

Simon studied his eggs carefully, nudging them with a fork. The eggs were the product of his son's favorite chicken. The fork was a long-ago wedding present from his parents, part of an exquisite silver set that was locked up every evening, guarded as carefully as though they were crown jewels. It still made him nervous, a bit. The eggs, not the fork. The chicken had been laying in a tree, oddly enough, and it had been weeks before they discovered this.

"Are you quite sure—" he began, not for the first time.

Mary, seated across the table, smiled at him. "Still quite sure, dearest. The cook was very careful."

"Mm," said Simon, thoughtfully.

"And if you don't hurry up a little," suggested Mary delicately, "we are going to be late."

Simon nodded. "Of course, love. I know." He poked at the eggs. The eggs didn't poke back. He cut a long vertical slice through them, watching yolk bleed into the white, contemplating. Perhaps in some universe the chicken's eggs were rotten after all, and on some subconscious level he knew that, and perhaps that was why he felt strange about eating them. That didn't explain why he felt strange about everything else, of course, but there was undoubtedly an explanation for that. There was an explanation for everything. He didn't know what they were, but he believed in their existence.

He felt as though there were shadows everywhere even in the bright light, as though he was being followed. He felt as though he should go back to bed, pull the covers up over himself and Mary, and not get out till they were ready to give Andrew a sibling. He hadn't noticed her stand up, or even noticed her move at all, and only knew it when she dropped a kiss on his left ear on her way past.

"It's quarter till," she told him gently.

"Just one moment," said Simon, distracted, dumbfounded, confronted by possibilities. He didn't eat the eggs after all, left the plate there with its attendant sausage and rashers of bacon, hurried through the house to his wife's bedroom and tried to convince her of the validity and value of his views. She laughed at him and, shortly thereafter, turned him out with a soft-spoken reproof, an admonition to put first things first.

"You can remind me later," she said. "It's just a theory, so I'll need your most convincing arguments."

He took it to heart, and tied his cravat crookedly in his haste.

Andrew was afraid of heights, of open doors, and of getting too close to the fireplace. He came down the stairs haltingly, one step followed gradually by another. He was small for his age and pleasantly neurotic in a manner that suggested he, too, would have to find an accommodating wife, such as his father had; someone who would look after him and put up with his myriad idiosyncrasies. He met his father at the foot of the staircase and they adjusted each other's cravats, brushed each other's shoulders off. Andrew did not time travel. It was not hereditary.

He had, on the other hand, inherited his father's black hair and his mother's soft green eyes, his father's mannerisms and his mother's delicacy. He suggested gently that his father comb his hair. His father did, brushing his fingers through it impatiently, pulling his pocket watch from his vest with the other hand and squinting at it.

"We're going to be late," Simon announced.

"We've got time," said Andrew serenely.

The wife, the mother, the lady of the house descended the stairs regally, smiling at both of them. She pronounced them little gentlemen, favoring her husband with a sly look from underneath her lashes and turning a brighter, livelier countenance on her young son, who offered her his arm. She took it and the two of them walked towards the door with grace and composure, as though entering a ballroom. Simon stood behind, watching them, his head beginning to pound. He grasped the ornamental ball of the railing tighter in his hand, counted his pulses. He was too young for a heart attack, he considered, but there were other things he could fall prey to; and perhaps there had been too much going on lately. Or perhaps he should have eaten breakfast; yes, that seemed the most likely.

Relieved, he shook the weight of premonitory gloom off his shoulders briskly, and followed his young family out the door and to the carriage.

It was a misty morning, full of dark grey fog and unfound as yet by sunlight; the driver was lighting the lamps on the outside of the coach, one by one illuminating only small patches of the world, not the whole.

The streets were populated almost entirely by Sime, later and later versions in different clothing and occupations, some of them running towards him and shouting, some of them trying surreptitiously to bog the carriage down in some way or another, bribe the driver, lame the horse. None of it ever worked, and Simon never noticed. There was something else at work here, something that contravened Okasina's Theory and everything else. This was Sime's one true reality, and myth, reasoning, and hindsight couldn't touch it. It was a high tower in time, unapproachable. There was as yet nothing that came afterwards, for as far as his time was concerned, it ended here.

"Stupid," murmured Sime, watching himself from the street corner.

"It's just life," said Sev. "Just the way things work."

"Well, I hate it."

"Yeah. So do I."

They stood together and watched as Simon of long ago helped his wife into the carriage first, then gave his son a boost. He took a few glances around the street before getting in himself. Sime shook his head.

"And I still don't know why," he said helplessly. "Why this needs to happen. What did this make me, that was so vital?"

"Brave," said Sev, taking his hand. "Wise. Strong. Resourceful. Sime."

He wiped his eyes with the back of his other hand. "In a few minutes," he said, "it happens. And when it does, I'll meet my time line and be me, the real Sime— Simon— again. For the first time in so long— I'll start to age again. I'll start to—" He sniffed, breathed in deep and let it out slowly. "I've never made it this far," he said, and she understood what he meant only after she saw the different versions of himself disappearing, everywhere she looked. Pop! went one, and pop! went another. She blinked. In a world full of things stranger than she'd ever seen, this took the cake.

"Why?"

"I was afraid of running back into myself, and continuing my history." He nodded slowly, watching as all around them the time-changing versions disappeared until he was the only one left. "This was the last minute I made it to. I don't think—"

She held his hand tighter. "You can't leave now, Sime. You have to do this. Believe me, I'd do it for you if I could, but—"

"It may take some time," he said, "but I will hurry. I'll be as fast as I can."

"Just do what you have to do," she told him.

She looked at him full on for the first time since they'd

arrived here, and it broke her heart to see the expression on his face: the slow anticipation, the knowing. The heartbreak over what was going to happen, the ache over knowing there was no way to stop it. *Maybe there was.* The thought shone out of the clouds and illuminated her brain in an unexpected shaft of light. *Maybe there was.*

Maybe she was being too optimistic. This still didn't seem like reality.

She squeezed his hand tighter. Out on the street in front of Simon's house, the horse began to walk, the carriage to move.

"I should have done it a long time ago," he said. "I should have done it the first time. I shouldn't have left—only I couldn't take it. I couldn't."

"And now you can." She let his hand go, and he left her side, moved forward, squaring his shoulders. She watched to see if there was anything any different in the real Sime, the Sime of this time line, of this history, anything that changed from reality to reality, as he skipped the universe where he'd left and melded it with the universe in which he stayed, stayed till the end, stayed forever as far as his family was concerned. There by their sides. He couldn't save them but he could watch them die.

It really was horrible, she thought, and was so engrossed in consideration of how she would feel in this particular situation that it startled her badly when the second coach came thundering past, turned the corner that she stood on, barreled onwards. She got a brief glimpse of the men on it, one driving, hustling and urging the horse onwards with a whip, the other on the back, holding on for all he was worth, face turned to one side and cheek pressed against the back of the carriage. His eyes lighted on Sev for the brief second they were level, abreast; they were gone before she could call out to them to stop or to slow down, and though she tried very hard to shout after them, somehow the sound never made it past her throat.

It hurtled past, apparently bound for a course that led it very close to the other carriage, rocking and moving unsteadily on the cobblestone streets. It turned at the last second and the wheels on one side left the ground slightly, sending the coach up on two only and brushing the top of the one against the side of the other. There were screams from both coaches. The running horse veered off and as it passed Simon's coach up, the man on the back reached out and kicked at Simon's horse; startled as it was already, that was all it needed. Rearing back in the traces, eyes rolling and flashing, it shrieked and ran, no preliminaries, started racing; hurtled around in the narrow streets, towing the coach; the driver was tossed from his seat, screams came from inside; the traces broke on the next turn the horse tried to take and as the terrified animal rushed off, the carriage overturned, one wheel breaking and the others spinning frantically in the air. It turned over to the right, trapping the single door closed steadfastly beneath it. The glass broke, the wood caught fire as the wind whipped up, the screams increased.

Sime stood in the middle of the road, tears streaming down, his face set and grim. His hair blew into his eyes but he was almost blind from tears already.

"*This is now,*" he said.

Simon takes a breath and finds himself breathless. From the interior of the carriage to the cold of the street in a second, in less than a second, in nothing. How is he going to explain his escape? How is he going to explain why he left them behind?

All he has is now.

He throws himself at the coach, burns himself on the burning wood, shouting and shrieking. His silhouette in the false light of the fire moves against the flames, looking like a minor demon, a dervish, a djinn. There are strangers going by, and they pause and are dumb and silent. Then they rush and are violent and loud. There's nothing to do. Everything's already been done.

This has already happened.
It happens again.

Sev was watching, her hands over her mouth and trying not to be blinded by the tears streaming from her eyes, wiping them away with determined hands. She looked from the over-turned coach to the path the other horse had taken, which must lead to the hospital. They would have to go there, after— oh, who knew how long? Sime had to do what he had to do. Sometimes, she told herself, you really only get one chance to make your history. It was a familiar thought, having popped into her head various times over the years, but she'd dismissed it from her mind ever since she'd broken into Matthew's house and ended up in 1856. The dismissed thought was making a comeback when it suddenly dawned on her who the driver of the other carriage was, and who was the man who crouched on the back, staring at her with baleful eyes.

It wasn't possible, of course it wasn't possible. But it had happened, just the same.

The other horse, magically, had come to a stop in its frenzied dance of terror nearly in the same place it had started out from: just at the bottom of the steps leading to Sime's house. She rushed impulsively towards it, remembering only when she got closer that it would be best to approach it slowly. She tried her best to calm it, walking to it with her hand held palm out, letting it smell her and feel her intentions.

The horse had been well trained and was ashamed of its recent conduct; it stood still, muttering slightly in apology. Sev backed it up slightly, then stood on the lowest step and got very carefully on. She hadn't ridden a horse since classes she'd taken the summer she was sixteen. Fat lot of good those classes had done her, considering how little she'd used her expertise since then. Well, now was the chance to make up for it, to vindicate what her parents had spent on them.

It was highly uncomfortable on top of the remnants of the traces; she shifted slightly, and when the horse took two steps forward she tangled her hands deep into its mane and held on. This wasn't getting them anywhere fast enough, though, so she leaned down, whispered something friendly in the horse's ear, and jabbed it viciously in the sides with her heels.

It worked.

The hard part was steering.

She could see the path that the run-away carriage had taken. It seemed to be leading to the hospital after all. She would have thought, considering the drivers, that there was something else, some bigger game afoot; but if they were trying to protect the last remaining member of the board, presumably they'd want his mother to give birth in a safe environment. At least, as safe as hospitals were in the 1800s.

She thundered up towards the building, which was large and looked every bit as cold and institution-like as the asylum across the street. The horse didn't appear to want to stop, now that it was going, and she tapped it with her foot, yelling "Left! Left!"

The horse, against all expectation, obeyed, running up towards the double doors.

"Good boy!" she panted into its neck. "When we get done here, you get an apple— *whoa!*"

The reference to an apple apparently excited the horse beyond all measure, and it reared up on the steps and struck the door open with its hooves. Sev hung on, crashing back down on the horse's back as it came back to all four legs, and buried her face in its mane. *Splinters.* It rumbled on. She could feel it moving underneath her, at a slightly more decorous pace, now, stepping more carefully on the slick hospital floors.

All hospitals, regardless of their age and orientation in time, smelled the same, she decided.

The horse was going where it wanted, wandering by

whimsy, and she gave up trying to control it. It was trotting slower now. This would be the time to try and dismount, before it sped up again. She didn't want to. She had a little argument with herself for a moment or two. It culminated, like all such arguments, in calling herself names.

That did it.

She lay flat on the horse's back, moved her left leg over to join her right, then turned herself carefully till she was horizontal across the beast. She slid off in a rush, landing on her feet, staggering and wincing at the impact. The horse trotted merrily on, relieved of its burden; Sev moved back the way she'd come, looking for the way to the maternity ward, if there was such a thing. This was obviously before helpful little signs had been invented, and she knew if she had to rely on her own instincts she would soon be completely lost.

There was a nurse standing at the end of the hall, looking a little shell-shocked. Because of the sight of a horse in a hospital, or something more sinister? Sev grasped her arm and shook her slightly.

"Where are the babies? Where would I find all the newborns?"

The nurse's mouth moved up and down a few times, soundlessly, and a faltering, twitching hand lifted to indicate the corridor to the right. Sev nodded.

"Thanks!" she said breathlessly, and pelted off down the hallway.

The doors were all closed. She opened each one to look into the room behind it, ensuring that it didn't contain what she was looking for. She saw brief scenes of bloodlettings and a leech, a comatose patient strapped to the bed and wearing a face-mask like Hannibal Lecter, a patient raving wildly about visitors from the stars. Someone like that wouldn't be in an institution in her day, she told herself firmly, marking the differences that medical advancement had made over the years. Someone like that would be winning literary awards, was all, or making television shows.

The last door in the hallway revealed a distraught looking woman who was still breathing hard and shiny with sweat. Her hair stood up every which way, escaping merrily from its entrapment in a bun at the back of her head, and she had the unmistakable look of someone who had just given birth in recent moments and was, therefore, not feeling too well. Sev pushed the door open all the way and rushed in, over to the side of the bed.

"Where's your child?" Her voice came out wrong. She'd been going for strength and authority, something to convey the urgency of the situation. Instead, she got a squeak. The woman looked dazedly at her.

"Why?" she asked.

Sev faltered.

"Emergency!" she blurted out. It was the first thing that came to her head, not to mention being true, which was an added bonus. "There's a major emergency— um— an epidemic, and we need to know where the baby is so we can, er, take care of him in this time of great, um— emergency."

"What's an epidemic?" said the mother, with the carelessness of someone who's undergone great pain and, having come through it, no longer cares for anything else but her own comfort.

Sev took another tack. "Look, I'm the owner of this hospital," she said, "and I need to know the whereabouts of your child at once. Right now. This instant."

The mother settled back against her pillow, wiping at her forehead. "The doctors took him off to be cleaned."

"What?"

"The doctors." She flapped a hand in the direction of the door. "Both of them."

"*Both* of them!" said Sev, and since that was likely all she was going to get out of the mother, she bolted for the door. Suddenly overcome with remorse and a desire to be helpful, the mother began to sputter details.

"Broad-shouldered, the big one," she said. "Nattily dressed, carried an umbrella. The other one a bit smaller, in a black jacket, with good cheekbones— " but Sev was already out of the door and racing down the hallway.

She wasn't sure where she was going.

She just hoped she would get there, wherever it was, in time.

Chapter Seventeen

There were shapes at the end of the corridor, which seemed with the sickening suddenness of a dream to stretch out far beyond the reaches of physics. The shapes were misty, unresolved, transparent. Sev wiped sweat from her eyes as she ran and as a result nearly tumbled headlong over a chair in her path. She skipped past and over it on one leg, grateful to be as tall as she was, and ran on. Even with her eyes clear, though, there was still something strange about those figures.

It was Tendence and Cavile, that much she was sure of. Tendence had his hands in his pockets. Cavile was holding the baby. They'd stopped and were waiting for her to catch them up now, looking loose and relaxed and still somewhat transparent. She could see the lines of the wall behind them.

She reached them at last, panting, and doubled over, hands on her knees.

"You've got— to stop! I— need that—"

"Catch your breath first," advised Cavile kindly. Tendence said nothing for the moment, merely looked on at her, head tilted to one side. His shark-like mouth was relaxed and slightly open. Within, she could make out glimpses of rows of jagged teeth.

"You did surprisingly well," he said at last. Sev nodded, swallowing hard and dry.

"Surprise!" she managed, lifting her hands from her knees and waving them.

"Ha ha," said Tendence politely.

"Yay!" said Cavile, and cast his partner a look of confusion.

In the back of Sev's mind it was registered that the last time she stood before these two, they had been very close to killing her. However, the rest of her, caught up in courageousness and ready to martyr herself, informed her this was not worthy of consideration. She was sure that it was, actually, but not only does courage seldom listen to reason, courage also bullied the part of her concerned with self-preservation into silence and submission.

"How are you guys here?" she asked. "You were pretty well out of it. Did you come to? Matthew wasn't able to stop you, was he?" She nodded slowly, suddenly convinced in her own mind. "You killed him, didn't you? Oh. Oh, God. I didn't want that to happen."

"In truth," said Tendence, spreading his arms out to the sides to demonstrate the vague transparency of them, "we are not really here at all. Regardless of what you do to the body, there is little that can stop the mind from going about its business." His mouth opened further and he grinned at her. "You should have killed us when you had the chance, Madam. Or at least, tried. I confess I'm not sure if it can be done."

"If you're not really here," she said, pointing at Cavile who stood by waiting patiently, "how is he holding that baby?"

"With my hands," rumbled Cavile.

"Oh, the mind does wonderful things," Tendence assured her. "And the stronger the personality, the stronger the mind, the stronger the manifestation of it. We will, perhaps, never understand what goes on in the human psyche, though studies are made of it years past your time.

One instance in which a sleeping man killed his wife leaving no apparent marks and with no obvious modus operandi, suggested that our sleeping consciousness can still get about and do things. Finish lists, do housework, have arguments, kill people."

"Do the shopping," put in Sev.

"Absolutely."

"Don't you think it's more likely they just haven't discovered how he did it yet?"

Tendence bowed slightly. "No matter how you choose to rationalize things, miss, we're still here. If we defy explanation then so be it: we'll defy it with everything we've got. That's hardly the point, it is?"

"No, it's not," said Sev, realizing she'd allowed herself to get distracted far too easily. "I need you to give me that baby."

"What are you going to do with it?" asked Cavile, who'd said hardly a word during the interim but had listened avidly.

"I'm going to change its destiny," said Sev self-importantly.

"But by definition, you cannot change such a thing," objected Cavile. "Destiny is about who we're meant to be, not who time and circumstance makes us."

"Very good, Cavile," said Tendence approvingly. Cavile smiled and preened.

"It doesn't matter," said Sev, rolling her eyes. "I don't actually believe in destiny anyway, okay? I don't believe that I was meant to be here, or that I was meant to meet Matthew so I could save him, or meant to meet Sime so I could comfort him. Everything's running into everything else, that's true, it's all this series of concentric circles that I don't seem to be able to do anything about because none of the decisions have been mine. But I'd rather believe that I'm doing what I choose because I believe it's for the best, even if it turns out for the worst, instead of believing that I'm being controlled by some force I can't escape. It doesn't matter what I do in any other universe. It only matters what I do right here, right now, in this reality. All I've got is the present. I don't know what makes me *me*, I'm going to be myself, just as hard as I can be."

In the silence as she paused for breath, Cavile lifted one leg, laid the baby carefully on his broad knee, and began to clap. He had admirable balance, for he clapped with enthusiasm, vigor, and articulation, and neither wobbled nor threatened to overturn. Tendence joined in quickly, his beautiful hands moving rapidly and producing a louder, sharper sound than that of his confederate. Sevannah stared at them, and they stared back at her, and they clapped harder and harder and Cavile shouted, "Bravo!"

There was clearly nothing to be done in this situation. She refused to do it. Instead, she took three steps forward, caught the baby up from his knee, and began to run.

"Come back with that baby!" screeched Tendence, pelting after her.

"Didn't expect *that* to happen, did you?" she called back over her shoulder.

"Bravo!" said Cavile jovially, still clapping even as he began to run.

The baby squalled jarringly as she ran; she tucked it up on her shoulder and under her chin, trying to make it more secure, muttered anything comforting she could think of into its tiny ear. As she ran past the open door of one room the mother called out, "Is it clean yet?"

"Not yet!" Sev yelled, and ran on.

It was fairly ridiculous— no, more than that, it was absolutely and incontrovertibly ridiculous, patently so, and she knew it. Running through a hospital carrying a newborn chased by time-travelling psychopaths. Yeah, that was right up there on the ridiculous list. She started to chuckle and stopped: it used up her breath and it seemed to disturb the baby. This made her wonder what sort of child would be bothered by laughing; then she remembered what sort of child this turned out to be. What kind of adult, more importantly. She knew why she was doing this, as stupid as it might seem.

Sime was waiting for her at the end of the hall. She didn't see him, but crashed on by. He caught her arm and swung her towards him, enveloping her— and the baby, in an incidental manner— in a bone-crushing hug. The baby yelled in his ear.

Sev was babbling, she knew it. She said, "No time! No time!" like the White Rabbit.

Sime took her hand and pulled her along, towing her in his wake as though she was a raft strapped to a speed boat. All she could make out of his face, turned away from her, was the streaks of tears, now dried: almost as though they never were. But she remembered—

"I didn't bring the chair!" she shouted.

"Good thinking!" Sime shouted back.

"I said I *didn't* bring it!"

"I know! That was sarcasm!"

"Oh!"

He pulled her out the double doors of the hospital and down the steps, stumbling and slipping but managing despite everything to stay upright through it all. The baby threw up on her shoulder at this point, though she didn't realize it till later. Every time she glanced over her shoulder, Tendence and Cavile were closer. First thirty feet away, then twenty-five, then twenty—

They were running grimly, silently, their heads lowered. Their eyes were lit with the thrill of the chase.

Sime pulled her down the street, running back in the direction she'd come, racing past the mental asylum now on her right, dodging between carts. There were shouts from people on the street, calls of consternation, encouragement, and disbelief. The horse was nowhere in sight; presumably he'd found some other equines to visit with. She paced herself as best as she could, feeling her breath already coming raggedly, thinking of how the last time she'd run like this, she was in track at school and had something to blame it on. She tried not trip over the cobblestones; any false step and it would all be over.

Sime glanced over his shoulder. His eyes caught at hers as desperately as fingers, for just a moment, then slipped onwards. He was looking at Tendence and Cavile, measuring the distance between them, judging how long they had before they would be caught up. Tendence and Cavile ran like dogs, low to the ground and loping, eyes narrowed and teeth at the ready.

"I've got to go," Sime shouted back at her.

"*What?*" She couldn't believe it, couldn't trust her ears. He couldn't do this to her.

"I'm sorry!" Wordless now, he melted in front of her, his hand turning to nothing in her grasp. He could take no one with him. *No one*, she thought. Most of her breath was used up in the first few sobs, and she faltered. Somewhere in her something caught and held, though, and she got hold of herself and ran, and the tears poured down her face but she could breathe; it constricted her heart but not her lungs. This was control. She was going to run until she couldn't run any more, and that was all. That was all she could do.

Sime reappeared in front of her with the chair, just then, just now, so close to her that she barreled into him, knocking him and the chair over, and when it reached the ground they were in her year, her present year, in Matthew's basement, familiar and wearied.

"You've been very brave," said Sime.

"Well, I *tried* to run away," said Sev, diffidently, shrugging her shoulders, "but something in me just wouldn't let me."

He grinned at her. "Because you wouldn't be you if you did."

"Maybe," she allowed. "Or it could have been sheer cold terror froze my feet to the ground."

"Nonsense! You managed it later on."

"When I was running for my life, yeah."

"You were running for all of our lives," he reminded her.

She took a deep breath. "Yeah."

They were watching as a family on the wrong side of the tracks in New York, 1846, discovered a brand new baby. There were exclamations of surprise and delight, there was the hustle and bustle of finding some blankets for the baby, finding the baby a warm place to rest. Sev grinned.

"Good thing for him he's cute at that point."

"Definitely," Sime agreed. "We would have had a hard time getting him adopted later on. He went bald, got some tattoos—"

"And it's all right? I mean, he'll age and everything?"

"Yes. It's all his time line, just happening in a different place, is all."

"So the Corporation—"

Sime leaned back against the building, waved a hand. "Poof. Gone, just like that."

"Just like that. It's too bad—" She hesitated.

"What do you mean?"

"I mean, I would have liked them to know."

He considered this for a moment, smiled, even laughed a little. "Even when you collapse universes all over the place, even when it's as commonplace as popcorn, people still know. On some level, they know. That's why Matthew was so horrified when we rescued him; he hadn't technically experienced it, but deep down in the dark heart of his cowboy boots he knew the reality of his own mortality, knows how close he's come. It's a ghost memory, sweeps you up, gives you nightmares." He swallowed, nodded. "Trust me, they know. They know what they had, they know what they lost, it's there at the edge of their minds and they'll spend their entire lives thinking about it."

She nodded. "That makes me feel better."

"Vindictive little devil."

"Yes I am."

"At least you know it."

"Been told it enough times." She watched the family with their new baby, shook her head. "And Tendence and Cavile?"

"I'm not sure," he said, thoughtfully, and stood up. "Shall we find out?"

"You always take me to the nicest places."

It was back in the assembly of Anarchists at All Saints, though they weren't, strictly speaking, Anarchists any longer. There was nothing to rebel against now, no reason for anarchy beyond the sheer joy that it held for some people. That being more than enough reason, nothing had really changed. Almost everyone they'd seen before was still there, drawn by the thrill, the allure, the inexplicable awesomeness of the concept of time travel. Anastasia was still keeping the minutes, and they made their way down to her side at the table.

"Need to ask you something," shouted Sime above the din.

Anastasia gave him a sidelong glance. "Should you be here? I mean, shouldn't you be somewhere else?"

Sime frowned slightly, and one hand reached out unconsciously to find Sev and tuck her closer to his side. "I don't think so. Where else should I be?"

She wrote it on a slip of paper, handed it over to him. He glanced at it, and the thoughtful expression didn't leave his face, but only grew.

"Can't get there with a machine," said Anastasia helpfully, glancing at Sev. Sev shrugged.

"I need to get home anyway. Matthew will probably be wondering where I am— or— wait a second!" She clutched Sime's arm. "If Tendence and Cavile never came after him, we never rescued him, he never told himself to date me so I could save him—"

"He told you to date him so you could save him?"

repeated Anastasia in stark disbelief. "What a cad!"

"That's what I said! Practically. I should have said it. I'd like to go back and say it to him." She turned back to Sime. "Does he know who I am? And— come to think of it, how on earth am I here anyway?" She spread her arms to engulf the whole room, people and all. "How did I ever make it here if I was never engaged to Matthew in the first place? Did I just randomly break into his house and find a time machine and decide to take a little whirl?"

"I told you," said Sime simply. "Paradox. It's not a religion exactly, but it certainly is a way of life."

Sev sagged slightly. "But I don't get it."

He took her hand and spoke to her earnestly, softly urgent. "Ever come to a decision in your life based purely on instinct, only doing something because if you didn't do it, it would be wrong? Ever come across a scenario, a circumstance, a relationship that just didn't make sense? It's all paradox, Sevannah. People are changing themselves beyond all reason, all the time."

She thought about this, and nodded.

"That's ridiculous."

"I know."

"But I suppose that most of the problems I have with life come from my assumption that there's a logical reason for everything." She frowned. "It's faulty, isn't it?"

"What is?"

"Life. Everything. Never mind, don't answer— you look like someone who knows, and I don't want to. Not really. Am I going to show back up at Matthew's if I hit the recall, or not?"

"I'm not sure," said Sime, though he probably was. "Just give it a try."

She nodded, moved the chair a little ways away from people, sat on it, leapt back up like she'd sat on a pin and clutched his arm.

"You'll come and say goodbye to me."

"If you're sure you won't stay."

"Yes. Yeah, I'm sure. I can't, Sime."

He nodded. "I understand completely."

"Good. That's good."

"I'll try to convince you again when I get there."

She laughed, and sank back down into the chair, wiping at her eyes. "Alright. You do that."

The recall button was within easy reach. She was casting a last glance around All Saints when Sime pressed it for her.

Well, it was Matthew's chair; it made sense that she would end up back in Matthew's basement. Sort of. As much sense as anything else, she supposed. She got off the machine, wandered out of the room and towards the stairs. The hallway clock announced it was just after 9. There was flickering light coming from the living room.

She couldn't help herself. It was a case of purely natural curiosity; she was drawn towards the light like a moth. She reached the edge of the hallway, peered cautiously around it and into the front room.

There was Matthew, on the couch, snoring slightly, mouth open. There was the expected woman, cuddled up against his side, head resting on his shoulder. Matthew's arms were up on the back of the couch, and a ring on his left hand glinted dimly in the light. Sev grinned in spite of herself and chewed on a fingernail. That was one way to end an unwanted relationship: go back in time and make it so it never happened.

The woman shifted, sat up, leaned forward, and for a moment her face was bathed in the glow of the television. She turned slightly to smile lovingly at Matthew. It was a profile so well-known to Sev that it could have been her own; in fact, it was reasonably similar to Sev's, because that was what family resemblance was all about.

Sevannah had to race from the house, clambering out the bathroom window and trying to hold her breath, to get out of earshot so they wouldn't hear her hysterical laughter.

Sime was waiting for her at her house.

"Can't stay long," he started immediately, grabbing her

up in a hug. "You would not believe what's going on over by the Carpathians."

"The what-thians?

"Remember we had that discussion about Dracula?"

"Er— yeah—"

"Somehow he got hold of a time machine. There's already reports of women across time giving birth to his children."

"Oh yeah? I read about some when I was in line at the supermarket. What are you going to do about it?"

"I don't know," said Sime grimly. "But definitely something."

"Send him to Hollywood," Sev advised. "He'll fit right in and he'll be fantastic."

"What about Matthew?"

She laughed. "It's great! This is great. He's married to Taylor. You know, my sister Taylor?"

Sime gave her a single shocked look and then burst into laughter. Sev nodded emphatically. "That's what I said! So where did you go?"

He sobered quickly, and smiled just a little. "Assembly of Bukados, in North Africa. Newer than the Assembly of All Saints. Smaller, too; it's just for Adepts."

She grinned, and tugged at his sleeve. "There's more of you?"

"There's many of us. Defenders of Time. Trying to keep things in their proper place. Failing, for the most part," he admitted, "but still trying. And—" He gave her a sly grin. "Guess who else is there."

"Tendence and Cavile!" The fact that she guessed correctly right off the bat made him considerably less happy, but he recovered soon enough and acknowledged it.

"They're keeping the minutes, like Anastasia does for All Saints. They're very good at it."

Sev laughed so hard her knees buckled, and Sime caught her, sinking both of them to the floor where he looked at her seriously.

"Thank you," he said.

"For what?"

"For just— being there. Through all of it— my family— near death experiences— thank you."

She smiled a little; nodded, ran a thumb around the perimeter of his chin, and hugged him.

"Are you sure you won't come with me?"

"No. I'm not sure about it. All I know is that I can't right now. I'm back in my life the way it was three months and twenty lifetimes ago— I'm going to give it a try. I've got it all ahead of me, right?"

He nodded.

She kissed him on the chin.

"But don't stop asking. There's always someday."

"Right. I'll skip ahead to then," said Sime (In Time). "As long as I know it's there, I can find it."

"Like steering by stars?"

"Like guided by light," he agreed, and it was.

It was fairly quiet at the minute.

Tendence noted this down.

"We need a diversion," he said, tickling his chin with the quill pen.

"In what way?" rumbled Cavile at his side. Tendence had written out the letters of the alphabet in large, clear script, and Cavile was copying them, his tongue sticking out the side of his mouth as he concentrated.

"Something to do," said Tendence. "Something to say. Something for me to write down."

"You write down what happens," said Cavile. "That's the rules."

"Oh, I agree," Tendence assured him, "it's just that it would be nice— I would appreciate it, I mean to say— if you would do something drastic, something out of the ordinary, something amusing. Something so I could write it down, do you see—"

Cavile laid his pen down, and turned to him

thoughtfully. "I don't think I'd be able to think of anything like that, Tendence. That's just not what I'm here for."

"What do you mean?"

"I mean, God put me on this earth to do one thing, and one thing only."

"And what is that, pray tell?"

Cavile shrugged.

"I don't know. Nobody's told me yet."

Tendence considered, then pushed his chair away from the table slightly, put both feet on the seat of Cavile's chair, and heaved. The chair, and Cavile, went over backwards. Cavile lay on the floor, feet waving in the air, still clutching the pen, his face dotted with ink.

"There you are," said Tendence, cheerfully, "now you've accomplished something, don't you think?"

He settled down to write, happily.

D. T. Kastn is a writer and compulsive blogger from the wilds of Northern California. Her short stories and poetry have appeared in a variety of publications, both online and in print, including the first *Arcane Anthology*, *Danse Macabre*, and the *Dan River Anthology*. This is her first novel. You can find her blog online at the Unboxed Project, where she writes about writing. It's all very meta.